THE GIRL IN THE WOODS

A.J. RIVERS

The Girl in the Woods
Copyright © 2021 by A.J. Rivers

THE GIRL IN THE WOODS

PROLOGUE

PUFFS OF WHITE BREATH HUNG CRYSTALLIZED IN THE SHARPLY cold air around them as they pushed onward down the heavily wooded path. Their boots crunched through the thin layer of sparkling ice that had formed over the snow by the slight melt of the afternoon sunlight. It was not strong enough to battle back the cold the previous evening had ushered in, but only enough to grant them a little glimpse of mercy.

They laughed to keep their lungs from freezing.

It was the punishment and reward of the hike. They pushed themselves hard to get through the snow and fight the chill, but as soon as they warmed up and the intensity made them draw in a hard breath, the cold took over again.

Even through the sharp pain, they carried on. It wasn't too much further: the trees ahead should open up and they would see the trail in front of them. If they could only get through the next step and then the next. If they could only keep moving forward before the coating of ice settled over them as well, they'd make it.

They talked to keep their minds from giving up.

Holly growing out of the snow, red berries bright like specks of blood; holly draped on the mantle, red berries bright like tiny ornaments.

The twinkle of the stars appearing just on the edge of the horizon, and the twinkle of lights on tree branches.

A fire they would build when they got to their site to warm their hands and heat instant coffee, and a fire glowing in the fireplace when they got home to warm their hearts and heat slow mulled cider.

Memories from this place that brought them back each year.

They should have started out earlier. They always should have started out earlier. Every year they walked further into the gathering dark as if testing to see if it would actually come. Every year, they laughed to keep their lungs from freezing. Talked to keep their minds from giving up. It was, in its way, a memory. Another tradition.

In a time of year that meant frantic chaos to so many, they made sure this was just about them. The two of them alone carving out two nights just for themselves.

This year, they weren't alone.

They reached the tree line; both felt the rush of relief and hope that came just as the hike seemed too long and worry started to creep in, making them ask themselves if they really knew the slant of the shadows and the arch of the tree branches as well as they thought. If they could have gotten lost.

Maybe that was what happened to the girl on the other side of the trees. She thought she knew better and ended up lost. She had nothing to laugh at, so her lungs froze. No one to talk to, so her mind gave up. But what brought her here? What left the specks of blood around her mouth like holly berries in the snow?

⟳

"Did you touch anything?" the officer snapped.

His face was red like he'd been trudging through the snow for hours, but the smell clinging to him when he stepped out of the passenger's side of the cruiser had come from huddling around a fire with a cup in his hand. A little bit of egg nog with his rum.

He wouldn't tell the precinct if they didn't.

His partner came around the front of the car to meet them. She had brighter eyes and a more focused stare. Ben couldn't help but wonder if she had been sitting behind a desk when the call came in. It was easier to not feel so alone at this time of year when there was an excuse. Telling herself the cot in the back room of the department was the only option to catch a few hours of rest might have felt better than sleeping in a bed alone.

"Detective Simon," she said.

Ben nodded and the first officer closed his eyes briefly like the lids would keep them from rolling.

"Yes, this is Detective Simon, I'm Wheeler, good to meet you. Didya touch anything?" he asked.

It all came out as more of a stream of sound with the occasional accent than multiple words. Ben didn't bother to introduce himself or his wife. The officers likely didn't really care right then anyway. He knew this wouldn't be the only time he would talk to them. They wouldn't see the campsite that year. They wouldn't carve anything to add to their favorite tree.

"My wife put a sleeping bag over her," he said.

This time, Wheeler didn't bother to try to stop his eyes from rolling.

"Shit," he muttered. "Why would she do that?"

"She said she looked cold," Ben said.

"She's dead," he snapped.

"Wheeler, why don't you take a second? Go back to the car and get some more of that coffee into you," Detective Simon said. "I'll take a look."

The older officer looked bitter, resentful of being spoken down to by the younger woman, but there was a look in the back of his eyes that admitted he knew what she was telling him was right. He was too on edge. He needed to get himself together.

He turned away from them and made his way back to the car. The inside was still clinging to some of the warmth of the heater and he wrapped his hands around the tumbler of coffee that was supposed to cut through the fog and bring him into his reality. He tucked his face down to it and drew in deep breaths of the steam to chase the ice crystals out of his blood.

He didn't want to be out here. The quickly dissipating heat wasn't a replacement for what he left for it. The furnace and rum and body heat. If this dragged on, by the time he got back, all would be gone but the furnace. That wasn't enough. Not even with the curtains pulled tight across the windows to block the colors of the lights from across the street.

Out of the corner of his eye, he watched the young detective follow the hikers toward the stand of trees a short distance away. By the description they gave, he could imagine what they were going to see on the other side. He'd join them when the joints of his hands loosened up and the heat was gone. He'd follow the footsteps they'd already cracked into the snow and listen to the details Detective Simon had already collected. He hoped it was over quickly. He didn't want lingering loose ends. He preferred a tidy end to the year.

⌒

The couple moved closer together as they walked toward the trees until they were pressed together, walking almost like one person. Detective Simon followed behind them. Never put your back to anyone at a crime scene. That was one of the first things she'd learned when she'd put on the uniform. It didn't matter where she was or what she thought she was handling.

Never trust anyone. Never make assumptions. Never think you know everything that's happening in any situation.

She still had the faint scar along the bottom of her belly and her hipbone as a reminder.

But that was the only scar she allowed it to leave. It wasn't going to darken her, to take away her motivation for taking up the gun and badge in the first place. She learned her lesson from that day and let it change the way she handled her daily interactions, but she didn't want it to take away why she was there. Not everyone she encountered was inherently brutal. She had to remind herself of that. To believe it.

After she sent Wheeler away, she got the names of the couple. Ben and Laura. Sweet and simple, just the way they seemed to be. They clutched hands through thick gloves and occasionally glanced over at each other like they just needed the reassurance.

Detective Simon swallowed down her disappointment at Wheeler so she could be present for the couple. They called for help and she needed to give that to them. They didn't need her to be preoccupied with the way her partner was slowly spiraling away. They'd only worked together for a handful of months; she knew that meant she didn't know him well. There was plenty about him she'd never heard; questions she had that she hadn't even asked, much less gotten the answers to.

But that didn't stop her from being frustrated at him that night. He was on call. He knew what that meant. She stayed at the precinct when she was expected to be available, and sometimes when she wasn't. The second she was needed, she was there.

Wheeler disappeared as soon as he could. He waited for a phone call. Sometimes more than one. It had gotten worse as the weeks passed. Not bad enough to be relieved of his position, but enough to create the edge he could very easily fall on.

That night he appeared with frustration in his eyes and anger on his tongue. He didn't appreciate being dragged away from his festivities. He denied the burn in his breath. But it was the way he lashed out at Ben, a young man wanting his help, that made her send him to the car. That wouldn't help anything. It wouldn't make this any easier for any of them.

As she walked toward the trees, she wondered if she'd made a mistake.

Wheeler wasn't in the state of mind to handle a body in the snow, but he was another person. He was another set of eyes and another set of hands. She hadn't turned her back, but she had made herself vulnerable.

Detective Simon didn't show a moment of hesitation. She still wanted to believe they only needed help and that she could offer it to them. So she followed. She kept her hand close to her radio and her awareness sharp, but she followed.

It was the first time in her career she felt relief at the sight of a body.

Her stomach would later turn at the thought.

A dark green sleeping bag covered the body, but the shape was unmistakable. It told her the person beneath was fairly small, but definitely the size of an adult. Ben and Laura stopped in front of her and she stepped up beside them.

"You said it's a woman?" she asked.

They both nodded.

"Yes," Ben said.

"And other than covering her, you didn't touch her or change anything?"

"No," Laura shook her head. "I'm sorry I covered her. I just couldn't bear her lying there like that."

The detective nodded but didn't say anything. She understood the compulsion to cover the woman, to preserve her dignity, and in a way, protect her from the elements. But the truth was, having that sleeping bag over her was a problem. That one simple gesture changed the entire investigation. Now everything they found on the body or in the area had to be analyzed through the lens of that intrusion.

"Did you notice any kind of injury?" she asked.

"No," Ben said, shaking his head the way his wife had. "But we didn't look too closely. It seems like she might have just gotten lost and the snow got her."

That reply struck Detective Simon as strange. She hadn't expected him to offer up his own explanation for what might have happened to the woman.

6

"Why would you say that?" she asked.

"Just look at her," Ben said.

She took pictures of the sleeping bag first. It was part of the investigation now and needed to be documented. Right at the moment, she had no idea what had happened or how the woman had ended up there in the remote location. It very well could be just what Ben said: an unfortunate accident caused by the elements. But they could never set that in stone from the beginning. Deaths like this always had to be considered suspicious.

Guilty until proven innocent.

Homicide until proven otherwise.

She asked the couple to step back. Even with the discomfort and fear in their eyes, there was a second of hesitation. They'd become protective of her. Simon waited until they were a few feet away, but still in front of her so she could see their every move and reaction. She took hold of the corner of the sleeping bag and pulled it back, revealing the body for the first time.

Pale blue eyes stared up at the sky as the last of the light died around them.

Detective Simon took out her flashlight and swept the beam over the woman. The long skirt tangled up around her exposed thighs made her shiver. Slim arms lay bare on the ground to either side. It almost looked like a moment of summer printed on a sliver of glass and laid over the winter night.

This woman should have been lying among wildflowers with a warm breeze sliding along her legs and rustling through her thick dark hair as she searched for shapes in the soft clouds drifting overhead—not sinking into snow with the last thing she saw now only stars reflected in her eyes.

The rustle of boots in the snow brought her attention away from the body long enough to see Wheeler making his way toward them. He walked with determination, focused on nothing but the scene in front of him.

"CSU on the way," he announced. "What do we got?"

Simon didn't know what happened to him in the time he was sitting in the car alone, but he had changed. The fog was gone, the angry edge put aside. He'd packed up whatever was going on within him and put it somewhere where it couldn't affect him. She had no doubt it would come back. She didn't know when or how it would show itself, but it hadn't dissipated into nothingness. But she was thankful for the reprieve. All that mattered now was finding out who this woman was and what happened to her.

"Female, white. Appears to be in her late twenties or early thirties," Simon told him. "No obvious signs of trauma. Small amount of blood coming from her mouth."

Wheeler looked down at the woman's body, then snapped his attention up to Ben and Laura.

"And you two just found her here?" he asked. "Just like this?"

"Yes," Ben nodded.

"What are you doing out here? This place ain't near anywhere," Wheeler demanded.

"It is," Laura replied. "There's a campsite in the middle of the next tree stand."

"A campsite?" Wheeler asked, the disbelief in his voice far from hidden. "You make it a habit of coming out in the middle of the night to sleep in the snow?"

"Yes," Ben answered. "As a matter of fact, we do."

The sweet simplicity that was there when she'd first started speaking to him was melting away under Wheeler's harshness. Lemon juice on cotton candy.

"We camp here every year," Laura added. "The same dates."

"Our first trip was the year we started dating," Ben told him. "There's a tree in the campsite with carvings from every year if you need proof."

Simon watched Wheeler straighten up, his spine hardening at the resistance. He wanted to cast suspicion on the couple. He wanted there to be something nefarious about them being out in the cold field on a late December night.

It was like he didn't see the packs on their backs. The sleeping bag tossed aside. The familiarity in their stances as they stood without fear even in the dark. This was a place they knew. He just didn't want to see it. That was the way he was. Wheeler wanted things done fast. He liked them smooth. Above anything, he hated to be fooled. Even without knowing him for long, Detective Simon knew that. He despised people trying to get something over on him or missing what was right in front of him.

In a way, it was an admirable and beneficial quality. She'd seen even hardened cops fall victim to an unassuming suspect. But it could almost drill him deep into something that wasn't there.

Before he could launch into them again, the detective leaned down and rested a hand on the woman's arm. It confirmed the suspicion the faintly blue cast created.

"Wheeler, she's frozen," she said. "There are blades of grass in her hand. She's been here a while."

∽

"Any luck?"

Detective Simon walked up to Wheeler's desk, sipping her way through her fourth cup of coffee. She put one next to him and he gulped it down as fast as he could without trying to taste it. It was only heat and bitterness at this point. He didn't bother with the sugar or noxious powdered creamer. All he cared about was getting the caffeine into his blood so he could keep going. It had pushed him through nearly two straight days. It needed to get him a little further.

"Nothin'," he sighed. "No ID on her. No cases that fit her description. The news ran that sketch, but none o' the tips that came in panned out."

"Did you hear that one of them claimed she was Lisa Marie Presley?" she asked.

"Did she die before or after the time machine brought her from the nineties?"

"By the clothing, I'm going to go with after," Simon said.

Wheeler nodded. "Well, that was our most promisin' lead so far. Accordin' to everythin' else, this woman plain don't exist."

He knew that wasn't really the case, obviously. She was someone. She had a name. A past. A wasted future. This woman was born to someone. She likely had friends and family. There was no ring on her hand or line that showed there once was one, so she probably wasn't married. But she'd been beautiful. She still was, even coated in ice crystals. There was someone out there who missed her.

But so far, they hadn't been able to find any link between the body left in the snow and the world of the living that kept churning on. He finished the coffee and took another bite of a breakfast biscuit far past its prime.

He wiped his fingers on his pants and reached for a copy of the sketch that had been distributed to the local news stations. There was a good resemblance to the body lying on the slab in the morgue. The planes of her face were slightly off, but the dark hair hung around it like it had in the field. The sketch made her lips too thin and her eyes too close together. It was as if the artist wanted it to be recognizable, but didn't want to make her look too pretty.

It was a strange phenomenon he'd witnessed many times through his years of service. Artists always had to use their discretion when recreating the face of the dead. Sometimes they had very little to go on and had to rely on their knowledge of physical structure as well as cultural and social cues suggested by details of the body or the crime to make predictions about what the person looked like in life.

But even when they were more or less just drawing what they saw, there was a tendency to create an image more attractive than reality. Maybe it was a compulsion to honor the dead or maybe it was the artist's own vanity, not wanting to seem as though they didn't have the skill to create art.

But then the opposite also happened. Beautiful people made plain. As if instead of not wanting to offend their memory, they didn't want to exploit them.

It didn't matter why it happened or what kind of misguided intentions went into it. These were the kinds of inaccuracies that drove Wheeler crazy during investigations. He wished they were allowed to just show the actual pictures when the victims weren't decomposed or badly damaged. But it was considered too traumatic, too ghastly and inappropriate.

Murder was ghastly. Murder was traumatic and inappropriate. But they had to show manners. They had to be polite.

Even if it meant identities were never uncovered. Secrets were never found out. People remained just bodies in the morgue.

But that wasn't the case with this one. As much as he believed a shock was sometimes exactly what was needed in a murder investigation, this time the sketch—along with details about her age, her size, and where she was—should have been plenty to have someone recognize her. Again, she was beautiful. She was young, but not the age of a childish runaway. She was well-kept, healthy, unblemished. This wasn't someone cast aside by society. She wasn't forgotten.

Her clothes weren't right and the blood on her mouth was still a mystery, but this wasn't a victim who should go unnoticed. Her not being identified meant something. He just didn't know what.

"How about the tattoo?" Simon asked. "When do you want to release that?"

"Not yet," Wheeler said. "I want someone to tell us who she is first."

"But that's a pretty unique tattoo. I don't think I've ever seen one exactly like it. Maybe that's the piece of information someone needs to know it's her," she said. "It could help get her identified."

Wheeler shook his head. "No. There's enough out there already. Someone knows who she is, they just ain't tellin' us. I want someone to mention that tattoo to me. If someone can tell us she's got a giant mermaid all up her back, we'll know we're onto something."

Three more weeks passed and there was still nothing. No name. No hint at who she might have been. No suggestion of why she was out there. Detective Simon buried herself in the tips sent in about the woman. There had to be something they missed. Someone said something or did something they weren't thinking about. Something that seemed right or inconsequential at the time. She just needed to find that one little thing and figure out what it meant.

Paper coffee cups piled up in the corner of her desk. Notes she'd started and tossed away in frustration filled the basket beside her and tumbled out onto the floor. But she didn't stop. She had to keep chasing.

It sounded like the ultimate cliche, a phrase she used to think detectives used to dramatize a case. Whether they wanted to bring more attention to the case or to themselves didn't matter. They said the same thing.

They felt a connection.

Sometimes it came with an explanation. They had children the same age. The couple that was murdered reminded them of themselves and their spouse when they were young. They went to the same school. They had a similar name.

Others didn't have the explanation, so they came with more vague descriptors. It was a mysterious connection. Or a strange one. Sometimes a spiritual one. Often unexplainable.

Simon didn't put a lot of stock into those. It wasn't that she was cold or unfeeling toward them. She hadn't slipped so far as to become as jaded as Wheeler. It was that she wanted to think every case was meaningful and important. Every victim was a person whose story deserved to be told. She didn't want to think that she would somehow start to play favorites or get more wrapped up in any one situation than any other.

But she had.

She'd let this woman get under her skin. There was something about her. Simon couldn't exactly place what it was, but it was enough to make this woman all she could think about. She wanted to know who she'd been and why she'd been there in the snow, not dressed for the cold weather around her, lost and forgotten.

She wanted to know what the mermaid tattoo meant.

They'd gone through every missing person report for the surrounding area, and when they'd found nothing, they continued to expand until they were scouring departments on the other side of the country, desperate to find something that matched her. But there was nothing. No reports of anyone missing even close to matching her description.

No one had reported her missing. People knew she was gone. They had to. She didn't fit the profile of the women who went unnoticed, the ones who were able to slip out of view and never surface again. Those women existed. It was horrible to think about, but it was true.

Everyone wants to believe that every human life is valued. It should be an inherent right as a person, a simple reality born purely out of the merit of being human. By coming into this world, a person should have worth and importance, and there should be others who uphold that worth and reflect it back to them. No one enters this world alone and they shouldn't walk through life alone.

As a concept, it's sound. It means every person was significant. It creates the sense of safe surroundings even in dark moments, like the world isn't truly as empty and hopeless as it could feel.

It doesn't always work out that way. The facade is beautiful. The structure behind it is flawed.

Some people are invisible. They could be there or not, it wouldn't really make much of a difference. It's usually easy to identify them. Just as it's easy to identify the ones who aren't like them. The visible ones. The loved. Or at least the known.

This woman was one of them. She was not invisible. There was someone out there very aware they were no longer seeing her.

But they hadn't said anything. Something was stopping them from reporting her missing.

Simon felt like she was losing her grip until she went back to the beginning. Rather than continuing to try to push forward, she went all the way back to the call that came in to emergency services and went from there. It brought her back to the early hours of their investigation when they'd barely started canvassing the area.

Then she saw it. It had been sitting there the entire time and she had gone past it over and over. Notes from two different officers, stuffed away in rambling statements. Two people who saw the woman before she was found. She gathered the papers and stalked over to Wheeler's desk.

"Why haven't we looked into this more?" she asked.

He glanced at the papers. "Into what?"

"The missing woman. The officers who canvassed the area asked around at all the nearby businesses. Two of them reported seeing her a week or two before she was found," she explained.

He didn't look impressed or even like the words meant anything to him.

"No. They saw a woman who looked like her at some point before she was found," he countered. "They didn't know for sure if it was her, couldn't tell us who she was, and didn't have any idea why she was around."

"That's not true," Simon replied. "Both of these men own convenience stores within a five-mile radius of where she was found. Both of them were able to clearly identify her as a customer who came in, and both of them were positive it was her because of her strange behavior. They both said that she came in seeming out of it and confused. Both of them said she asked for directions to the prison. She said she was going to see a friend there."

"So there was a woman ramblin' her head off at a convenience store, another store owner heard about it an' reported the same thing," he shrugged.

"They reported it in separate instances far too close together for either of them to know what the other was saying. It wasn't the same store or the same person. It was two completely different places."

"Yep," Wheeler said. "Two different locations of the same chain."

"What?" she asked.

"Look at the names of the stores. They were two different locations of the same chain of stores. The owners are brothers. You don't think it's at all possible that one of them could have had some woman come in acting strangely and told his brother, who decided he wanted the attention of bein' helpful, so he told the same story?" he asked.

"Even if he did, at least one of them saw her. They were able to describe her clothes and talked about how she was acting. They said that she mentioned the prison over and over. She was going to see a friend. She had a visit coming. But there wasn't any visitation that day."

"You just happen to know that?" Wheeler raised an eyebrow.

"The prison was on lockdown. They hadn't allowed any guests for a month. Anyone who actually had a friend at that prison would know that. Each inmate has a list of approved visitors. Anyone who is not on that list cannot visit. They have to fill out a visit application and have it approved before they come for a visit. That means that woman would have been told the facility wasn't allowing visits at the time," Simon pointed out.

"Maybe she didn't know that. Not everyone's smart enough to understand procedures. Or she might've thought she was too important to follow them. For all we know, she coulda been one of those disturbing women who whore themselves out to inmates through letters, thinking they're gonna win their undying love and devotion when those men are playing them for money on their books and fantasies for shower time.

"On her end, she thinks she has found the man of her dreams and it's just so romantic that they are kept apart by the so-called in-justice system. They trade a buncha sappy nonsense back and forth, she pines for him, she thinks that they are deeply in love. Maybe he even tells her they're gettin' married and when he gets out, he'll be a changed man. She wants to surprise him, so she drives all the way out to the prison for a visit. Only then does she find out they aren't taking visitors, she didn't apply for a visit, she isn't on his list… whatever the case may be. He gushes apologies and keeps her devotion. Or she finally comes to her senses and leaves him. He sweeps her away and moves onto the next desperate woman on Murderers Mingle dot com or whatever the fuck it is. And life goes on," he said.

"Except life didn't go on," Simon fired back. "Not for her. And I saw her. She didn't look like the kind of woman who would get caught up like that and do something that ridiculous. She was too polished."

"Dumb and impressionable comes in all kinds of packaging. I'll admit she don't look like the disposable kind, but do this job as long as I have, you find sometimes it's the ones who look the most like they have their shit together who are actually teeterin' right on the very edge. They focus so hard on making sure they are perfect, they need something to make them feel wild. They need to feel like someone else is in control. After too many of the professional type who bore them to tears and get flustered deciding what kind of wine to have with dinner, they crave a bad boy to light their panties on fire."

"Is that why you didn't look into it?" Simon asked. "Because you thought she was that kind of woman? That she wasn't worth it because maybe he was in love with a prisoner?"

Wheeler looked at her with eyes that could have once held true intensity, but now only held the shadow of it. The look was worn around the edges, like it was getting difficult even to have just that. He was resigned, tired.

"I looked into it," he said. "That's how I knew the men are brothers. I didn't look into it any further 'cause it wouldn't do any good. No credit card, no ID. They didn't see her in a car. What else was there to look into? All those statements did was tell us what we already knew. She existed."

⌒

It took another four weeks to have the papers in his hands. Early in his career, it had always stunned him how slowly things could move. Answers they needed desperately, pieces to the puzzles they were trying to solve, were held like breath on the results of the materials they sent to the lab. From there, it was out of their hands. That was the moment when they had to relinquish control.

They had to give up the grasp they had on the investigation and entrust the next steps to someone else. It was always difficult. The investigation would be rapidly moving forward at full speed, and then slamming into a wall. He'd always hated feeling tethered by having to wait for the results that held the next key to figuring out the truth.

But eventually, they got their control back. Eventually, they could move forward.

And that day had come.

He didn't bother to wait for Detective Simon to read through the findings. He saw the woman's death differently than Simon did and he knew he would see the results differently as well. He read through them a few times to make sure he understood what they said, then got up to go to Simon's desk.

"D-lysergic acid diethylamide," he announced, dropping the folder of results down onto her desk.

The detective looked up at him, surprised and incredulous.

"LSD?" she asked as she reached for the folder.

He nodded. "Her blood was full of it. No wonder she was actin' strange at the corner store. She was on a powerful hallucinogen. Nothing she said made any sense 'cause her mind was scrambled. Then she wandered out into that field, passed out, an' froze over. I really thought that couple had something to do with it, but it looks like she was just a junkie who got on the wrong side of a nasty acid trip."

He started to walk away, but Detective Simon called after him to stop him.

"We still don't know who she is," she said.

"And we probably never will. We got fooled this time, Simon. We thought she was someone who'd be missed, but it turns out, she was just another addict lookin' for her high."

CHAPTER ONE

"**I**'M BACK."

My hand tightens around the phone until my knuckles ache and it feels like I could snap it in half. The voice on the other end slithers into my brain and down my spine. Anger surges through me.

How dare he? How dare he do this?

I end the call and storm back through the door into the reception hall. The music and happy voices fade into white noise around me. My eyes scan the room, piercing into every shadowy corner, behind every support beam. I don't register any of the faces. Like water poured over paint, they all blend together. I'm not looking for any of them. I don't need to know they're there.

I stalk across the room toward a small hallway leading away from the room. Shoving the door open, I confront the dark space. Nothing there. I move on to the space behind the stage, stepping over the crossed and tangled wires on the floor and straining my ears to hear past the buzz of energy from the equipment just beyond the curtain. Nothing.

I move on to the front door where just hours ago, Sam and I walked through, holding hands and beaming at the announcement of our names. We've been married for several days already, but our ceremony was private. Just us and a small handful of the people closest to us.

At least, I thought.

Tonight is supposed to be about joining with our other friends and the members of the community that is so important to us. It's to celebrate us finally getting married. I didn't think anything could get in the way of the joy I was feeling this morning. The pure elation of finally getting to this place in my life. I've been waiting to marry Sam since I was seven years old and now I have it. It's mine.

And I don't take kindly to anyone threatening what is mine.

Pushing through the doors, I take several steps out onto the porch and scan the darkness beyond the building. I force myself to focus, to take in every single detail. I want to see something. I need to see the leaves of a tree shake or hear footsteps. Anything to tell me I'm close.

But it's silent. There's only stillness.

He's here. I know he is. He wouldn't come and leave early. He wouldn't bring someone else into it by having them leave the gift on the table.

This is about me. It always has been.

You look beautiful.

The words twist in my stomach. I loved this dress when I found it. As soon as Sam and I decided we were going to do a private ceremony in Florida and then have a large reception for all of our friends in Sherwood, I knew I needed two dresses. I wanted my ceremony dress to be separate and special, worn only for that experience. The dress for the reception needed to be more about the fun and celebration of the event. This dress was everything I wanted and I couldn't wait to wear it.

Now I just want to rip it off and cast it aside. I don't want the feeling of his eyes on it and to know he was watching me. He isn't supposed to be here. He was never supposed to see me or share this moment with me. He doesn't have the right to have this experience.

But he stole it. He took it for himself without me knowing. He's here. It's the only way that red box could have shown up on the gift table. It's the only way he'd know to call me right as I was opening it. It's the only way he'd know how I look.

He's here. I have to find him. I can't let him take this from me.

I search every corner of the reception hall. I look behind every door and around every corner. I know he's watching me. I can feel his eyes. Every step I take, he can see it. He knows where my eyes are falling and he's able to stay one step ahead. He's letting me chase him. He's somewhere I haven't thought of; the anxiety and anger coil up tighter and tighter within me the longer I search.

Suddenly, there are hands around the tops of my arms. Fingers grip me and my name pulses in my ears. It's his voice. And then it's not. It melts away until I'm in this moment again and I can see. I look at Sam. My Sam. My new husband. He looks directly into my eyes and blocks everything else. He stops the thoughts spinning out of control and forces them to quiet as he holds me in place as much with that stare as with his hands.

"Emma," he says again. "What's going on? What's wrong?"

"He's here," I say.

Something flickers across those eyes. I can see him flipping through memories, the moments burned into his mind like they are mine.

"What do you mean?" he frowns.

I take him by the hand and pull him to the gift table. The red box is still sitting there where I left it. I pick up the framed picture and show it to him.

"I just opened this," I explain.

"It's our wedding ceremony," he notes.

I nod. "Look at the angle. No one was over there. At least, no one we realized was there."

He shakes his head. "You're just on edge. It couldn't have been him. He wasn't there. He couldn't have been. You know that. The fact that this picture is still sitting here is enough to convince me of that completely."

"What do you mean?" I ask.

"Think of the way he operates. He wants your attention. Just yours. He wouldn't just leave something like this sitting around where anyone could see it. Even if he did intend on you finding it and somehow got it here, which I still don't think is possible, he would make sure someone got it out of sight as soon as you walked away from it."

"No," I shake my head. "I understand what you're saying, and in other circumstances, I might agree with you. But that's not what I think is happening here. He's not thinking about anyone else. He wants me to have this. It's a gift, not a taunt."

"Emma," he says, running his hands down my arms gently.

Before he can say anything else, Xavier and Dean appear at the door and notice us standing there. They walk toward us, Dean's expression becoming more curious as he gets closer.

"Is everything okay?" he asks. "Emma, I saw you walking around. What's going on?"

I look at Sam. I can tell he doesn't want me to say anything, but also that he knows there's nothing he can do to stop me. I pick up the picture and hand it to Dean.

"This was sitting on the gift table," I say.

"If you were going to open your gifts, you should have gathered everyone around," Xavier says.

"It's not a birthday party, Xavier," Sam chuckles. "We don't have to open our gifts in front of everyone."

Xavier nods slowly. "Weddings don't involve the same obligatory hell of gift-receiving displays of enthusiasm. Duly noted."

I shake my head, turning my attention back to Dean. "He called me."

Dean's eyes snap to me. I can see in that look he already knows the answer to the question he's about to ask, but he needs to hear it.

"Who?"

Breath slides out of me.

"Jonah."

CHAPTER TWO

"**H**OW THE HELL WAS JONAH AT YOUR WEDDING?" DEAN ASKS through gritted teeth.

"I don't know," I say.

"How did he come here and leave this?" he asks.

"I don't know."

"Why did no one tell you he is out of prison?"

"I don't know, Dean," I snap, my voice getting angrier. "But he took that picture. He framed it, wrapped it up, and left it on my gift table without anyone seeing him. So, either no one has noticed that he's not in his prison cell and just hasn't noticed for probably a week, or they have noticed and just haven't bothered to tell me about it."

"Maybe he's not out," Sam offers. "He could have had someone else take the picture and bring it here. You know how powerful he is, even from prison. There are countless people who would do absolutely anything he said without question, and we've both been so wrapped up in the wedding we might not notice someone who came here to do his bidding."

"Someone would have noticed," Dean replies. "Someone would have noticed an unfamiliar person."

"Just about everyone here is unfamiliar to at least someone here," Sam points out. "It's a wedding. The whole point is bringing together different people."

"It was him," I insist. "He did this himself."

"How do you know for sure?" Sam asks.

"He called me."

His face goes cold. "He called you?"

"Yes," I nod. "I came out here to get some fresh air and noticed the red gift box on the table. It seemed out of place, so I came to look at it. It only had my name on it, which I also found odd, so I went ahead and opened it. The picture was inside and as soon as I opened it, my phone rang. I answered it and it was him."

"What did he say?" Dean asks.

"He said," I take a deep breath and gulp, "'You look beautiful, Emma. I'm back.'"

A wave of uneasiness settles over everyone. Dean and Sam trade a few furtive glances.

"He's back?" Sam asks.

"Yes," I confirm. "That's what he said. 'I'm back.'"

"There you go," Xavier offers brightly, gesturing with his hand like he's presenting the words I just said. "He was letting you know that he came out to bring you a wedding gift, but now he is safely back in prison where he belongs."

"I don't think that's what he meant," I reply. "I think he meant he's back as in he's back in my life, ready to mess everything up again."

"Oh," he sighs. He lets out a breath. "Well, that was all my optimism. I'll let you know if I get another wave."

"It's okay," I tell him. "That was plenty. I don't think this situation really warrants optimism."

"Did you see him?" Dean asks.

"No. I looked everywhere and I didn't see him. I can't believe he's doing this again. He was there. He was at our ceremony, and I didn't know. He came here tonight, around the people I care about, and I didn't know. What the hell else is he going to do? How far would he go to make sure he has our attention?"

"And get us back for putting him away," Dean adds, his voice lowering.

"Sam," I start, looking through the doors at our guests dancing and laughing. They have no idea what's happening. That they may be in danger.

It's a familiar feeling. I look back on moments in my life and feel like I'm seeing myself looking into a snow globe. Into those seconds before horror. I can remember how the people looked. Happy and carefree. Distracted. Focused. Bored. Whatever they were, those last seconds in my memories felt tenuous and fragile because I know what comes next.

That's what I feel like now. I'm watching. All the people who are here are here for me. They are here to share in the happiness Sam and I share, and to celebrate us. Each of them is here because of me. They don't know the danger lurking in their midst. They have no idea someone responsible for the torture and deaths of countless people—of my mother—is among them.

I'm waiting for the moment to shatter.

"Emma, look at me," Sam says, turning me toward him. "Listen to me. This place is crawling with police officers and FBI agents. Let me talk to the guys and let them know what's going on. They'll keep an eye out and make sure everything is secure. Okay?"

I nod and he kisses me, then walks inside. I watch him go over to one of the officers from the Sherwood Sheriff's department where he's sitting at one of the tables sipping a drink. Sam leans down and whispers in his ear. Caleb stands and they walk over to the next table to another officer. Savannah has the same immediate reaction as Caleb and they move on to the next. Two other officers join the group before they go to the side of the room to talk, then fan out.

They don't call attention to themselves. They don't make it seem like they are doing anything different than enjoying the reception, but I know what they're doing. They're doing a perimeter, checking over the surroundings, and making sure they don't notice anything I might have missed.

While I wait, my neighbor Janet from across the street comes up to me.

"Emma," she smiles. "I feel like I haven't had a second with you all night."

I accept the hug she's offering out to me. "It's good to see you, Janet. Thank you for coming tonight."

stress about work. I don't have to think about everything else. I can just relax and be something I don't often get to be.

Normal.

I look forward to a time when those nights are possible again.

Across the room, I see Sam gesturing at me. I join him off to the side where our guests can't hear us. But they can see us. He wraps his arms around my waist and pulls me close so it looks like we're just sharing a moment as newlyweds.

"So?" I ask.

"He's nowhere around here," he whispers. "We checked everywhere and got in touch with the officers still on duty today to make sure they know what's going on. Everything is fine. As I said, he probably came only long enough to drop off the gift and leave, or he had someone here do it."

"Which means one of our guests is doing his bidding," I offer.

Sam shakes his head slightly. "Or one of our guests thought they were talking to your father and took the gift to make it easier on the father of the bride."

"I didn't think of that," I admit.

There was a time when almost no one, including me, knew that Jonah existed. I grew up thinking my father didn't have any siblings at all, much less an identical twin. I only became aware of his existence by digging deep into the recesses of my mind, allowing me to remember the terrifying night my world clashed with his when I was just a little girl. When he came for me and tried to take me away because he believed I was his daughter.

But I didn't remember him. It wasn't until ten years after my father's disappearance, when I thought my mind was slipping because I started seeing him around me, that I learned the horrible truth of who he was and what he was capable of doing.

I've been fighting him ever since.

That fight earned him many lifetimes in prison, and though I knew I would never entirely escape the mark Jonah left on my life, I thought I wouldn't have to deal with him anymore. With him caged, he couldn't continue to torment me and the people I love.

Everyone else believed the same thing. Which meant no one who saw him would question they were actually seeing my father. It had to be Ian. Their minds wouldn't allow them to think of anything else. They wouldn't even consider the friendly, familiar face they saw wasn't the one they knew. They would be so sure, so confident in who they were seeing, they wouldn't even see the scar that differentiates him from his brother.

"Everyone is safe," I say.

It's part a statement, part a question.

"Yes," Sam confirms. "Now, I want you to relax and enjoy the night."

I look at him incredulously. "Are you serious?"

"Yes," he says without hesitation. "Emma, listen to me. Jonah has done enough damage in your life. Don't let him take this from you. From us."

"But…"

"How long have we been waiting for this?"

I let out a long breath. "Our whole lives."

"Exactly. We've been through so much to get here. And whether you want to admit it or not, Jonah got in the way of it happening before."

He's right. On both accounts. Jonah's interference with my life definitely did keep us from getting to this point much sooner. And I really don't want to admit it. Not just because I feel horrible for it, but because I hate thinking he can influence me that much. And that I hurt Sam that much.

"I'm sorry," I say.

Sam shakes his head, cuddling me a little closer again. "You have nothing to say you're sorry about. You did what you had to do. I know that. Probably better than just about anybody in this world, I know that. You took up a burden that shouldn't have been yours when you were far too young to know what to do with it. But you figured it out. And you became the woman you are. Who just happens to be the woman I love more than anything on this planet."

I nestle my head against his broad shoulders. I will never get tired of hearing him say that.

"Even with all of this?" I ask.

"I hope so. I mean, I just promised to spend the rest of my life loving you. Kinda stuck now."

I exhale a soundless chuckle, then wrap my arms around him and tilt my head back to look directly at him.

"You already promised that, you know. When I was nine. We were at the playground. You looked at the sandcastle I made and said that one day we were going to have a house even better than that when we grew up," I tell him.

Sam smiles. "And you asked if we were going to live together. I told you that we were going to get married. We just had to get old enough and we would love each other forever. Then you asked how you could be sure, so I held your hands and we promised each other."

"Forever and ever," I say.

He leans forward for a soft kiss. "And that hasn't changed. It doesn't matter what we had to go through or how long it took us, we got here. And I'm not going to let anything stand in my way of enjoying every single second of knowing you are finally my wife."

I kiss him again, wanting to dissolve away the feeling of Jonah anywhere near me.

"You know the guys at the station got you a shirt that says 'Mr. Emma Griffin', right?" I ask.

Sam grins. "I will wear it proudly."

CHAPTER THREE

I DON'T KNOW HOW LONG WE HOLD EACH OTHER, WORDLESSLY swaying to the music, but it isn't long enough. It could be a lifetime and it still wouldn't be long enough.

Sam plants a tender kiss on my forehead. "Just enjoy tonight," he says. "Relax. Have fun. Savor all the attention from everyone who has gathered around to admire and adore us."

I let out a soft laugh. "I'm not entirely positive that's how wedding receptions work, but I'll go with it. You're right. I've dreamed of this for far too long to let him ruin it for me. Tonight is about us. And that's all I'm going to think about."

Sam takes my hand and we make our way back toward our guests. Bellamy notices and rushes over, one hand holding up the skirt of her dress so it doesn't tangle under her feet. She flashes a grin at a couple of guests as she goes by. I recognize that smile. It's the forced casual one that she thinks looks like everything is just fine, but is obviously a cover for something going wrong.

"Are you okay? Dean told Eric and me. Is everything alright? Did you find out where he is?" she asks.

"Everything is fine for now," I assure her. "Sam's officers and a team of agents searched the building and the surrounding area. There's no sign of Jonah anywhere. The on-duty officers have been alerted, and for right now, that's all we can do. And so, everything is fine."

"Are you sure?" she asks.

"I am," I nod. "I have to be. Jonah exists. That's something I can't get around. As long as he's alive, he's going to be a reality in my life. That doesn't mean I have to let him, or the idea of him, or any of the little minions of his who might still be running around, control me or anything I do. I won't let this slide. If Jonah is out, I will find him. If he escaped, I will make sure he goes back. But tonight isn't for him. It's not about him. It's for me and for Sam. It's for my father and my mother. It's for all of us. We won't let him take it away."

She embraces me in a tight hug.

For the rest of the reception, I savor every moment and make every memory I might never have had.

I have the dances with my father I thought I would never have in the long years I didn't know where he was.

I listen to stories about my mother and smile through tears that are mine to cry and that I wouldn't trade for anything.

I laugh with my best friends, who have all been willing to lay down their lives for me, and who many times I've thought I would never see again.

I watch Xavier and try to see and hear and feel what he is.

I eat far more than I probably should and enjoy every bite.

I slow down and look into Sam's eyes as he feeds me wedding cake, not forgetting even for a second how lucky I am to have those eyes see me the way they do.

The night could continue on for days and I would be happy. But soon Xavier and Bellamy come up to us.

"I think it's about time for the happy newlyweds to say goodnight," Bellamy says.

"We will even continue to suspend our disbelief and pretend tonight is your wedding night," Xavier adds. "Congratulations!"

"Thank you, Xavier."

"Getting out of here sounds good to me," Sam comments. "I think if we stay too much longer the officers are going to put me back on duty."

31

"Yeah," I nod. "We should probably dip out before the agents get it in their minds to start asking me about the case I'm working on."

"Which one?" Sam asks.

I point at him. "Exactly."

"Oh, dear lord, we'd never leave," he laughs.

"Good," Bellamy says. "Come on. We'll get everybody outside with their bubbles and sparklers so you can run out to the car."

"Give us just a minute to say a couple of goodbyes," Sam tells her.

"It is our wedding," I point out. "People kind of have to do what we say. Besides, there's no major rush."

"Xavier and I decorated your hotel room for you," Bellamy blurts out.

"That was supposed to be a surprise," Xavier says in a loud whisper as he looks over at her.

"I thought telling her might encourage her to go," Bellamy fires back in the same whisper. It seems she's picked up Xavier's tendency to use stage whispers in the apparent belief people around him actually can't hear them. We generally humor him.

"When did you do that?" I ask.

"We snuck out during some of the dancing," Bellamy says.

"Sneaked," Xavier says.

"What?"

"Sneaked. You said we snuck. We sneaked."

"Sneaked? That's not right. Is it? That definitely doesn't sound right. Sneaked is not a word."

"Definitely is. According to the language committee at the Oxford dictionary, sneaked is the correct past tense conjugation for the verb 'sneak' when considering said verb as regular. However, in all fairness and full disclosure, they have recently shown flexibility and leeway of which I do not approve and conceded that the verb can also be viewed as irregular, and as such, 'snuck' would be the accepted past tense conjugation," he rambles. "After all, it has been used in informal settings since the 1800s."

Bellamy swings her head over to look at me. "Did I just get considered irregular in comparison to Xavier?"

"I think you did," I say.

"It also makes an appearance in *How the Grinch Stole Christmas* when the dastardly green guy enters the Who homes without welcome. What's troublesome to me about that is the use of an irregular conjugation for that word, but not for others within the same text. Accounting for whimsy and artistic license, it seems to me there would be more adherence to the irregulars. Of course, the use of snuck does help to reinforce the cadence later utilized with 'stink, stank, stunk' and it would be needlessly cumbersome to try to shoehorn 'stinked' in there and have an audience accept it."

I blink and wait for a second, then look at Bellamy. "There it is."

"We went in and decorated a little while ago," she says, carefully avoiding unruly verbs.

"Thank you," I tell her. "That was really sweet of you. I can't wait to see it. We just need to say goodnight to some people and then we'll be ready for our big send-off. It shouldn't make that much of a difference, right? As long as you didn't light anything on fire, there shouldn't be a problem." I start to turn away, then stop and look back at them. "You didn't light anything on fire, right?"

Bellamy shakes her head, but Xavier is looking distinctly uncomfortable. His eyes shift back and forth and he seems to be contemplating the fastest way to get out of the room.

"Xavier?" Bellamy says.

His head snaps over to her. "Hmmm?"

"Did you light something on fire?"

"You put down candles," he admits after a couple of seconds of silence. He says it as if it's a foregone conclusion that if someone places a candle somewhere, it must be lit.

"Oh, no," Bellamy mutters.

"You put down candles?" I ask.

She sighs. "I thought they would be romantic."

"Not if they weren't lit," Xavier says. "Then it just looks like a commentary on their relationship."

"How many candles?" I ask.

"I left matches right there on the table," Bellamy points out.

"I know," Xavier replies. "That's how I lit them."

"How many candles did you put down?" Sam groans.

"And where exactly is 'down'?" I add. "On the floor? The table?"

"When did you do that?" Bellamy deflects, turning the heat onto Xavier.

"When you were doing the rose petals."

"Just give me a surface texture," I say. "Carpet? Laminate?"

"How many candles?" Sam repeats.

"Did you light all of them?" Bellamy asks. "In the sitting area and the bedroom?"

"And the bathroom," Xavier admits.

"Oh, damn," I say.

Bellamy and I hurry toward the small room to the side where I'm supposed to change out of my dress into the getaway outfit she insisted I get even after I pointed out I wasn't really getting away to anything after the reception. Sam and I are spending tonight at the hotel in Sherwood and our honeymoon doesn't start for another four days.

"I added the candles because I thought they would be pretty," she tells me. "I didn't think he would actually light them."

I'm already kicking off my shoes and reaching around to unzip my dress by the time she closes the door.

"You didn't account for whimsy and artistic license," I say.

CHAPTER FOUR

THE HOTEL WAS STILL STANDING WHEN SAM AND I GOT TO IT LAST night. We accepted the well-wishes and congratulations of the staff and other guests as politely but quickly as possible as we checked in and then moved through the lobby toward our room. I was trying to sniff out any signs of carpet singing on the way and was relieved that everything seemed perfectly fine as we approached the door.

Fortunately, when Bellamy and Xavier were talking about decorating the room with candles, they were referring to tealights. Most of the tiny candles didn't make it long enough for us to get there, with only two still managing to hold onto the littlest hint of a glow by the time we opened the door. But there was a very nice trail leading from the door through the sitting area and into the bedroom, where it forked off and also led to the bathroom to sit on the side of the sunken tub.

I have to admit it was beautiful, especially when I envision what it would have looked like with all those little flames actually flickering.

"This seems like a very Bellamy thing to do," I pointed out, showing Sam the few inches of water in the bathtub and sink, both with rose petals floating lightly on top.

I was back out in the bedroom area, starting to unpack the suitcase put there for us earlier, when Sam called out to me from the bathroom.

"Well, Xavier definitely had something to do with it."

"Rose petals in the toilet?"

"Yep."

And that is how we came to decide if we are ever to decide to try our hand at songwriting, our first breakup ballad already has a title.

He's at the heavily laden breakfast buffet filling up a second plate while I sit at a table in a picture window alcove, reading through the texts on my phone. I woke up to a screen full of them. Mostly more congratulations and thanks for having people at the celebration. But also a few from Dean, Eric, and my father checking in on me.

I scroll through them several times, making sure I didn't miss any. I'm waiting for Jonah's name to pop up on one of them. Even though it hasn't been there any of the other times I've gone through the list, it feels like it's going to show up. Like he's going to manage to sneak one in. I hate the creeping feeling on the back of my neck. The way the edges of my awareness now seem like shadows for him to hide in.

Throughout my career, I've taken pride in my observation skills. In my instincts and my ability to detect when something isn't exactly right. I tend to rely on those more than protocol and training in a lot of circumstances. It's gotten me into a considerable amount of trouble over the years, but it has also saved my ass more times than I care to count, so I'm not exactly inclined to change my ways.

But despite those abilities, Jonah got through. He followed me throughout my entire life without me even knowing he existed. Everyone thought he was dead. Deciding it was for the best, my grandparents put all mentions and reminders of him in a room in their attic and sealed it up. I understand why they weren't able to bring themselves to destroy those things. No matter what he did or what he was capable of doing, he was still their child. They still remembered him when he was just a baby and a little boy, well before he tumbled down a dark path. Before my mother came along. Before his mind changed and he started seeing the world as something he could take for himself.

I try not to, but I wonder all the time about what times in my life Jonah could have been there in the shadows, with me completely unaware. My wedding day went by without even a second of me thinking he was there. It was a private ceremony with no invitations sent, no reception, minimal vendors to have any idea what was happening. Yet he found out about it. He was there and none of us knew. What else has he witnessed?

I know there were many years when he was imprisoned and others when he was not in the country. But there were plenty that he was here, lurking just beneath the surface of our perception. My father's disappearance made it more difficult for him to follow me around as much as he once did. Having a replica of Ian Griffin's face made for a convenient mask when moving through my life. It's easy to blend in when you look like you should be there.

But when my father disappeared just after my eighteenth birthday, Jonah lost that protection. My father's face was no longer a part of my daily life, except in the memories and nightmares that haunted me, so he couldn't use it to seamlessly drift in and out of my orbit.

Now I know that was part of the reason my father left. After years of thinking his brother was dead, he discovered he was alive, burning a wide path of pain and suffering everywhere he went. My father left his own life to go to battle against Jonah and Leviathan, the massive network of terrorists aimed at creating chaos and stirring up torment and horror.

I thought I would never get him back. It was the hunt for Jonah that brought him back.

"Anything new?" Sam asks, breaking me out of my thoughts as he comes back to the table.

He's carrying three plates and looks like he's concentrating with everything in him to not drop them as he carefully lowers them down to the table.

"No," I tell him, setting my phone aside. I look at the plates. "Did you leave anything up there?"

"I thought you could use a second round and I didn't want my new bride to have to get up and get it," he says with a grin.

"Ah," I grin as I pick up a fork and spear a strawberry from one of the plates. "Is this what they call the honeymoon phase?"

"That starts in a couple days," he says with a wink.

I shift in my seat. "Sam, about the honeymoon."

"No," he replies without even letting me finish the thought. "We're not canceling. We're not delaying. We're not changing anything."

"But until we know what's going on..."

"It doesn't matter what's going on," he counters. "Emma, you're doing it again and you have to stop. You have devoted everything to fighting crime so that you could have a life and protect the ones in it, but you're forgetting to live."

"You make me sound like a superhero," I say.

"Yeah," he nods. "And sometimes I feel like you think you are. You've put the entire world on your own shoulders. You're always willing to put yourself right in the path of any kind of danger that might come your way. You would rather be at risk than know that anyone else could be hurt or harmed in any way. You are incredible, Emma. It's why I love you. It's why so many people love you. But you have to remember to just live. You aren't that angry teenager who doesn't know where to go or what to do anymore. Your life isn't careening out of control. You need to be willing to slow down and see what exists outside of the fight. If there is nothing else, then there's nothing to be fighting for."

I draw in a breath and let it out slowly.

"I know," I admit. "But you said it yourself. He's taken so much from me. I've lost so much to Jonah's bullshit. I lost my childhood. My mother. A decade with my father. Years with you. Greg. A good part of my faith and trust in humanity. So many people."

"But you didn't lose yourself. And you can't. I won't let you lose yourself. I won't lose you. I did tell you yesterday that Jonah has taken so much from you. I also said not to let him take more. I understand that you're upset and angry and frustrated. I am too. But I'm not willing to let go of this experience with you. I've been dreaming of marrying you for so long. And I've been dreaming of our honeymoon for just as long. I want this time with you, Emma. Just you. Just the two of us. Away from everything and everybody. I want to remember what it was like to not have anything to do," he says.

"That sounds really nice," I say.

"And think of it this way. No one knows where we're going except for Bellamy, Eric, Dean, Xavier, and your father."

"No one knew about the wedding, either," I point out.

"There were a lot more people involved there," he says. "This is just us going away together. Those are the only people who know where we're going and what we're doing, and even they don't have all the specifics. We'll be just fine."

"I still don't know," I attempt, but Sam already has an answer for that.

"What's the alternative, then? We stay at home in Sherwood, where he absolutely does know where you are? If anything, we're safer away for a while. It will get us away from the spotlight and allow everyone else to try to catch his trail."

"Alright," I finally relent.

"Alright?"

"Yes," I tell him. "You're right. This is our honeymoon. Jonah is not going to ruin it for us. And you're also right that I don't need to put it entirely on myself."

"Wow," Sam says. "Right about two things in the same conversation. Maybe this really is the honeymoon period."

I shoot him a look while I take a sip of coffee and nibble on the cinnamon roll that's been sitting untouched in the middle of the table. It feels strange eating one that I didn't make. It isn't nearly as good as mine.

"It can't possibly be that we're the only ones who know he's not in prison anymore. Someone else has to have noticed," I comment.

"Speaking of which," Sam says. "We're going on this honeymoon and it's going to be absolutely amazing. But that's still a few days away. Until then, you go to the Bureau, you find out what the hell is going on, and you do everything in your power to find that son of a bitch and make sure he doesn't hurt anyone else."

There's an unsaid implication at the end of his phrase. "And then?" I try to draw it out of him.

"And then you put it down be a newlywed with your wonderful husband," he winks.

CHAPTER FIVE

MY BRIDAL MAKEUP REPLACED WITH A FEW SWIPES OF MASCARA and a coat of lip balm, my hair slicked back into a tight ponytail, and my credentials around my neck, I walk through headquarters with a determined stride. I'm focused directly ahead of me, not paying attention to anyone or anything else around me. People are waving and I'm sure some of them are calling out to me, but I don't stop. They'll have to hold their congratulations and excited shouts of how good it is to see me back.

I'll be able to talk to them later. But for right now, I need to get to the office and find out what's going on.

Eric is already there when I walk through the door. He contained himself well when he found out about Jonah, but I've known him long enough to know when he's swallowing down fury. He's still the interim supervisor at the Bureau after Creagan was taken down, which means he should have been kept aware of anything developing. And Jonah no longer being in prison is definitely something developing.

"Who's going to tell me what the fuck is happening?" I demand when the door hasn't even closed behind me.

Worried, tired eyes come to me. These are the eyes of people I don't know as well as the people at my wedding. I've worked with some of these people and I've encountered others in passing. But I don't care who any of them are. All that matters to me is knowing why I ended up feeling like a truck hit me in the middle of my wedding reception.

"Agent Griffin," Eric says.

He stumbles slightly over saying my name for the first time since I got married. I don't correct him. I feel like it's the perfect reflection of the conversation Sam and I had this morning over breakfast. In my life, away from all of this, I'm Mrs. Emma Johnson, the wife of Sheriff Samuel Johnson. I'm proud of those three letters and will happily use them every chance I get. But when I put the gun on my hip and the shield in my pocket, I stand behind another three.

Here, I am and will always be Agent Emma Griffin, FBI.

"Most, if not all, of you know I recently got married. Saturday night was my reception. While I was trying to celebrate with my friends and family I found out that Jonah Griffin, a maximum-security federal inmate with several life sentences, had not only been there, but at my ceremony days before. Now, which one of you cares to tell me how that could possibly be?" I ask.

Eric doesn't try to stop me. He technically has the authority, but he knows better than to try to get in my way right now. I'm not going to throw my weight around or play the card that if I wasn't tangled up in a complex case also involving Jonah, as well as our former supervisor, Creagan, I would have been the one to take the role. The general consensus is that I will still one day take that position.

That's still yet to be seen. For right now, it's not even on my radar. I have enough to think about, enough to try to untangle. When it is all settled, there might be a decision to make. Until then, I'm more than happy to have Eric in charge. I trust him, quite literally, with my life, and I know he has the skill and intellect to handle the pressure and make the right decisions.

It's not something he wants to do permanently. He joined the Bureau not as a field agent, but as a research and cybercrime expert. He has been indispensable in countless cases, and I have a feeling he looks forward to getting back to his office and losing himself in cyberspace again.

"Sit down," Eric says. "We need to talk about this situation."

I don't want to sit. I am buzzing, the tips of my fingers tingling with energy. I want to pace, to do something. But I lower myself into one of the empty chairs at the conference table. My eyes lock with each of the people sitting around the table. None look happy to see me.

"Alright," I say. "I'm sitting. Now, tell me what's going on."

"It came to the attention of the Bureau that Jonah was not present for an inmate check two days before your wedding," Eric starts.

"Two days?" I ask incredulously. "He was missing from prison for two days before my wedding, a week at this point, and no one said anything to me?"

"You weren't on duty," one of the agents quickly tosses in my direction, like that's going to assuage me.

Somehow he thinks it's going to make me feel better to know they kept this critical news from me because I was on leave at the time of the escape.

"I don't care if I wasn't on Earth," I say, struggling to keep my voice calm and even. Now is not the time to lash out, even if that's exactly what I want to do. "Anything pertaining to Jonah Griffin is information I need to know about immediately."

A couple of the men at the table stammer like they are trying to come up with something to say. Finally, Eric takes a breath and looks at me intensely.

"I take responsibility," he says.

"What?" I ask, confused and a little shocked by the declaration. "You were just as surprised as I was when you heard that he was out. You didn't know."

"Exactly," he nods. "And I should have. As supervisor of this unit, Jonah is under my jurisdiction. The charges against him in Greg's murder case are still pending and he's been tapped for interviews regarding the conspiracies of the Order of Prometheus and the Dragon. Investigation into the scope of Leviathan is ongoing. Anything having to do with him and his movements should have been on my radar and it wasn't. I dropped the ball on this one."

"This isn't your fault, Eric," I tell him. "You weren't here. You took vacation to be with me. That doesn't mean everything here should completely fall apart. I understand Creagan's arrest has sent this place into chaos, but this is inexcusable. Jonah is an unimaginably dangerous criminal with a history of being able to fake his death, move undetected, and manipulate a huge array of people. He was being held in a maximum-security prison. I need to understand what happened and why."

"That's the problem, Agent," one of the men, Zane Melling, says. The others look at him with a hint of admiration for being the one to jump in and say something first.

"What do you mean?" I ask.

"No one knows what happened," he says.

"No one knows what happened," I repeat slowly, making sure I heard the words correctly.

"The prison is investigating his escape, but they haven't been able to figure out how it happened," Eric explains.

"Let me get this straight," I frown. "Jonah is brought to trial for a list of offenses that amounts to the fucking Wilton Gold Box assortment of crimes against humanity and is sentenced to more time than entire civilizations existed on this planet. But the fun surprises didn't stop there and we find out he was all wrapped up with the Dragon and the Order, which led to the murder of a federal agent, Greg Bailey. Because just holding him and torturing him for two years just wasn't enough entertainment. He had to also dangle him around like a cat toy in the sick initiation game with the Order. And after all that, he doesn't feel like he's done quite enough to screw with the world and my life, so he just disappears from prison. No one knows when. No one knows how. No one knows where he is. And to top it off, I wasn't informed either in a victim notification or in my professional capacity."

There are a few seconds of tense, uncomfortable silence.

"Essentially," Melling admits.

I press my lips together and pat the top of the table as I give a single nod of acknowledgment. "Great. Good to know I'm up to speed and we're all on the same page."

I stand up and Eric steps toward me. "Where are you going?"

"To the prison," I say. "They lost Jonah. Now, I get to find him."

"We've been in touch with the prison officials," Zane pipes up as I walk away.

I turn to face him, staying silent as I stare him down, dragging out the moment just too long.

"You've been in touch?" I ask. "Really? So, can you give me a bulleted timeline of Jonah's movements for the days leading up to his escape, the names and records of all staff working for those shifts, details of all disciplinary actions for the last month, and contact information for all outside vendors contracted by the prison for the past year?"

He shakes his head. "No."

"Thank you. So, as I said, I'm going to the prison. Eric, can I assume there is now a task force for locating Jonah and returning him to custody?" I ask.

He nods. "Yes. You have my full support. Any and all resources and manpower you might need are at your disposal."

"Thank you. I'll keep you updated."

CHAPTER SIX

ANYONE REALLY NEEDING VALIDATION AND TO FEEL LIKE PEOPLE are happy to see them should be sure to cross 'working for the FBI' off their list of potential careers. While there are definitely people who are happy when federal agents come in and take over an investigation, and there are plenty of people who are happy when a criminal is apprehended, investigations tend to be chock full of people who cringe as soon as they see that badge.

Such is the case when I walk into the prison. I'm not expecting anything less. They didn't just allow the escape of an inmate. They allowed the escape of a mastermind who arranged for the brutal murders of my mother, her bodyguard Eli, my ex-boyfriend and close friend, and countless others.

I am the stuff of their nightmares.

"Agent Griffin," Warden Cutler starts as I walk into his office. "It's good to see you."

"Somehow, I doubt that is a genuine sentiment considering the circumstances," I reply.

The expression on his face drops. He obviously hoped this would be more civil and we could ease into the more unpleasant talking points in front of us. I really don't have time for that and it's sinking in for him.

"Right," he says, lowering himself into the big chair behind his desk. "Have a seat."

"I don't feel much like sitting right now," I say. "I want to know what happened with Jonah Griffin and why I didn't find out until the day before yesterday. At my wedding reception."

"You what?" he gasps.

"Yeah. He walked into my reception and left a box on my gift table, then called me to make sure I knew he'd found it," I say.

"He had the balls to go to your reception?" Cutler asks as if the meeting is going to turn into a gossip session.

"I'm more concerned about the balls it took for him to escape from the prison on your watch," I fire back. "And why I wasn't notified as soon as the escape was detected."

"The investigation is still ongoing," he starts, heading down the path of the boilerplate statements used to cover just about any situations that might arise.

"Don't give me that," I tell him. "This is me you're talking to. If there's one thing in this world I don't need to have explained to me, it's investigation. I want to know how a situation like this could possibly go to hell this spectacularly."

"We tried to notify you," he defends himself. "Your phone wasn't on."

I'd done my best to unplug and go a bit off the grid while I decompressed from my second visit to Windsor Island and went forward with my wedding. I didn't want my phone ringing nonstop. I didn't check my email. I disconnected. But that didn't mean I was unreachable.

"You could have gotten in contact with my father. He would have relayed the information to me. You could have contacted Eric Hernandez, the interim supervisor and one of my best friends. You could have contacted the Sherwood Sheriff's office, which would have gotten in touch with my husband. This is a man who has proven himself extraordinarily dangerous to me, my cousin Dean, my father, and anyone else who gets in his way. Not informing me he was no longer in custody put my life in imminent danger, not to mention gave him the opportunity to reconnect with his followers, which puts anyone and anything in his path at serious risk," I say.

"I understand the significance of this situation, Agent Griffin," he says. "Remember, this isn't just about you. This is a prison security issue as well. Informing you of the escape is important, but frankly, it was not my primary focus in the time immediately following the correction's officer noticing Jonah was not in his cell. Our first efforts were to locate him, and then when the prison and grounds were thoroughly searched without finding him, we turned to finding out how he managed to escape so that he could be more easily tracked. We did our due diligence notifying local law enforcement and the Bureau, and we did make attempts to notify you personally. I regret they weren't more successful."

"Fine," I say. "I'm here now. Right in front of you. Can't miss me. Notify me."

He looks incredulous, like he's not sure whether I'm being serious. I am. I wait for him to say something, but he just continues to look at me until I widen my eyes and lean my head toward him slightly, showing him I really do expect an answer.

Cutler leans forward, clasping his hands on his desk in front of him.

"Agent Griffin, I need to inform you that Jonah Griffin has escaped custody and is currently at large," he says.

"For how long?" I ask.

"Nine days."

I don't let him see my shudder.

"And why was I not notified earlier? As the primary complainant for several of Mr. Griffin's charges, one of only three living relatives, and the federal agent responsible for his capture, I am entitled to notification of any and all changes to his custody, placement, and status."

"I'm aware and I can assure you, efforts were made to make you aware of the situation. These were not immediately successful and I regret that the chain of communication did break down, resulting in…"

His voice trails off as if he has run out of words and doesn't know how to finish the thought.

"Resulting in him running around unchecked and getting the opportunity to stalk me again without anyone challenging him?" I complete the sentence. "I also want to know why this hasn't been publicized. This man poses a huge threat to the public. He is responsible for large-scale attacks and a list of murders we are still building as we find new evidence. But I haven't seen a single news report about his escape or warning people about him."

"We made the decision not to release the information to media outlets," he says with an effort at finality.

He doesn't want me to ask anything else. He doesn't want me to push it. Around here, he's on top. People don't question anything he says and the decisions are his to make. Unfortunately for him, that doesn't have any impact on me. I'll show him professional courtesy, but the courtesy ends where negligence and incompetence begins.

I'm definitely feeling like we're at that place now.

"You made the decision to allow a sociopathic murderer and terrorist leader to escape custody and go out among a completely unknowing public? To let him freely walk among people who don't know who he is, what he's capable of, and how critical it is to protect themselves from him?"

Cutler stares at me, the muscles at the sides of his jaw twitching.

"I felt it was an important strategic move to keep that information confidential," he replies. "As you've just emphasized, Mr. Griffin is an extremely dangerous, calculating, and connected man. I thought releasing the information about his escape could cause panic, but would also alert those who might be loyal to him and provide him with more assistance. I decided it was better to keep the escape confidential and focus our energy and attention on finding him."

It might sound like good reasoning to some people. But they don't know the full extent of Jonah and the actual implications of staying silent. I don't bother to emphasize this to Cutler. He's stubborn and arrogant. Whatever decision he makes is always going to be right in his eyes. Even if he says he recognizes the flaws, he doesn't really internalize them.

And it doesn't matter, anyway. He might not realize it, but this isn't in his hands anymore.

"How did he get out?" I ask.

The team has already told me they didn't have a clear idea of how

Jonah was able to escape from the prison, but I need to hear it from Cutler. The warden may be able to give me more information than he's already shared with the others at the Bureau. Or he might say something that has significance they don't immediately recognize. But the look on his face isn't giving me a tremendous amount of confidence.

"We don't know," he answers.

"That's it?" I ask. "You don't know?"

"Yes," he says. "He was present for inmate counts and reported for his work detail. By all reports, he was accounted for at all points throughout the day before his escape. The next morning, he was not there for the count."

"How long were there no eyes on him?" I ask.

"Somewhere between twelve and sixteen hours," he says.

"How could there possibly be such a big gap if he was accounted for at all points?" I ask.

"The last inmate count of the day was after dinner. There was optional programming in the evening and then lights out. The next count was not until the next morning after breakfast. The guard assigned to his block thinks he saw him returning to his cell after the evening programming, but is not completely positive. He didn't see his face clearly and didn't scan his identification band."

"So, he didn't just escape from the prison. He quite possibly escaped from a locked cell after lights out," I say.

"We're trying to figure out how he did it."

"I suggest you try harder." I stand up. "I will be back. I want to be able to see the cell, everywhere Jonah would have had access to, and any evidence you actually do have. Are you going to make that difficult for me?"

"No," he says. "The prison will cooperate with any Bureau investigation."

"That's a good choice."

CHAPTER SEVEN

"**U**P TO SIXTEEN HOURS," I SEETHE, FLATTENING MY HANDS ON THE conference table in front of me. "He could have been out for up to sixteen hours before the prison even noticed he was missing. And that's if Cutler is telling me the truth."

"You don't think he is?" Eric asks. "Do you think he's hiding something?"

"At this point, everything is still a possibility. He wasn't acting like he knew more than he was telling me. He actually seemed humiliated that I was confronting him about it. But that doesn't necessarily mean he isn't playing us. We both know how well Jonah can manipulate. If he got under Cutler's skin…" my thought drifts off and I shake my head. "No. I don't think that's what's going on here. I don't think Cutler is smart or conniving enough to act the way he was if he was covering for Jonah. He was pissed. And embarrassed. He was definitely not happy to see me there."

"Well, that's not all that unusual," Eric comments.

I glare at him. "You're so sweet."

"Hey, if I had allowed Jonah to escape from prison on my watch and hadn't let you know for more than a week, I wouldn't be happy to see you, either."

"Fair enough." I let out an exasperated sigh and straighten up. "He's been out nine days. Nine. Do you have any idea what he could do in that amount of time?"

"Yeah," he says solemnly. "I do."

I nod, starting to pace back and forth across the conference room we've turned into a war room for the Jonah task force. As soon as I got back from the prison, I requested files from the records department and set up residence in the conference room. I only have four days before it's time to leave for my honeymoon and I need to make the most of it.

"The prison officials have gotten nowhere since he got out. They still don't have any idea how he managed to escape, and if they don't even have that, they aren't going to have a place to start to look for him," I say.

The two other agents sitting at the table watch me carefully. They haven't said a word. It's probably for the best. At this moment, I have no need for their input. They are bodies. Labor. The task we have ahead of us is going to take work, and as much as I'd like to handle it all, I know I can't. There's only so much I have the physical capability of doing with the restraint of time and available resources. That means to get this done I'm going to need boots on the ground, and these men are those boots.

"We don't know how he escaped, either," Eric points out. "We have no idea how he got out or where he could have gone. We don't know anything more than Cutler does. So, where do we start?"

"That's the thing. We do know what he doesn't know," I reply.

"What?" Eric raises an eyebrow.

"Cutler knows Inmate Griffin. Number 98559083. We know Jonah."

He nods. "Yes, we do."

"So, we start there. The first thing we need to do is to make it as hard for him as possible to move around," I say.

"Don't we want to capture him?" Zane asks.

I stay silent for a few seconds, reminding myself he hasn't been a part of an investigation involving Jonah before this. He really might not understand what we are up against.

"You don't set out to capture a wild animal with the first goal of getting a chain around its neck. First, you have to close it in," I tell him.

Eric tilts his head to the side to look at me. "You were channeling Xavier with that one."

"Who is Xavier?" Zane asks.

Eric and I look at each other. There's really no clear way to answer that question.

"He's a member of Agent Griffin's family," Eric finally says, bringing a smile to my lips.

That is exactly who Xavier is.

"Does he say things like that a lot?" Zane asks.

"He's essentially a human fortune cookie. Crack him open and a whole bunch of little strips of paper would go falling out all over the place," Eric says.

That is also exactly who Xavier is.

"My point is, yes, obviously we want to find Jonah and bring him back to prison. But we can't just have that as our only aim. It's not going to be that easy. Maybe with other escapees. Maybe with other criminals. Not with him. We have to use what we know about him to control what he does while he's on the outside and close in on him until we're able to capture him and bring him back. That means recognizing who he is," I say.

"He's Jonah Griffin," Zane says.

Eric is looking at me with heaviness in his eyes.

"No," he says. His voice changes. He's only talking to me now. "He's Lotan."

I give a single nod.

"Leviathan is alive and well. Jonah going to prison didn't stop the devotion of his followers. I'm sure some of them were able to wake up and leave the cult behind, but for every one of them, there are likely half a dozen others who are just as devoted to him or even more. That means he has the world at his disposal."

"If he's really that powerful and has that many resources, it's going to be impossible to find him," Zane says. "He got out of prison. I doubt he wants there to be any chance of going back. He's going to disappear into the vapor."

"Maybe other people. Not him," Eric tells him. "He's going to do everything he can to stay out of reach, but as long as Emma exists, he's not going to fade away completely."

"And Dean," I add. Eric nods. "So, we go back to basics. Contain him. We know he has a lot of options, but we take as many from him as we possibly can. We need to get in touch with the travel administration and make sure his name and description are on every list we can get him on. If he tries to use any type of mass transit, planes, trains, boats, someone needs to notice and stop him.

And we'll need to have my father use his contacts to put failsafes into place. If Jonah tries to use his identity to use transportation or if he comes in contact with law enforcement, there needs to be something in place to alert them that it is Jonah. We can't rely on any type of picture identification or customary documents. Jonah is a master at falsifying that type of information. By now he probably has an entire assortment of documents that make it seem like he's Ian Griffin rather than Jonah Griffin."

"They can probably establish a code," Eric says. "Secure passcodes are used in all kinds of situations for clearance. They'll set a code that only Ian knows and that will be required for anything that uses his identity."

"Perfect. I'll call him. You get on the phone and get him on the lists for every airline, rail, boat, hot air balloon, anything you can think of. Stop him from having easy access to travel."

"I'm on it."

"What can we do?" Brad, the second agent at the table, asks.

"Start calling hotels," I say. "Identify yourself as Bureau agents and ask if Ian or Jonah Griffin have checked into the hotel or have reservations. Then tell them if they get a reservation for either of those names, flag the account and get in touch with us."

"Which hotels?" Zane asks as I head for the door aiming for the records room.

"Start in the heart of D.C. and work your way out," I tell him.

"How big a radius?"

"The Continental U.S. We'll go from there."

CHAPTER EIGHT

E VEN THOUGH YEARS SEPARATE ME FROM GREG'S DEATH, SEEING HIS handwriting still sends a chill through me. I know so much of the reaction is because I still haven't gotten the chance to fully grieve and move on. There have always been questions. New details coming to light. New pain and anger to add to the layers that started building the day his body was found on the beach after he disappeared from the hospital.

He was my friend and he was murdered. That should be enough to allow me not just to grieve for him, but eventually be able to move past it. But it isn't that simple. Greg was my friend—and was once something more—but he also became one of the biggest mysteries of my career. He became the case that has followed and haunted me.

I've only just uncovered the truth about how he died, but I know there are secrets I may never fully uncover. I might never know everything that happened to him over the years Jonah kept him captive. I may never know everything he was forced to do and what he might have witnessed and gone through. Part of me is glad for that. I already know so much. I've already borne witness to some of the horrors he endured. I don't really want more of that in my mind.

And yet there's another part of me that feels like I owe it to him to know everything. Not just because Jonah and Creagan deserve to pay for everything they did, but also because Greg chose to be brave. He could have left. He was offered a chance to escape and instead he chose to stay so he could continue his own fight. Because of that, we know as much as we do about Leviathan. Lives were saved. Horrific acts of violence that could have wreaked havoc and caused extensive destruction never came to pass.

He offered up his life and saved so many innocent people. He took the hard way, not the easy way, and helped strike a heavy blow into a vast criminal network. I have the chance to continue the fight because he was brave.

The very least I can do to repay him is ensure that Jonah doesn't slip through our fingers.

And I'll start again where my knowledge of Jonah began. With Greg.

During his time in the hospital after being dragged back from the edge of death, he wrote out notes about everything he could remember from the time he was held. He described the places he stayed and where Jonah brought him. He wrote lists of names and aliases. There were sparsely drawn maps and pages of bullet points, many of which he was never able to explain to us.

He wrote them down as the thoughts came to him, but there was too little time. I didn't have the chance to talk through everything with him, so much of what he wrote down remains a mystery. It's a code I return to occasionally to see if anything stands out to me.

Every time I learn something new or a piece of evidence comes up, I compare it to what he wrote down in hopes there will be a word or a hint that will just click and everything will unfold. So far, that hasn't happened. But that's where I am today: with everything he wrote spread out on the conference table in front of me.

There are a couple of notepads, but most of it is on loose pieces of paper tucked into acetate sleeves to protect them from fingertip oils and wayward spilled coffee. I have a fresh notebook in front of me and a pen poised, ready to write down anything that comes to mind.

"We need to find as many of these locations as we possibly can," I announce to the group. "These are all places Jonah held Greg, which means they are places important to Leviathan. We need to figure out what and where they are, and go to them to see if they are still being used. Identify their use, clear them if needed, and secure them."

"If he's hiding out, do you think he'll go back to the places where he's already known to have been?" Zane asks.

"People are creatures of habit. Even if they don't realize what they are doing, they tend to follow the same patterns and return to what is comfortable to them, especially during times of stress or challenge. Knowing a place or action or tendency well enough means it's one more thing that their mind doesn't have to process or focus on, so they can put all of their energy and concentration into other things. It's one of the reasons why you see the concept of an MO with serial killers.

"The same method of killing, the same type of victim, the same general area. Sometimes it's an intentional thing—a signature or a message—but a lot of times it's just because those are the things that the killer is comfortable with.

"I don't honestly believe he's feeling much stress or anxiety right now. He would have to have far more normalcy and humanity for him to feel those things. But he does know that he doesn't want to go back to prison and it's an annoyance to him to have the authorities pursuing him. Going back to the places he knows would be convenient, comfortable, and easy. It's also just a compulsion, something that comes to mind without thinking about it.

"And even if he doesn't return to one of these locations, we need to be there. If his followers are still out there, they need to see uniforms, badges, and guns. They need to be aware that we know where these places are and are watching them. If his followers are still in any of these locations, our presence there will flush them out. The fewer safe places they have, the more nervous and vulnerable they become," I say.

"And unpredictable," Zane says.

"Yes," I respond. "Hence the guns." I look at each of the men in the room. "I make no promises that this is going to be easy. In fact, I'm much more inclined to promise this is going to be hard as hell with the potential of being one of the most dangerous cases you've been involved in during your career. Jonah is not your average criminal. He's not to be underestimated. One of the most important things to remember about him and that he doesn't think he's done anything wrong."

"Most criminals don't," Brad points out.

"That's not true. The vast majority of criminals you'll encounter have a clear understanding of the difference between right and wrong. They just choose to do wrong. There are also those who don't know what they're doing is wrong, but also don't claim that it's right. They believed they were forced or called by a higher purpose to commit their crimes. They're not culpable for them in the same way because they didn't choose to do them of their own volition.

"Jonah is different. He is among a much smaller segment of criminals who truly feel justified and righteous in what they do. Jonah believes in the mission of Leviathan. He understands that chaos and destruction cause pain, but he believes that's what the world needs in order to continue to function. His philosophy is that without danger and turmoil, without the unpredictability of disaster and the brutality of sudden and unexplained death, that there can be no compassion and happiness.

"He believes in power and control. He believes himself to be an arbiter of society; that society will be happier and more fulfilled rather than going through life asleep and unfeeling. In ancient mythology, Leviathan is a sea monster, one of the servants of the sea god Lotan, described as the head. There is a theory in political philosophy that when the entirety of a group of people agree to submit to the leader as their sovereign, following their rule without question in all things in exchange for security and a peaceful existence, they become the body of the being with their ruler as the head. It's called a Leviathan.

"Jonah twisted those concepts and created his own version of them. He creates chaos so people will appreciate peace. He shows his power by causing destruction and mayhem, but also stopping it."

"That is one fucked-up interpretative leap he took," Zane mutters.

"Yes," I nod. "Yes, it is. But it's one he believes in wholeheartedly and will stop at nothing to defend. He believes that anyone who comes up against him is an enemy to his vision of beauty, to the creation of the body of Leviathan. He will destroy anyone and anything he thinks stands in the way of him achieving that. Then justify it to himself and to everyone who will listen to him as doing righteous work."

"Why does that matter when it comes to finding him?" Brad asks.

"Because he's going to go back to his work. And he won't just disappear. He can't bring himself to do that because it would mean separating from me again. He won't do that. His fixation on Dean and me will never go away. We are part of his plan and he will continue to pursue us. He's already reached out to me. He will use every resource and connection he has to make sure he can continue his plans without being detected. When he feels threatened, horrific things happen. So, we don't go for him directly. We move around him. We narrow down his world until he's trapped."

"Where's our first stop?" Eric asks.

"I'm going to get in touch with some people in Feathered Nest. I doubt he's going to go there. It's too obvious. But just in case, I want to let them know what's going on. The new police chief isn't as familiar with everything, so he's going to need a bit of a rundown to get up to speed. Eric, I need you to get in touch with the Crystal Valley police department. Greg spent part of the time he was with Jonah in a house there.

"When he still thought Jonah was my father and he was being treated well, he lived with some of the other members of the group in a white Victorian with black shutters. He didn't write down the address, but he described the area. Take that information and find the house. It needs to be searched."

"You never found that house before?" Zane asks.

"No," I say. "There were other locations that took precedence. Particularly, the scene where Greg's body was dumped. We've identified some of the other locations and they've been secured already. We'll have to go back through them, but we can't skip anything. I didn't think it was as important to find this house because it wasn't one of the locations where Greg was held captive. Now I realize that was an oversight. I should have focused there since it was the first place he went."

"You can't change it, Emma," Eric says. "We do it now."

CHAPTER NINE

"**W**HAT DID I DO TO DESERVE YOU?" I ASK WITH A SIGH AS I SINK down onto the couch and accept the cup of hot coffee Sam presses into my palms.

"Tried to kill me by bouncing a ball in front of my bike," he says. "And failed."

"Well, I guess it worked out for me, anyway," I say. I lift my face up to him for a kiss. "Thank you."

"How did everything go today?" he asks.

I take a sip of the coffee and hold it in my mouth for a second. I love the heat of it. The strong, bitter taste washes away all my stress and my body relaxes. Some people only reach for the java first thing in the morning to get their bodies moving and their brains pumping. Coffee both wakes me up in the morning and calms and soothes me in the evening. I'm convenient like that.

"Jonah isn't back in prison, so not great," I admit.

"You didn't actually think you were going to be able to find him that easily, did you?" he asks.

"No," I say. "But a girl can dream." I let out a sigh. "We're casting a wide net. No pun intended. Once I got back from the prison we spent the rest of the day making sure he can't travel easily using his or my father's identities and alerting as many hotels as possible so if he tries to make a reservation, we'll know about it. I spent far too much time on the phone with the police chief in Feathered Nest and dug through Greg's notes trying to identify any locations and people I could. Eric is getting a team together to go to Crystal Valley tomorrow to search for the house where Greg went first with Jonah."

"Does that mean you're letting him take over the investigation?" Sam asks. I swing a look in his direction and he shrugs. "A boy can dream, too."

"I still have three days before our flight leaves," I defend myself. "There's a lot I can do in that amount of time."

"I have no doubt about that," Sam says. "But I hope you're penciling in at least a little bit of sleep at some point."

"I will," I say.

"Considering it's almost three in the morning and you just got back, I don't have a whole lot of faith in that statement."

There are several containers of takeout from my favorite Thai place stacked on the coffee table, but now that I've sat down, I can't even muster up the energy to lean forward and get any of it. Sam notices my longing stare at the food and goes into the kitchen to get a plate and fork. He sits down beside me and dishes out portions of all my favorite dishes.

This food is one of the things I've missed the most since moving to Sherwood. Every time I'm back in Quantico for a couple of days, I make sure to get my fill of the incredible pra ram tofu and sesame noodles. I guess in a way that speaks volumes.

When I first considered going back to what I consider my hometown, I had no intention of it being a long visit. I'd actually thought I would never return. In fact, I had made that promise. Just before going into the Academy, I told myself I had to make a choice. It was either the life I had in Sherwood, the life with Sam and the comfort of the small town my grandparents loved, or the life I believed I was called to lead. The one dedicated to law enforcement.

I chose the FBI and closed my heart off to the option of anything else. I made my life in the house my father bought when I first went to college thinking my future started with art school. I built my existence around the friends I made in school, with only Bellamy a link to a time before the Bureau.

I didn't want to go back to Sherwood. I definitely didn't want to see Sam again. It would be too hard. I made the decision to go only because I told myself it would be a brief visit and then I'd be back to my real life. Only I found my real life there in Sherwood. And as much as I thought I'd never be able to pull myself from the life I had just outside of D.C., I realized there was more for me in my grandparents' old house, on the street where I used to play, with the man I claimed for myself when I was seven years old.

Bellamy and Eric could easily come visit. The Bureau could send me on assignment from anywhere. All that was left for me to miss was the Thai food.

"Think of it this way," I say, taking the plate and fork from him. "Our flight goes out of Dulles, so we were probably going to come stay here the night before anyway. We are just getting a jump on that trip."

"I know wait times at the airport have gotten longer with the tighter security in past years and all, but I think three days is a little much," Sam counters with a chuckle.

I finish my first bite and look at him. My new husband. The man who is willingly spending the second week of his marriage at his father-in-law's house because I can't leave this investigation in someone else's hands. At least not yet.

"I'm sorry," I say.

He looks at me strangely. "Why are you sorry?"

"For this," I say, looking around the room. "For all of this. For not being able to let this go."

"You have no reason to be sorry," Sam says. "I know who I married. I love *you*, Emma. Not some version of you or some memory of you. I loved the you when we were kids and I loved the you when we were apart and I love the you I know now. This you is my favorite you. I can't imagine you in any other way. I know you have to do this. I don't expect anything less of you. If you were to just completely ignore this and let somebody else

62

take over the search, it wouldn't be you. I don't want you to let this take over your life or take these important moments from us. But that doesn't mean I think you should stop."

"Really?" I ask.

"Emma, I've seen what Jonah has done. He needs to be found. And if there is anyone who can find him, it will be you."

"I love you," I say.

I finish eating and get changed for bed. Sam is already deeply asleep beside me when I climb into bed and tuck my phone under my pillow. After a few seconds, I take it back out and pull up a text to Dean.

Me: Are you doing okay?

I hope he's asleep and I won't get a response from him for a few hours. Instead, the screen blinks, and the message from him appears within seconds.

Dean: No.

Seconds later there is another.

Dean: Where is he?

CHAPTER TEN

THERE'S NO ANSWER.

The phone has already been disconnected.

I didn't really expect anything different. It couldn't be so simple as to pick up the phone, call Jonah back, and have him answer. But I had to try.

At this point, he's likely already discarded the burner phone he would have bought to call me and moved on to another. It means I can't use the number to get in touch with him. If I'm going to speak with him again, it has to be on his terms.

I hate that. I feel like I've dangled from Jonah's fingers for enough of my life. I pried myself out of them. But now I'm right back there again. All I can do is chase him and wait to see if he'll reach out to me again.

My computer chimes, letting me know a video call is coming in. I click to connect and Eric's face fills the screen.

"Hey," I say.

"Hey," he says. "How did the visit to the prison go?"

I sigh, running my fingers back through my hair. "It was all but useless. I went through every area Jonah had access to trying to figure out how he might have connected to other areas of the facility. It's a maximum-security prison. It's not like he had a lot of freedom of movement. The only time there aren't eyes on him is when he's in the bathroom and when he's sleeping. And trust me, I checked both places and there was nothing. There's no damage to any of the walls. No broken or missing windows. Nothing that gives any indication of where he might have gotten out."

"So, he didn't physically break out of the building," Eric notes.

"Well, I can't go that far quite yet. But it doesn't look like it. At least, there weren't any signs of the classic escape methods."

"He didn't dig himself out with a spoon?"

"Not even one of those scary grapefruit ones with the points at the end," I say. "Right now the evidence suggests he vaporized, but I don't think that explanation is going to fly."

"What's next?" he asks.

"I requested schedules for staff and other inmates, information about any vendors or volunteers who might have been in over the last few months, and tattoo information for the inmates. I'm waiting to get all of those so I can review them."

"Tattoo information?" Eric raises an eyebrow.

"If any of the inmates were Leviathan members in good standing when they were arrested, they would have the sea serpent tattoo on their back. Because Leviathan isn't a recognized gang or terror group yet, prisons don't isolate members from each other the way they often do with others. If there are any of his followers in that prison, they could have helped him. Or have information."

"They aren't going to tell you anything," Eric says. "They would have thought it was a gift from God to have Lotan put in prison with them. If they were able to help him get out, they would be honored. They are going to protect him with everything they have."

"I know," I admit. "But looking at their movements and activities might give me a clue. And there is always the chance that one of them is disillusioned by his precious Lotan not delivering him from captivity as well. Betrayal is a powerful motivator."

"That's definitely true," he acknowledges.

"How about you? Did you find the house?"

"Yes," he says. "I'm almost positive. There were only a couple of places in the town that fit the description Greg gave. Of those, only two of the houses weren't continually occupied by distinctly non-Leviathan families over the last several years."

"And those two?" I ask. "Who owns them?"

"Well, that's where things got interesting. One of them was listed as being abandoned and one was owned by a woman who has been diligently paying her taxes and maintaining the home for forty years. Despite being dead for fifteen of them."

"Well, that would certainly make the postage requirements on her payments higher," I muse. "Is that the house you went to?"

"Yes," he says. "But it was in complete disrepair."

"I thought you said she had been maintaining it," I say.

"That was what we were told. She always paid her taxes on time. The property had never been cited for having an overgrown lawn. But when we got to it, there were broken shutters and the lawn was a mess. It's at the end of a personal driveway, so there are no neighbors to ask about it. So, then we went to the other house, the one that was supposedly abandoned."

"It was in great condition?" I ask.

"It wasn't there," he says.

"What?"

"Yep. Apparently, it burned to the ground years ago."

"How many years?" I ask. "How did it burn down?"

"And now you've caught up with me," he says.

"Great. Alright. Keep digging."

"I will. Let me know what you find when the prison gets you that information."

"I will."

We disconnect and a few seconds later, I start another call to him.

"I've already sent it," he says when his face appears on the screen.

As he says it, an email appears in my inbox. It has the addresses and scans of notes from the houses.

"Thank you," I say.

"Bye, Emma."

I read through the information, but don't let myself get too sucked into it. Plenty of other things need my attention. I have stacks of papers in front of me, pictures spread out across the table, and an email inbox waiting for messages from several different sources. I'll have to trust Eric. At least for now.

That's not easy for me. I've never been the greatest at delegating to other people. If something needs to get done, I'd much rather do it myself. I want to know it's being done the way I think it should be done. Not that I'm the only person in the world who can do anything right. It's just that I know what I'm thinking, the ideas and instincts I have, and how to follow them. Trying to pass that along to someone else and trusting they will follow through with them the right way is challenging at best, impossible at worst.

And if something goes wrong, if something falls through the cracks or there's a bad outcome, there is always the question of how it was done. Maybe they missed something. Maybe they had a wrong assumption. Maybe they didn't understand what needed to be done. Whatever the reason, if something does go wrong, I want it to be because I made the mistake, not because I put the situation in someone else's hands.

But that has led to so many problems of its own and I've had to force myself to learn that I can't do everything on my own. As much as I want to follow every hunch, listen to every instinct, follow through with every step of every investigation, I can't. I need to be able to truly see the people around me as my team and trust that they will do the best thing for each investigation in every case.

I can't say I'm fantastic at it yet. I'm still working on being willing to step back. But I'm far better at it than I once was.

And for now, I'll step back from the houses. I'll focus on deciphering more of Greg's notes and trying to track his movements, pinpointing where he might have been and what he might have been doing during those two years while I wait to hear from the prison.

Or from Jonah.

Sam is asleep on the couch when I get back to my father's house. There's a massive salad covered with plastic wrap on the table next to a plate with a slab of lasagna. A note beside them tells me to look in the refrigerator. A few moments later, I'm curled up at the end of the couch with Sam's feet tucked up against me and a plate of tiramisu in my lap.

I try to watch TV for a little while to make my mind relax, but it keeps going back to the files sent over by the prison. It's not everything. Cutler said it will take several days to get all the information I asked for. I told him I don't have that kind of time, but he said there was nothing he could do. He offered me pictures of the tattoos of current inmates and a list of the programming for the last two months.

I examined each of the pictures, checking the hundreds of inmates for signs of the Leviathan tattoo. It isn't as simple as just finding a singular image. The organization operates under a strict hierarchy, with all of the followers eagerly seeking out Jonah's approval and favor. Early on in their acceptance into the organization, they get the first bits of the tattoo. It grows larger and more detailed the higher in the hierarchy they climb, or the more they please Jonah.

Those who have proven themselves valuable, who have been deemed worthy to enter into Jonah's closest circles have elaborate, highly detailed depictions of sea monsters covering their backs. The ultimate insult for those who are cast out of the organization is having their tattoo torn from their body.

So I'm not just looking for the sea monsters. I'm looking for simple sketches that might develop into sea monsters. Smaller images that hint at very early stages of assimilation into the group. Scars that suggest the rare instance of escaping with their lives.

It will take more than just going through the images once. The first pass lets me sift out those very few with empty backs and those with tattoos unrelated to Leviathan, as well as inmates who are too old, too young, or otherwise don't fit with Leviathan. After that, I have to examine each more carefully to determine if what I saw during the first pass might be a link or could be eliminated. And so on and so on.

So far, I've been through all of the images five times.

Now I've divided them into two stacks. One I still need to go through more and one that seems to contain definite links to Leviathan. I have two inmates in the second stack.

I'm going to need more tiramisu to get through this.

CHAPTER ELEVEN

"**E**MMA."

"Where are you?"

"Listen to me."

"Tell me where you are, and I will."

"You know I can't do that."

"I want to know where you are and what you are doing."

"Emma, you looked beautiful."

The phone clicks and I scream into the silent line. Eric rushes into the conference room and sets the coffee he went to get down on the table.

"What is it? What's wrong?" he asks.

"He called me again," I say.

"Jonah?"

"Yes. Just now."

"What did he say?"

"Nothing," I sigh bitterly. "He said my name and I asked where he was. He wouldn't tell me, he just said to listen to him, so I asked again. He said he couldn't tell me and when I asked again, he just said I looked beautiful and hung up."

"Why didn't you listen to him?" Eric says.

"Excuse me?"

"He called you for a reason and you wouldn't even give him the chance to tell you what it was," he says.

"Are you serious right now? You want me to sit here and have a pleasant conversation with him? A little afternoon chat?"

"What harm would it have done?"

I can't believe what I'm hearing. He can't actually be telling me to carry on a conversation with Jonah

"Do you not remember who we're talking about?"

"I know exactly who we're talking about. I also know you want to know where he is and what he's planning. You're not going to get that out of him with demands," Eric points out.

"He's an escaped felon with the blood of dozens of people on his hands. I'm an FBI agent who has already taken him down once. This is happening on my terms."

"It can't always be on your terms, Emma."

"Why not?"

"Because you're the reason he is who he is." As soon as he bites off the words, his face falls. "Emma."

I scoop up everything off the table and put it back in folders, then stuff it all into my bag.

"No," I say. "I don't really think there's anything else for you to say after that."

"Emma," he says again. "I didn't..."

"Yes, you did, Eric. But thank you. It's good to be reminded sometimes who I really am."

I walk out of the office and head for the parking deck. Eric doesn't come after me. He knows better. At this point, he doesn't want to be near me any more than I want to be near him.

I get to my car and throw everything into the backseat, climb behind the wheel, and slam on the gas. It's nothing short of a miracle that I make it back to the house without smashing into anything or running anyone down. At least, I hope I didn't. When I get into the driveway I realize I don't remember anything about the drive from headquarters.

I've done the drive so many times before I don't even need to think about it. It's muscle memory, like breathing or blinking. My mind is racing in too many directions to have room to pay attention to something so automatic. My lungs are burning and I wonder if I even took a breath after leaving.

I take a second to gather myself, then go inside. Sam is finishing packing his suitcase. There's the hint of a smile on his face as he tries to stuff one more rolled-up pair of socks into the corner. Usually watching Sam pack for a trip is one of my favorite forms of entertainment. He always starts out with the best of intentions. I've even known him to lay out all of the outfits he needs for all of the days of the trip ahead of time so he can make sure he packs efficiently.

But somehow extra articles of clothing make their way into the mix and he ends up playing a game of Tetris in an attempt to make the suitcase accommodate far more than its size was designed to allow. I have to admit, I've been impressed with what he's been able to accomplish during some of those packing missions.

I've also been the person who went to the store to replace all of his clothes when his suitcase zipper exploded during handling at the airport and it came around the carousel with nothing but a couple of pairs of underwear, a shoe, and his shaving kit.

Today I'm too angry to enjoy it.

"Hey, babe," he says when he notices me. "You're back early. And not just on the same day you left. I mean actually early. You must be even more excited about getting our honeymoon started than I thought." He comes up and slips one hand around my waist, pulling me in for a kiss on the side of my head. I don't react and he gives me a questioning look. "You okay?"

"Not exactly," I say.

"Did you find out something about Jonah?"

"Only that I am apparently the root of his evil," I mutter.

"What?" he asks.

I tell him what happened with Eric.

"He tried to backpedal, but I had to get out of there. I just couldn't stand there anymore."

"Babe..."

Before he can say anything else, my phone rings. I snatch it out of my pocket and am surprised at the name on the screen. It's not one I see often.

"Xavier?"

"Emma? Emma, are you there? Emma?"

"Xavier, take me off mute."

"If he's on mute, he can't hear you," Sam points out.

"Emma?"

"Text him," I tell Sam.

"Emma? It's not ringing anymore, but I can't hear you. Am I leaving a message?"

"Did you text him? He thinks he's leaving me a voicemail."

"I just sent it," Sam says.

"Emma," Xavier continues, "If you get this, Dean's in the hospital. He... my phone just clicked. Why did my phone click? Am I still leaving a message?"

My heart sinks.

"What's wrong with Dean?" I ask frantically.

"Dean?" Sam asks.

"Emma's voicemail, if you're still listening, Dean is at Harlan Memorial."

"What happened?" I ask. I remember he can't hear me and I let out an angry growl. "Xavier, learn to use your phone!"

I end the call and grab my car keys.

"Emma, what's going on?" Sam asks.

"I don't know. All he said was Dean's in the hospital. He's in Harlan. I've got to go."

"Hold on. I'm coming with you. And we're going to need to bring a bag. We won't make it back here tonight," he says.

"I don't have time to pack anything," I say. "We need to go."

"You don't need to pack. I already have our carry-ons ready. They have clothes and toiletries. Grab a couple of drinks and some snacks from the kitchen and let's get out of here."

"Thank you," I say.

My phone rings again as we're running out to the car.

"Emma? Did you get my message?"

"It wasn't a message, Xavier, you—yes. I did. What's going on?"

"Dean is in the hospital," he says.

"I know. Why? Why is Dean in the hospital? What happened?" I slam the door and latch my seatbelt in a rush.

"I don't know. We were at home. He had a case and needed to call the client. He stepped outside and that was it. He was gone."

"Xavier, I don't understand what's going on. What happened to Dean?"

"I fell asleep in my chair. I woke up and he wasn't home. He'd been gone for a couple of hours. My phone rang a few times."

"But you couldn't answer it," I say.

"I tried," he says. "But I couldn't. They left me a message."

"Who did, Xavier?"

His voice is steady, but I know he's upset. At this point, he's still processing.

"The police. Mine was the last number he called, so they called me. They said he was going to the hospital."

"Yours? I thought he was calling a client," I frown.

"I don't know what happened. Emma, I tried to answer."

The stress is starting to come through in his voice. I need to try to keep him calm. He's not used to being alone for long and it's going to be especially hard on him while he's worrying about Dean.

"I know you did," I tell him. "I'm on my way, Xavier. I'll call the hospital and see if they'll tell me anything. Can you get in touch with Ava?"

"She's not in town," he says.

"Damn it. Alright. Xavier, listen to me. I'm coming. Sam and I are on our way. You stay right there and we're going to be there as fast as we can. Do you want me to stay on the phone with you?"

"No," he says.

His voice has gone flat again. It's not reassuring. If anything, it makes me more concerned about him.

"I have my phone right here with me. If you need to talk to me, call. I'm not driving. Sam is. You can call me. Okay?" He doesn't say anything. "Xavier? Okay?"

"Okay."

"Don't leave the house."

"I won't."

"I'll be there soon."

I hang up and Sam gives me a quick look before getting his eyes back on the road.

"What's going on?" he asks.

"He doesn't know. They were at home. Dean said he was going to step outside and call a client. Xavier apparently fell asleep and when he woke up, Dean wasn't there. The police left a voicemail on his phone saying his was the last number called and they needed to let him know Dean was being brought to the hospital."

"He can't figure out mute, but he can check his voicemail?" Sam asks.

"I think it has to do with intentions and sequencing. The point is, Dean is in the hospital and no one knows why or what happened to him. He said he was going to call a client, but the last number he had dialed when the police found his phone was Xavier. Which means something happened to him after he walked out of the door, but before he could make a call."

"Don't panic," Sam tells me. "We need to get there and find out what happened. Getting worked up right now isn't going to help."

"What if it was Jonah?" I ask. "I know Dean went to see him at the prison. I don't know what he said to him, but..."

"Emma," Sam says. "You need to breathe. For right now, all you can do is call the hospital and see if they will tell you anything."

"And if they won't?"

"You wait. And you hope. There's really nothing else you can do."

I have never loved anyone like I love Sam. And sometimes I hate him. Usually, they're for the same reasons.

CHAPTER TWELVE

"**X**AVIER?"

I stuff my keyring into the pocket of my coat as I make my way into Xavier's house. He doesn't have an alarm system. No matter how many times we try to convince him it would be a good safety measure, he refuses. Just the thought of accidentally setting off the alarm and not being able to remember the code because of the sound makes him anxious enough to never want to open a door. He's reassured me he has his own ways of keeping the house safe. Considering some of the gadgets and gizmos I've seen that he's created, I have the utmost confidence that if he says no one would get away with breaking into the house, that's what he means.

As for me, I have a key. I actually have several keys. One to each of the various locks on the doors of the house. I have faith and trust that by merit of them unlocking the locks, these keys also deactivate whatever systems he might have in place. I don't particularly want to know what those might be. I feel it is in my best interest to keep all that a mystery. From both a mental health and a legal standpoint.

I don't ask. He doesn't tell. I continue to hope my key is magic.

"Xavier?" I call again.

He hasn't answered and my heart is beating faster with each step through the house. I'm terrified something has happened to him. Maybe I'm wrong about the protective measures in the house. Maybe I'm wrong about him being able to protect himself, despite stories to the contrary from his time on Windsor Island. Maybe he just couldn't handle the anxiety and stress of being there alone for so long without knowing what was happening with Dean.

Dean is his lifeline. He keeps him tethered to reality as much as is possible for Xavier, and in return, Xavier gives Dean some release from the rigid view of existence he once had. The levity comes along with a sense of responsibility and worth that were often missing in Dean's life. Knowing both men separately, there's no reason the two of them should have the bond that they do, and yet the fact that they are so very different is probably exactly what makes them integral to each other's lives.

Xavier once told me he feels like every day he has to find a way to live in a world that wasn't made for him. Sometimes he feels himself slipping, but when that happens, Dean is the other half of his Velcro. He helps him get a grip. It was one of the many moments in conversations with Xavier that I don't know if he's making a joke or not. And like most of those moments, it's both funny and heartbreaking.

"Where is he?" Sam asks, coming in behind me.

I shake my head. "I don't know. This house is so damn big. It's like a maze."

"I don't understand how Xavier gets around it. He can't explain to someone how to get out of our neighborhood," Sam says.

"This is his space," I say. "He knows it. I have seen him use the wrong light switch, though."

"Well, I do that," Sam shrugs. "It's confusing when there are a bunch of them together."

"Look," I say, grabbing Sam's arm and pointing toward the end of the hall.

There's a small room there with heavy curtains over the windows, a TV, and a recliner. Xavier's version of a decompression room.

The door is standing partially open and I can see light flickering in the darkness. I walk cautiously into the room.

"Xavier?"

There's no response. On the TV is a woman just from the mouth down in front of a microphone. Her mouth is moving, but there's no sound coming from the TV. The back of the recliner is to me so I can't see anything in it, so I walk around it slowly. Xavier is in the chair, leaned back with his eyes closed. There's a blanket draped over him so only his head is visible.

"Is he breathing?" Sam whispers.

"I can't tell," I reply.

I reach out to touch him, but before I can, Xavier's eyes pop open. I jump back as he gasps and sits up, flinging his blanket to the side so it hits Sam in the stomach. He grunts as it hits him and I notice the blanket sounds oddly like a rainstick as it pools onto the floor.

"What the hell?" Sam asks, leaning down to pick up the blanket.

Xavier claws at his ears and I realize he's taking out tiny earbuds.

"Emma?"

"I'm sorry that I scared you, Xavier. Are you okay?" I ask.

"Yes," he says.

"I don't know if I am," Sam groans.

"Honey, it was a blanket," I say. "You're going to be fine."

"It weighs twenty pounds," Xavier says.

"It what?" I ask.

"The blanket," he says. "It weighs twenty pounds."

"Why in the blue hell does your blanket weigh twenty pounds?" Sam asks. "Are you weaponizing comfort now?"

"It's for deep pressure therapy," Xavier says. "The application of concentrated pressure on the skin stimulates the release of certain neurotransmitters, including serotonin, which produces a sense of happiness and general well-being, and melatonin, which is relaxing and calming. Use of weighted or pressurized items can dramatically reduce sensations of overstimulation, create a sense of security and peace, and ease anxiety."

"Oh," Sam says with a nod.

Xavier looks over at me. "I call him Huggie."

"Oh, this is Huggie," I say, gesturing at the blanket, then reaching down to haul it up off the floor. "I've heard Dean mention that before. He said it calms you down a lot. Makes you feel safe."

"What did you think it was?" Sam asks quietly.

"I honestly had no idea," I answer slightly to the side.

"Did you talk to the hospital?" Xavier asks. "Is Dean alright?"

"They wouldn't tell me anything," I explain. "Not over the phone. But they said the doctor will update me when we get there."

"Let's go."

A thousand thoughts are running through my mind as it tries to figure out what might have happened. Dean isn't a small man, and his elite military special forces training means he's not easy to overtake. It's hard to imagine anything that would be able to take him so quickly, unless it was something truly horrific.

But there's no sign of blood or a struggle outside the house. Something occurs to me and I stop.

"His car," I say. "Is Dean's car here?"

"His car?" Sam asks.

"He said he was just stepping outside to make a phone call. But something happened to put him in the hospital. I don't see any sign of something happening outside the house and Xavier didn't hear anything."

"Unless he was plugged into the scary whispering woman," Sam offers.

"No," Xavier shakes his head.

"So, something happened after he stepped out of the house. Xavier, could he have gotten into the garage from the outside without you hearing the door?"

"No. The door is loud. And I have signal lights in the rooms where I spend most of my time. If the garage door opens, I know."

"Can we check anyway?" I ask.

He nods and we hurry through the house to the garage. I know it's hard for him here. He doesn't like to come to the garage and experience the memories that flood him every time he does. This is where his best friend was murdered, setting into action a chain of events that left Xavier in prison for more than eight years.

I open the door connecting the mudroom to the garage and immediately see Dean's car sitting in its spot. Stepping down into the room, I'm reminded of my own terrifying moments of being trapped in a garage. Not this one. One back home in Sherwood, at a house across the street. The car in that garage was on and the doors were locked, leaving me to breathe in the fumes.

I rest my hand on the hood of the car before thinking. It's been too many hours for the hood to still be warm if he did start the car, especially in the cold weather. I crouch down and look under the car.

"What are you looking for?" Sam asks.

"Water," I say. I point at the spot on the floor under the car. "Right there."

"Water?" Xavier asks.

I nod as I stand up.

"Dean has a habit I noticed the first winter I knew him. As soon as the weather gets cold, he turns on the defroster as soon as he starts the car. No matter what. Even if he doesn't see frost on the windshield, he still does it. This garage is insulated. It's much warmer than it is outside, and the air is dryer. So, frost won't form on the windshield. But Dean still turns on the defrost when he gets in. That automatically turns on the air conditioner, which causes water to leak from the bottom of the car."

"He turned the car on?" Sam frowns.

I nod. "Yeah. But the car didn't leave the garage."

CHAPTER THIRTEEN

THE DRIVE TO THE HOSPITAL IN HARLAN SOMEHOW FEELS LONGER than the hours it took to get from my father's house to Xavier's house. I'm even more confused and afraid now than I was when I first heard Dean is in the hospital. I don't understand what could have happened.

Xavier knows he walked out of the front door when he said he was going to call his client. Which means he walked into the garage through the door beside the main door rather than either going through the mudroom or just using the garage door opener to open the main door so he could drive out.

It leaves so many questions. I understand why he grabbed his keys on his way out of the house. Xavier has a tendency to lock doors when he walks past them and then disappear off into the recesses of the house. Dean quickly learned to take his keys with him even if he's just going to go out to the mailbox, especially when the weather is very hot or very cold. It's not so bad being locked out on a nice spring or fall day, but when it's near freezing and windy, it can get unpleasant fast.

Why did he go through the side door of the garage rather than opening the main door? Did he purposely not want Xavier to hear the door open and know he was getting in his car? If that was the case, why did he get in it at all? He would have to open the door to go anywhere. And what happened to him after he got in the car and turned it on?

We finally get to the hospital and I run inside. I'm at the nurses' station before Sam and Xavier catch up with me.

"Dean Steele," I say, gripping the side of the desk with both hands.

The nurse looks up at me. I don't recognize her, but the other times I've been at this hospital are mostly a blur.

"Emma Griffin?" she asks.

I nod. "Yes. I'm Dean's cousin."

"I'll let the doctor know you're here."

She picks up the phone beside her and makes a call, speaking in hushed tones as she tells the person on the other end I'm there. She hangs up and gestures to the side of the station where a small alcove holds several chairs and a coffee table with an out-of-place fake floral arrangement sitting in the middle. It's like the tiny room wants to make you forget you're in a hospital.

But that's not possible. The cold, astringent smell stinging my nose is unmistakable. I can almost block out the beeping and whirring of unseen machines in other rooms, but the smell stays with me. I've been surrounded by it too many times, and I have no delusion this will be my last time. It's part of the life I've chosen. That doesn't make it any easier to stomach.

It takes too long for the doctor to show up. When he does, I jump to my feet and close the space between us to shorten the time it will take for his words to get to me.

"Agent Griffin," he starts, extending his hand toward me. "It's good to see you again."

I don't remember ever seeing this man. I nod anyway.

"Where is Dean?" I ask. "What happened to him?"

"He's in a room. I had him sedated for a couple of hours, but he's awake now. You can go in and talk to him."

"What happened to him?" I ask again.

"I don't know," the doctor admits. "Emergency dispatch got a call earlier about a man on the side of the road. Police found him unconscious, propped up against a signpost. He has sustained a few injuries, but he hasn't explained what happened. I'm hoping you might be able to get more insight."

Xavier and Sam get up to follow us and the doctor stops, holding up his hand slightly.

"Family only," he says.

I gesture toward them. "They are family."

He looks like he's going to question me, but stops and continues down the hall. We follow him to a room in the back corner of the floor. Dean's name is scribbled in green marker on the dry erase board on the door and a bright red sticker across the bottom indicates his penicillin allergy.

It's a private room, but there's still a curtain pulled partially around the bed, blocking it from view from the door. A nurse comes out from behind the curtain and offers a hint of a smile as she walks past us. The doctor moves the curtain out of the way as he announces our presence.

"Mr. Steele, your family is here," he says.

Dean's head was turned so he could stare out the window when the curtain first moved, but now it turns sharply to look at us.

"Emma," he says. "You're here." His face drops. "Your honeymoon."

I shake my head as I walk up to the side of the bed. "The flight isn't until tomorrow night. It's fine."

He nods and his eyes move over to Xavier. "Oh, god. Xavier. I'm so sorry. I let you down. I'm sorry."

Xavier goes to the other side of the bed. "No, you didn't."

"Yes, I did," he says. "I left you alone. I didn't mean to. Did Emma call you and tell you what was going on?"

"No," Xavier says, shaking his head. "I called her and told her what was going on."

Dean looks over at me. "He did?"

"Yes." I nod, then give a half-shrug. "Well, kind of. Yes. Yes, he called me and told me you were here. I got here as fast as I could. Dean, what happened?"

He looks confused. "He called you and told you I was in the hospital? Xavier, how did you know?"

84

"The police called me."

Dean looks at me for clarification. It's a simple, straightforward statement, but coming from Xavier, that can make it even more confounding.

"They left him a voicemail," I explain. "They said they found you and his was the last number called on your phone, so they called it."

"His number?" Dean frowns, shaking his head. "But I didn't call him. Not today. I was home with him. Why would I call him?"

"I don't know. You said you were going to step outside a call your client," I say.

He nods. "I know. I remember that. I'm working with a man who suspects his sister-in-law killed his brother. I needed to ask him a question and I wanted to go outside because the reception has been spotty at the house."

"Did you call him?" I ask.

Dean looks in front of him, his eyes lost as he tries to think back on the morning. They come back to me filled with worry.

"I don't know. I don't remember. I don't remember anything after walking out the front door."

"You had another blackout," I say.

Dean has been experiencing the loss of chunks of time and lapses in memory since he was young. He's fought to minimize them, but the more stress and anxiety he faces, the more likely they are to happen. Now that he knows Jonah is out of prison and no one knows where he is, the pressure is coming down on Dean. The stress is getting to him and I'm worried.

"What happened this morning, Emma?" Dean asks.

I shake my head and reach for his hand to give it a comforting squeeze. When I look down at it, I notice something about his skin. Releasing his hand, I turn it over in my palm and look at it. It's tinged red, the lines of his palms and fingers caked with blood.

"Oh, Dean," I whisper. "What don't you remember?"

CHAPTER FOURTEEN

S AM GETS MY ATTENTION FROM THE DOOR AND GESTURES FOR ME TO come out into the hall with him. Xavier and Dean have been playing a game on Xavier's phone for the last twenty minutes, so I step away and join Sam. He takes a few steps from the door and I pull it most of the way closed.

"I talked to Bellamy," he starts. "Eric is obviously really busy, but since she has been working from home to be with the baby, she's available. She'll come stay with Xavier and Dean until we're back so that they're not alone. She doesn't know how to watch over or keep up with Xavier the way Dean does, but she can be there to make sure Dean doesn't…"

I nod to let him know he doesn't need to finish this sentence. I already know what he means. After what happened between Eric and me earlier, I wasn't the biggest fan of Sam's idea to call them. But they needed to know what was going on, and I need to know there will be someone at the house with Dean and Xavier. My father would have been my first choice, but he's working and investigating Jonah's escape as well. He's needed closer to headquarters.

"That makes me feel better. Until we get some clear answers about what happened, I just don't feel comfortable with him being alone."

"What did the doctor tell you?" Sam asks.

"Not a lot. But there's not a lot that they know. The police found him unconscious. But they don't know why. He doesn't seem to have a head injury of any kind, so they are not sure what happened to put him out of consciousness. He has some deep bruises and some cuts on his back and arms. There's a deep scrape along one of his thighs."

"Do they think that's where the blood on his hands came from?" Sam asks.

"They don't know," I tell him. "They think it's possible."

"And you?" Sam asks.

"That was a lot of blood, Sam. Enough to make his hands red like that and leave so much on his skin even after they tried to clean them up. And they didn't look like there were any smears or handprints on him where he would have been holding on to one of his injuries. I just don't know what to think. The officers who found him are supposed to come and talk to me. Maybe they'll be able to give more insight into exactly how they found him and what they think might have happened."

It takes another hour for the police to get back to the hospital. Xavier is still sitting in the chair beside Dean's bed but is leaned forward with his head resting on the mattress, sound asleep. I glance in at them to make sure they are alright before going into a small office with the officers and Sam.

"Agent Griffin, I'm Officer O'Malley," one of the officers introduces, holding out his hand to me.

I shake it with one hand and gesture to Sam with the other. "This is my husband, Sheriff Johnson."

"Nice to meet you," O'Malley says. "This is my partner, Officer Ramos."

We nod a greeting at the younger officer.

"What happened this afternoon?" I ask.

The officer looks at me with raised eyebrows. "I was hoping you would be able to answer that for me."

"Me?" I ask, confused. "Why would I know? I was at the FBI headquarters this morning. I only got here this evening after finding out my cousin is in the hospital and was apparently missing for a couple of hours."

"You were at the FBI headquarters this morning?" the officer asks.

"Yes," I confirm. "I'm involved in an extremely intense investigation and getting ready to leave for my honeymoon tomorrow."

"Busy girl," Ramos comments.

I slide my eyes over to him. "Excuse me?"

He gives an innocent look like he doesn't know what would have offended me about the comment.

"I'm just saying it seems like she's got a lot on her plate right now, is all," he clarifies.

I glare at him. "What is that supposed to mean?"

Ramos looks at O'Malley like he's hoping for backup, then sags when he realizes he's not going to get it. "Alright, look. I know who you are. I know what people think about you. But that doesn't mean you're going to be able to lie your way out of this or manipulate us into changing the story of what happened. O'Malley here might want to play good cop with you, but I'm not going along with it."

I stare at both men. "What in the living hell are you talking about?"

Sam slides one hand across the table toward the officers to get their attention. "I think we need to start from the beginning. Agent Griffin and I have clearly missed a couple of steps and need to catch up."

"The 911 dispatcher got a call from a woman saying she just witnessed a car pull up to the side of the road and a woman matching your description get out, drag a man out of the passenger door, and leave him there before driving off. She was able to describe your vehicle and give us a tag number that is registered to you," O'Malley explains.

"That's absurd," I say.

"Of course you think it is," Ramos replies. "Because you can't stand the idea that anyone won't let you get away with something."

I hold up a finger toward him. "Look. I don't know who you are or what you think you know about me, but I suggest you back off and back off quickly. This is ridiculous. I've been at this hospital for almost two hours with the man I supposedly dumped out of my car battered and bloodied, and you didn't decide to come and talk to me about it until now? Either someone is lying, or neither one of you is very good at your job."

"Emma," Sam warns, but I don't stop.

"I want Noah White here. Now."

The two officers look at each other. I can't really decipher what their expressions are supposed to mean, but O'Malley takes out his phone and makes a call, requesting Detective White come to the hospital.

I'm familiar with Detective White. We've worked together a couple of times before and I know how he operates. He comes into the room with a stern look on his face.

"Emma," he says. He nods at Sam. "Sam. Good to see you both." He eyes the officers. "I think. What's going on here?"

"Dean's hurt," I tell him. "He doesn't have any memory of what happened to him and when I spoke to your officers here about it, they accused me of being involved."

"What is she talking about?" Noah asks, staring the officers down.

"A 911 call came in earlier about a man being dumped out of a car on the side of the road," O'Malley tells him. "The caller said it was a woman who pulled him out of the car and described her as tall, athletic, with a blonde ponytail. It sounds suspiciously like Agent Griffin."

"Because those features are so rare in America," I say sarcastically.

"They said the caller also described her car," Sam points out.

"Her car?" White asks.

"The description of the car is consistent with a vehicle similar to the one Agent Griffin is known to drive," Ramos says.

I scoff at the ridiculousness of the statement. "So, you're saying the person was driving some sort of vehicle. Fantastic. Narrows that right down. And what about it having my license plate?"

"The caller gave several numbers and letters," O'Malley says. "She wasn't able to give the entirety of the plate number, but what she did give is consistent with characters that appear on Agent Griffin's license plate."

"You know what can give you the entirety of the plate number?" I ask. "The security cameras surrounding FBI headquarters. Several of them will have recorded me driving in there today. And the parking deck attendant. And the camera on her booth that records each license plate that enters and exits the parking deck. And the tolls on the drive from there to here. And, for a cherry on top, the son-of-a-bitch rookie who gave me a ticket for speeding on the leg when I took over driving."

"But you told her that the caller gave her full tag?" Noah asks.

"We wanted to see if she would give us any information," O'Malley says.

"She knows something," Ramos insists. "Every time she comes sniffing around this town, something bad happens."

"Maybe it's that shit keeps going wrong here and I have to come fix it," I say through gritted teeth. "My cousin is lying in a bed in there and no one can tell me what happened to him. Now is not the time for your little role-playing game. All I want to know is the facts. What happened? Where was Dean? Who called Xavier?"

Noah looks at the sullen officers. "Answer her."

"When we got to the scene, the 911 caller wasn't there. There was no sign of the car that dumped the victim. He was propped up against the signpost, unconscious. There were several wounds evident on him and his hands were bloody. He had no identification on him, so we used his cell phone and called the first number that showed up. We told the guy Dean was being brought to the hospital," Ramos says.

"You told him?" I ask.

"Yes," the officer says with a sharp, nasty edge to his voice. "We needed to make a notification and that was the best we could do without personal identification. The last person someone calls is usually going to be someone they know, so that's who we call."

"When you spoke with Xavier, did he have any idea what happened to Dean?" I ask, wording the question very carefully.

Sam glances over at me. I don't acknowledge the look.

"No," Ramos says. "Just said thanks and hung up."

"Alright," Noah says. "The two of you go back to the station. I'll talk to you when I get back. I'm going to stay here with Agent Griffin for a bit."

The two officers look like angry, sullen teenagers as they skulk out of the room and down the hall. Noah steps up to me.

"I'll get a recording of the 911 call and see what I can find out," he says. "I don't need it for me, but I'm going to request stills from those security cameras you mentioned. Just to have them."

"That's fine," I nod.

"What do you think about the blonde woman dragging Dean out of his car? Mistaken identity?" he asks.

I shake my head slowly, staring down the hallway. "A lie."

CHAPTER FIFTEEN

"**Y**OU THINK THE OFFICERS ARE LYING?" NOAH ASKS. "WHAT motivation would they have to do that? They would have to know it would be easily proven it wasn't you."

"Of course it wasn't me," I reply. "I'd have no reason to do something like that to Dean. And then pretend to come worry about him."

"Angels of mercy," Noah offers.

"Like the doctors?" I ask.

He nods. "They nearly kill their patients so they can bring them back to life and be celebrated and honored for their amazing skills."

I narrow my eyes at him. "Are you saying you actually believe them? You think I would purposely hurt my cousin so I could come to his rescue and... what? What's the end game there? I didn't find him by the side of the road. I didn't bring him into the hospital. He didn't need any resuscitation and if he had, I wouldn't have been here to do that. And if I was really trying to get attention for my skills as an agent, I would have to find the person who did it. So, what am I supposed to do? Slap cuffs on myself, walk into your office, and declare 'here I am'?"

"That's not what I'm saying," Noah says. "I just mean it isn't completely unprecedented. The officers might have acted rashly and gone far outside of their job descriptions, but maybe it was for the right reasons."

"The right reason being an FBI agent is untrustworthy and inherently dangerous?" I ask.

"The right reason being they want to do their due diligence and not be accused of having bias because you are in law enforcement. We've been taking a lot of heat recently from people accusing us of covering up crimes done by our own."

"Either that or it's an excuse to cover for overzealous uniform officers who want to take a shortcut to the top," I reply. "But whether I'm going to give the benefit of the doubt or not, I don't think it's the officers who are lying."

"You don't?" he asks.

"No. Being ridiculous and not taking the time to do some very basic research before launching into their gumshoe routine, but not lying."

"They did lie about your license plate," Sam chimes in.

"A little bit of contextual modification," I say. "You should be familiar with that interrogation technique. The fact that I wasn't being interrogated at the time should have dissuaded them from doing it, but they decided to shoot for the goal. The point is, it wouldn't make any sense for them to make up what they said about the blonde woman with the ponytail getting seen dragging Dean out of her car at the side of the road. All it would take is checking the 911 call log, just like you said you are going to.

And I think when you do, you're going to find that a woman did call and report seeing a blonde woman with a ponytail dragging a man out of a car at the side of the road."

"But she's the one you think is lying," Sam says.

"Absolutely."

"As you said, there are a lot of blonde women around," Noah says. "It could have been someone else."

"Who just happened to have a car that looks like mine with some of the same letters and numbers on the license plate?" I ask. "And think about this. The road where Dean was found isn't a major highway or anything. There isn't a lot of traffic. But a woman was dragging another person out of their car and dumping them, and didn't notice another car going slowly enough past that the driver was able to give an extensive description of the woman, the car, the license plate, and what was happening?"

Noah nods as if to acknowledge the logic. I'm thankful someone in this town is going to listen to me for once.

"And there's something about the way that the call was described that bothers me," I add. "I need to hear it. Can you get a recording of it tonight?"

Noah nods again. "Sure. It shouldn't take long. I can have them email me the file."

While he calls dispatch, Sam and I go to the coffee machine in the waiting area. The coffee comes out slow, like it's too thick for the spigot, but it hisses with heat and sends up a strong aroma with the steam, so I won't complain.

"I could really go for a cinnamon roll right now," Sam comments as he stirs noxious powdered creamer into his coffee cup.

"I'm sorry. I don't carry them around in my purse," I tell him.

"You also don't carry a purse."

"Which might be why I don't carry cinnamon rolls in it," I say.

"Well, maybe that's something you should consider."

"Just an emergency baggie of cinnamon rolls on my person at all times?"

"I wouldn't object to it," he grins.

"Emma," Noah calls from the doorway to the office. "I have the file."

Sam leans down for one quick kiss before we go to the office. I take a sip of the coffee and cringe as I realize the flavor does not live up to the aroma. I can't even imagine how my husband swallows the sludge swirling around in his own paper cup.

"Go ahead," I say, sitting down to listen to the recording. I listen to the woman's voice rattling off information to the dispatcher. When it ends, I shake my head. "Play it again."

I listen to it two more times.

"What did you hear, Emma?" Sam asks.

"When she's talking about Dean getting pulled out of the car, she says 'she's pulling him out of the car. She just dumped him on the ground and drove off.'"

"Yeah," Noah says.

"But Dean was leaned against the signpost when the police got there. He was sitting up, but unconscious. The caller didn't say the woman propped him up or put him against the sign. She said she dumped him on the ground and drove off. Did he wriggle himself over there unconscious? Or did he wake up, go over to the sign, sit down, and pass out again?"

"He could have," Noah offers.

"He used all that energy to move himself from the edge of the road all the way over to the sign post to sit upright, but didn't use the phone in his pocket to call for help? And the way she talked about him. She didn't say that the woman was dragging a person out of the car. Or a body. Or a man. She said 'him'. 'She's pulling him out of the car. She just dumped him on the ground and drove off.'"

"So?" Noah asks.

"It's familiar," I explain. "She's not just talking about some person. Or a person she identified earlier in the call. This is a person she knows, or at least someone she has come into contact with."

"She's outside."

The coffee I just sipped nearly comes right back out of my mouth. I turn a glare to the doorway.

"Xavier, how long have you been standing there?"

"Just the last two play-throughs," he says.

Throughout my career, I have been known for my skills of observation. I'm able to notice things other people don't. I'm excellent at reading people and picking up on quirks and characteristics. I take in what is around me and use it to unravel complex mysteries and solve crimes that have confounded teams of other investigators.

Xavier sneaks up and scares the bejeezus out of me just by existing.

"Noah, you probably remember, Xavier," I say, gesturing to him.

"Xavier Renton, of course," Noah says, reaching out toward Xavier. "It's good to see you."

Xavier just looks at his hand. I gesture toward Noah.

"Xavier, you remember Noah."

"Detective White, the man who cooperated with other law enforcement entities to construct an unlawful case against me and ensure I was trapped in the purgatory of prison for eight years. I speak metaphorically, of course. How are you doing?"

Well, that could have gone worse. Noah's hand drops and he gives a nod toward Xavier.

"What were you saying about her being outside?" Sam asks.

Xavier looks at him with a questioning expression, unsure of what he's being asked.

"That she's outside," he says.

"No, I mean, why do you say that? She's calling from her car, so, yes, she's outside."

"No, if she were calling from her car, I would have said she was calling from her car. She is calling from outside. As in, not on the inside. Of anything... Motor vehicle included."

"Why do you say that?" I ask.

"Her voice doesn't sound close to the phone. It's a little bit hollow. The sound isn't reverberating off of surfaces around her. And if you listen behind her you can hear wind and cars."

We play the recording again and I'm stunned to hear exactly what Xavier described.

"I didn't notice any of that before," I say.

"Because you weren't supposed to," Xavier says. "When someone calls emergency services and says they are driving past something that horrible, your instinct is not to question them. What you hear becomes what you think it should be. But that is not a woman who is inside a car driving."

"Play it again," I say. We listen to it again. "She's breathless. She's not driving, she's moving. Walking or running. She's outside, moving."

"So, if she actually is seeing what she's describing, she isn't seeing it from inside a car as she's driving by. She's outside on the side of the road with them," Sam says.

"And she doesn't do anything about it. She doesn't make any effort to intervene. Even if she doesn't know him and it's just a strange choice of words for her to say 'him' when she's describing it, think about how long it must have taken for this whole thing to happen. How long she would have had to stand there and watch this whole thing unfold."

"Well, if you take Dean's muscular density into account, and consider the average…"

Sam holds up a hand to stop him before he rambles into a tangent. "The point is, Dean is not a small man. If he's unconscious, it would take a massive effort to haul him out of a car, then walk several feet and dump him on the ground. That's if we just ignore that he was sitting up."

"He's unconscious right now," Xavier says. "He's not in a car, but we could still try it."

"That probably wouldn't be the best idea, Xavier," I say.

"That would have taken a long time," Sam continues. "Not just a quick pull-in, pull-out situation. And those are definitely cars in the background. Quite a few of them. With that many cars going by, someone would notice that whole thing going down and call the police. But only that one 911 call came in."

"From an unidentified caller," Noah adds.

"Of course," I say.

"What does this mean?" Sam asks. "Did the person who made the call actually do this to Dean?"

"I don't know," I say. "But she didn't witness someone who looked like me do it."

"Which means she made that up to put suspicion on you," Sam says.

"Pretty poorly planned out," Xavier adds.

"Or not planned at all," I point out. "It's entirely possible something happened with Dean and she knew he needed help, but didn't want to tell the truth about what was actually happening, so she made it up."

"And just happened to describe you?" Sam raises an eyebrow. "Whatever happened to no such thing as coincidences?"

"No. That was intentional. Whoever that is on the phone is someone who knows me, or at least knows of me and my connection to Dean." I shake my head. "But I didn't recognize the voice. I have no idea who it was."

"Now all we can do is hope someone saw something and is willing to come forward," Noah says.

"Or Dean remembers," I say.

CHAPTER SIXTEEN

THE HOSPITAL DECIDES TO KEEP DEAN FOR ANOTHER DAY FOR observation. Xavier wants to stay with him, but we convince him it would be better to go home and get some rest. He's resistant, but he finally lets us bring him home and we all fall asleep just before sunrise.

Bellamy arrives at the house a couple of hours later. She calls from the front porch and I hurry to let her in so she doesn't wake Xavier. The last thing any of us need is for him to be exhausted on top of worried about Dean. He'll do better if he can sleep as much as possible and close the time between him waking up and going to get Dean from the hospital.

Sam and I plan on going by to see him before getting back on the road, which means we don't have much time. Being this hurried and on edge definitely isn't how I ever wanted to feel the morning of leaving for my honeymoon. I should be excited and thinking only about long days and nights of just Sam. Instead, I'm writing notes, leaving instructions, and reminding Bellamy of everything she needs to do far more times than she actually has to hear it.

"Emma, you don't need to do all of this," she says. "He can tell me if he needs something. He's a person. Not an exotic plant."

"Oh, and make sure he drinks enough water and if you can get him out in the sun, that would be great."

"Emma," she scowls. "I'm a mother now. I can do this."

"Yes, you are a mother. You take care of a baby. Not a Xavier. It is very different."

"It's not like he needs actual care," Bellamy says. "Dean doesn't take care of him. He just watches out for him."

At that moment, Xavier comes into the room still in his pajamas, his hair sticking out at all angles. He says nothing to Bellamy or me but goes right for the baby in her carrier sitting on the kitchen table. Releasing her from the harness, he scoops her up into his arms and cradles her to his chest.

"Hi, Bebe," he coos. "I hear you're going to be staying with me for a few days. Come on. I'll show you around. We'll go get some books and crayons and stuffed animals. Maybe clay, as long as you won't eat it. You can sleep in my room." He's already headed down the hallway. "There's a rug to curl up on."

"Xavier," Bellamy and I say at the same time.

He turns around and gives us a little smile. "I'm not going to put the baby on the rug." Bellamy lets out a sigh and laughs. "That's for me. Bebe gets to sleep in the bed."

Xavier turns around and heads down the hallway. Bellamy watches him for a second, then looks at me.

"I'm going to need very clear instructions."

"Yep."

At least it's good to see that Xavier and Bebe have a better relationship now that she is born and no longer the fetus he had wary conversations with over Christmas last year.

I get through three cups of coffee before Sam and I have to leave. I hug Bellamy tightly.

"Call me if anything happens. Anything. You know where I'll be."

"Everything is going to be fine," she reassures me. "You go and enjoy your honeymoon. If there is anyone in this world who deserves that, it's you." She looks over my shoulder at Sam. "And you, Sam."

"Glad I factor into this, too," he laughs, then hugs her. "Thanks for doing this for her."

I say goodbye to Xavier and my tiny goddaughter, then head for the front door.

"Emma?" Bellamy says and I turn back to her. "Eric says he's sorry."

I draw in a breath. I can't bring myself to say anything, but I nod.

We get out to the car and hook our seatbelts. Sam looks over at me and I take a second before I meet his eyes.

"Are you sure you want to do this?" he asks.

"Do what?" I ask.

"Go," he says.

"It's our honeymoon," I say. "Of course I want to go."

"I know you want to go on our honeymoon, but I mean, are you sure you want to do it now? With everything that's happening…"

"Aren't you the same husband who told me I shouldn't let Jonah take more from me? Especially this?" I ask.

"Yes," he says. "But that was before everything that happened last night."

"Last night doesn't change anything, Sam. I know a lot is going on. A few years ago, I would have stopped doing everything, right down to eating and breathing if I could so I could focus every drop of energy I could possibly muster on this. And I'd be lying if I said I don't still have that compulsion. I want to know where Jonah is and what he's doing, or who he's doing it to. I want to know what happened to Dean and why I am being invoked in it. But do you know what I want more?"

"What?" he asks.

I reach out and run my fingers down the side of his face. "You. Just you. The truth is, there is always something going on, and there always will be. As much as I would like to think that there will be a time when there are no cases to investigate or criminals to chase, that's not going to happen. I'm not ready to hang up my shield. I don't know if I ever will be. But I'm not going to let him, or anything else, stop me from having these moments with you.

"I hate Jonah for what he's doing. I'm not afraid of him. I'm not afraid he'll hurt me or what would happen if he came after me. I've handled him once and I can handle him again. But I hate what he's doing. To you. To my father. To Dean. Whatever happened to him, he can't remember because of the stress and anxiety of Jonah being out.

"There are few people who can really understand how his escape affects me. But I'm not the only person looking for him. And I am going to put it in their hands. I'm going to trust that they will do everything they can to find him. I will do my part by holding onto everything he has tried to steal."

Sam smiles and turns his face to kiss the middle of my palm. "Let's go."

We stop by the hospital and find Dean looking more awake and aware than last night. He's cleaned up, the blood now gone from his hands and his injuries better wrapped. I give him a careful hug and when I pull back, he's already shaking his head.

"What happened, Emma?" he asks.

"We're still trying to figure that out," I say. "Do you remember anything? Anything at all?"

He takes in a breath and focuses on the blanket draped over his legs like he's trying to sink down into his thoughts. After a few seconds, his head swings slowly back and forth. His eyes lift to me.

"No. I remember waking up and having breakfast with Xavier. We made egg nog french toast."

"He had french toast this morning, too," I say.

"Doesn't surprise me. It's almost Christmas. He'll find as many ways as he can to fit in his flavors before the season is over. We had breakfast and were talking about what we were going to do in the afternoon. I knew I needed to talk to my client, but I've been having trouble with reception in the house, so I went outside."

"Yeah, you said that. Have there always been problems with reception? That kind of surprises me with all of Xavier's gizmos and gadgets and things. Can't he do something to fix it?" I ask.

"I actually think some of the problem is his gizmos and gadgets and things," Dean chuckles. "They interfere with the signal."

"Ah. Alright, so you went outside to make the call. Did you?"

"Yes. He didn't answer, so I left a message."

"You didn't remember that yesterday," I point out. "That's good. Alright, after that. What happened?"

He thinks again but ends up shaking his head. "I don't know. I can't remember anything after that."

"You went into the garage," I tell him. "Do you know why?"

"The garage?" Dean seems confused by the revelation. "How do you know that?"

"There was water under your car. You'd gotten in and turned on the defroster."

"Then Xavier must have heard the door open," he says.

I shake my head. "No. He says the door didn't open. You must have gone through the regular side door."

"I never use that door. I hate being in the garage with the main door closed. Especially if I'm going to get in the car, I wouldn't leave that door down."

"Someone got in your car and turned the defroster on the way you do," I say. "But the car is still there and the door wasn't opened. And you were found almost ten miles away. And at some point in there, you called Xavier."

"Did he answer?" Dean asks. "Did I tell him anything?"

"He says he didn't get a call from you. He did say he took a nap and that's why he didn't notice you were gone for a while, but he didn't mention a missed call from you. I mentioned it to him and he seemed confused," I explain. "But it was his number on your phone when the police checked your recent calls. That's how they reached him to tell him they found you."

He hesitates for a second. "They came to talk to me this morning."

"Ramos and O'Malley?" I ask.

He nods. "They told me about the 911 call."

"Emma," Sam pipes up from behind me. "I'm really sorry, but we have to get on the road."

"We have to catch our flight," I tell Dean. "But Bellamy is with Xavier. And I'm going to call Noah and have him come talk to you, okay?"

"I really don't think I'm going to be able to tell him anything else," he says.

"I know," I say. "But he has things to tell you. Call me if you need anything. I'll be back in a few days."

"Go on," he says. "Have an amazing honeymoon."

"I will."

I wave and start to walk away.

"Emma?"

"Hmm?" I say, turning back around.

"Be careful."

I smile at my cousin. "Don't worry about me. I can handle Jonah. And I'll have Sam. But I don't think it will be a problem. And if he does come for me, at least that means he's not here with you."

CHAPTER SEVENTEEN

HAD NO QUESTION WHETHER GOING ON MY HONEYMOON WAS THE right choice, but if there was even the hint of hesitation in my mind, it disappeared by the time the door closed on our hotel room. For those days, I was able to separate myself from everything for the first time in as long as I could remember.

I was happy. Really, actually happy.

That seems like such a ridiculous statement. It's so simplistic and cliche. But there's a lot of meaning behind it for me. Before now, there were glimmers of hope and moments of levity, but I wouldn't really describe my life, or myself, as happy. There is a difference between experiencing happiness and being happy. I was never truly happy.

Not until I found my way back home. To Sherwood and to Sam. And not until I found the family I've built around myself. I didn't think I could have a family, a life, and my career. I had to choose one type of fulfillment. One path.

It took time, but I finally realized those paths can converge. And now I can actually say that I'm happy.

I floated on that feeling throughout my honeymoon. It was all I wanted to think about.

Not that we lived in a complete bubble. I got my fair share of pictures from home. Bellamy somehow got roped into letting Xavier bake cookies with EmmaBelle—and somehow they got half the bowl of dough stuck to the ceiling. Dean got home and was doing well. Xavier even let him use Huggie. Dean didn't seem amused, but I was sure he appreciated the sentiment.

It didn't take long after getting home for reality to start to settle in again.

Maybe it was naive of me, but I hoped I'd come home to news of Jonah's arrest. I purposely didn't watch the news or go online while we were away. I didn't want even the slightest reminder of what was going on if it wasn't urgent. If there wasn't an emergency happening right at that moment, I didn't want to be a part of it.

I hoped I would get home and it would be over. The answers would have come and we could move on.

It wasn't that easy. It was never that easy.

∽

"Anything?" I ask, walking into the conference room where the task force sits at the table. I immediately notice it has grown by several people. That isn't a good sign.

It's my first day back at work and they look at me like they hoped I wouldn't be back for much longer.

"No," Zane mutters dejectedly.

I look at the new faces—a couple that are unfamiliar, a couple I know.

"For those of you who don't know, I'm Agent Griffin," I announce.

"They know who you are," Zane says.

It's hard to decipher the emotion in it.

"Then I suppose that saves the time from the Get to Know You talk," I say. I sit down at the head of the table. "We'll just go straight to catching me up on what's been happening while I was away."

The door to the conference room opens and Eric comes in. He pauses just inside when he notices me sitting here. We haven't spoken since the last time we saw each other. I don't know what Bellamy said to him or if she mentioned that she passed along his message to me. I also don't know what to say to him. Neither of us says anything.

He comes to the table and sits at the other end, setting down a stack of folders in front of him.

"What's happening?" he asks, sweeping his eyes over the other people at the table.

"Agent Griffin wants an update on the investigation," Brad says.

He shifts in his seat, then holds his hands open toward them as if in invitation.

"Go ahead," Eric says.

"We studied Agent Bailey's notes and used them to identify four more locations in addition to the house that is still standing in Crystal Valley. All have been thoroughly checked and cleared," Brad starts.

"Cleared?" I ask. "There was nothing?"

"Jonah Griffin was not present at any of the locations," Zane says. "We took several individuals into custody and questioned them, but there was nothing to hold them on. None were committing any crimes at the time of the raids."

"So, they were released," I say, resigned to the dead end.

"Nothing was happening that warranted arrests or charges. We have their information now and will be able to monitor them."

I nod. "At least that's something, I suppose. What else?"

There's an uncomfortable silence around the table. Eyes flicker to each other like they are searching for someone to be the one to say something. Finally, it falls on Eric.

"That's it," he says.

I look around the table, waiting for someone to say something else. Anything else. When they don't, I stare at Eric again.

"That's it? Still nothing about how he got out of the prison? No security footage, no rideshares from the area, no hits on any transportation?"

He shakes his head. "Nothing."

I don't know if I should lean more into my anger or my frustration. I knew realistically the chances of everything falling perfectly into place over the course of just a couple of days were next to nothing. The FBI isn't a magic wand, and just because the Bureau gets involved in a case doesn't mean it's going to suddenly unravel right at our feet. Especially something this complicated.

We've investigated prison escapes before. I've personally been involved in several of those types of investigations. But most of the time, it isn't a matter of the escaped convict disappearing into thin air. Even if there is a hunt for a fugitive, generally it begins with at least an idea of how they got out of the facility.

From there, there are sightings and clues that create a trail to them. It's extremely rare for someone to get out of a corrections facility at all, much less a maximum-security prison. The idea of an inmate simply vanishing without even the slightest indication of how is mind-boggling. And disturbing.

But that's Jonah. He wasn't just any other inmate, and he isn't just any other fugitive. His intelligence and creativity alone set him apart. The resources available to him push it farther. Knowing how he got out is a critical step. Finding that out can mean identifying people who helped him, tools he might have with him, or the direction he is most likely to have gone.

Without any of that, he's vapor.

⌒

"He had to have help," I say to Sam and my father that evening as we set dinner out on the table. "There's no way he could have just walked out without anyone knowing or making it possible."

"Did you talk to the prison again?" Sam asks.

I let out a sigh as I drop down into my chair. "Yeah. Cutler gave me a line about the investigation being ongoing and they would update me on any further information when it comes up. Essentially, he has no idea what to do either, and just hopes I'll leave him alone."

"So what now?" Dad asks.

"Now I keep searching. I still have the inmate records and vendor information to go through. The one useful thing Cutler did was give me the rest of the information I asked for, so I'm going to keep digging. There has to be something he hasn't noticed."

"Or doesn't know to look for," Dad points out. "You have to remember just how rare escapes are. Even if prisons say they are prepared for them and have taken steps to manage them, all they are really doing is following the lead of ones that have already happened. They can only take precautions against dangers they can anticipate."

"And no one can anticipate Jonah," Sam adds.

That strikes me. "Except for the people who know him best."

"Like us?" Dad asks.

I shake my head. "Like Anson."

CHAPTER EIGHTEEN

IT TAKES A WEEK BEFORE I'M ABLE TO GET INTO THE PRISON TO meet with Anson. I've been to the facility to talk to him before, so I know what to expect. But there's nothing comfortable about the experience.

I think there is a common misconception among people who have never been to a prison that all of these facilities are the same, like they were built from the same plans and have a cookie-cutter design. That's not the case. While there are some basic features you can expect to find across prisons, the actual layout, construction, and amenities vary widely.

The prison where Anson is set to spend the rest of his days is a stark contrast to the one Jonah escaped. He has a far higher degree of relative freedom, which can have both its benefits and its dangers. But that doesn't make my time with him casual. We don't meet in the visitation room. I'm not a visitor. I'm not here to check in on how he's doing or show him that he still has support on the outside. I'm not going to give him reassurances and tell him to keep his head up.

They bring him into the office in wrist and ankle shackles. The guard with him attaches his ankles to a hook in the floor, stopping him from being able to get up and launch at me if the urge came over him. I know it won't. There wouldn't be any gratification in that for him.

"You can take the cuffs off of him," I say.

The guard gives me a questioning look, cocking one eyebrow. "Are you sure?"

"Yes," I nod.

Anson lets out a short laugh as the guard releases the cuffs from his wrists and they fall with a heavy metallic thud to the cement floor.

"Feeling friendly today, Emma?" he asks, rubbing his wrists.

"You're attached to a floor and there's a man with several weapons behind you," I point out. "The handcuffs seem excessive."

"That usually doesn't matter to people coming to talk to any of us in here. They'd have us in a studded cage hanging from the ceiling if they could. Why does it matter to you?"

"Because I need your help," I tell him honestly.

He laughs again, looking me up and down. I don't show any reaction to the examination and I don't let myself think too much into it. If I do, I'll have to remember the ownership he feels over me. This man tormented me for more than a year. He infiltrated my life and played with me like his puppet, dangling bits of the past I always wondered about and the lives of people I love in front of me to keep me following along.

I would rather never have to interact with him again. I'll never be able to forget what he did, but I would happily tuck it all away into the back of my mind and not think about it. But I don't have that option. Right now, the information he might have is more important than my desire to blot him from my consciousness.

"This seems to keep happening. Could it mean you don't want to let me go? You have to keep finding reasons to have me in your life, don't you, Emma? You just can't get enough of chasing me."

The cadence of his voice makes my skin crawl. He isn't just teasing me. He's taunting me with our past, dragging claws across the recesses of my mind to open tenuously healed wounds and dredge up festering memories. The guard behind him doesn't understand what he's saying. Anson knows it. To that guard, he is just another inmate, another of the many murderers he has to watch over every day.

To me, he will always be Catch Me.

"I'm not chasing you," I say carefully.

He gets a more curious expression on his face and sits back in his chair.

"Which means you're chasing someone else. Who is it?" he asks.

I swallow down the hard rock of anger that has formed in the middle of my throat. It's a congealed mass of hatred and pride, and I have to force myself to get beyond it if I want a chance at getting something useful from him.

"Jonah," I say.

Humor dances in Anson's eyes. He drapes an arm over the back of the chair and runs his tongue over the edges of his teeth.

"Jonah," he says almost to himself. "I thought he went down for a while."

"Several lifetimes," I say. "He's borrowing on future evolutions of the species at this point."

"But he escaped."

I draw in a breath to keep myself calm.

"Yes."

The sound that comes out of him isn't quite a laugh, but that's the closest thing to it. There are far too many thoughts and emotions in that sound for it to be something so simple.

"How?"

The guard looks at me with a type of suspicious, condescending narrowing of his eyes that says there's a part of him that thinks I'm about to offer up a handbook of escape to a mass murderer.

"They don't know."

Anson's eyes widen and a smile comes to his lips as he leans forward, resting his elbows on his thighs like he's getting closer to share a secret with me.

"And you want me to help you figure out how he did it? Or you want me to help you find out where he went?" he asks.

"I need to know where he is. I want anything you can tell me," I say.

Silence stretches between us. He's drawing this out, lingering over it and savoring the feeling that he has me in the palm of his hand again. I'm not afraid of him. The fear he created in me has long since dissipated and been replaced only with scar tissue and steel. But that doesn't mean it isn't disturbing watching him sit there, seeing his brain work behind his eyes.

He's mechanical. There's no flesh and bone there. No warmth, no heartbeat, no blood. Anson is all gears and circuits. Cold, calculating, methodical.

He can create and project the image of emotion and connection, even love. He's fooled people before. But it's all for show. A ruse to get him to what he wants. In the end, he is a little boy who liked to dismantle toys to see how they worked, who grew up to be a man who does the same to human beings.

"I wish there was something I could tell you, Emma," he says. He loves to hear the sound of my name on his tongue. He loves even more that he knows he has no right to say it, but does anyway. "I'd like to help you, but I don't know anything."

"You don't know anything?" I ask. "You didn't know he was planning an escape or that he got out?"

Anson looks around the stark cement block room.

"This isn't a spa retreat where I've come to find myself, Emma. I'm in prison. Inmates aren't allowed to communicate with each other through the mail. Especially ones at other facilities," he says.

"Not necessarily," I say. "Prisoners who are co-defendants are permitted communication. You are technically co-defendants."

"Even if we were to attempt to use that loophole, every piece of mail that comes in here is read by the staff. Men have the birthday cards their children make them sliced up and run through tests to make sure no one has dissolved drugs into the paints or hidden dirty pictures between the layers of the paper. There are people whose entire jobs consist of reading through letters and making sure there aren't any potentially dangerous or suspicious sentiments in them. Do you honestly believe Jonah and I would attempt to send messages to each other planning a prison break?" he asks.

"Yes," I say without hesitation. "I believe both of you think you are smart enough to get away with it."

"And if we did, then we've proven ourselves right, haven't we?" he asks.

My teeth grind against each other and I can feel the pain and tension building up through the sides of my jaw and down along my neck.

"What happened, Anson? How did he get out and where is he?"

He holds up his hands. "As I said, I don't know anything. I have not heard from Jonah since coming in here. And I haven't heard anything about his escape. We don't get a lot of news in here. On the rare occasion the TV in the dayroom works, it's usually set on the true-crime channel so guys can wait around to see if their cases show up." He shakes his head and gives a dismissive snort. "Narcissists."

"You know how he thinks. You know the kinds of things he plans," I say.

"No one knows how he thinks," Anson clarifies. "I only know what he let me see, and all of that happened when he never could have imagined someone putting him back behind bars. Remember, Emma, I lost my favor with him a long time ago. I tried to pull away. Jonah wasn't who he claimed to be."

"But I am exactly what he claimed me to be, except for his child."

He gives a single nod. "In many ways, you are. But I still can't help you. I haven't been a part of Leviathan for years."

"What about the tattoo on your back?" I ask.

"Feel free to have a look," he says. He glances back at the guard. "I'm going to stand up now. There's no reason for panic."

He stands and twists his body as much as the ankle shackles will allow. Taking hold of the bottom of his shirt, he lifts it to reveal the mangled scar where the sea monster once was. I bite back the gasp that comes up my throat. The shirt drops back into place and Anson sits down again.

"Who did that to you?" I ask.

A hint of a smile twists his lips. "It was an accident. I fell into a bottle of bleach and spontaneously burst into flame."

He's not going to tell me the truth. That doesn't go over well within these walls. I nod my understanding.

"I hear that kind of thing happens a lot once you've tangled with Jonah."

Anson gives a half-shrug. "Never underestimate the power of Leviathan's hold. Once you're marked, that's it for life."

CHAPTER NINETEEN

February

"IS IT THAT MUCH OF A SURPRISE THAT THEY AREN'T TALKING?" Dean asks.

I grab up another handful of little heart candies from the crystal candy dish on the table in front of me and look down at the words imprinted into them.

"No. It's not a surprise at all," I acknowledge. "But that doesn't mean it doesn't aggravate the hell out of me." Xavier uses one fingertip to poke a pink mylar heart balloon bobbing around beside him. It bounces away from him, then floats back. "These people are sitting in prison. Not even jail. Prison. Dark, dank, grimy, violent prison. Many of them for the rest of their lives. And they still won't say anything."

"You can't forget that Leviathan is still not recognized," Dean points out. "You said it yourself. It's not like one of the big gangs or terror organizations. It's out there, right in front of people, and it goes unnoticed. Legally speaking, these people are in prison for crimes they committed of their own volition."

Xavier pokes the balloon again.

"But they didn't," I say. "They might have chosen to do it. They might have agreed to do it. Hell, I will even give it to them that in some situations, they might have come up with the idea themselves. But the real reason they did it—the only reason—was for Jonah. For Lotan. It was for the mission of Leviathan and to build up their rank."

"And if they start talking about it, Leviathan is at risk. They know the FBI and the CIA are hot on their trail. But they also know that there are too many missing pieces to complete that investigation and finally bring them down. So Leviathan still lurks in the shadows. All these criminals are way more afraid of Jonah than they are of the Feds. No way they'd be the ones who gave those pieces up."

"And what about Anson?" I ask. "The sea monster tattoo was melted off of his back with what essentially amounts to a prison flamethrower, and he still won't say a word. He's admitted to not having loyalty to Jonah and to wanting to be disassociated with the organization."

"But he still aspires to the same thing," Dean counters. "It wasn't that he didn't believe in the mission anymore. He pulled away from Leviathan because he thought Jonah wasn't doing enough for that mission. He's still a true believer in their twisted goals. If Jonah hadn't put so much focus and attention on finding us, Anson never would have lost faith in him. He'd still be devoted to the cause. And he probably wouldn't be in prison."

I know he's right. The only reason Anson got disillusioned about Jonah was because he felt like the great leader who had once been so powerful and driven on his quest had gotten distracted. He felt that Jonah had lost sight of their grand ambitions, and turned on him in an internal power struggle that nearly left me dead—several times.

Jonah had his own mission at the time: he wanted to bring Dean and me into his fold so we could rule alongside him. In his deluded mind, I am his daughter. Despite being told the truth countless times, he won't accept that I am not a baby he conceived with the one woman he ever really loved—my mother. His brother's wife. He pretended to be my father so he could rape her, but my mother quickly figured out what he had done. She took measures to ensure she would never give birth to a child belonging to Jonah.

The fact that I was conceived shortly after was a twist of the Universe. It gave my parents something they dearly wanted, but also offered Jonah something more to cling to, another bit of what he saw as validation for the obsession he had with my mother. It would culminate in the men he hired to kill my father cutting her down instead.

And my father and I went on the run.

Jonah wouldn't let me go. In his eyes, I was his daughter and I had been stolen from him by the same man who had stolen the woman he believed he was meant to be with. He wanted to bring me home, to teach me about who he believed I really was, and to give me a life of power, wealth, and privilege.

He wanted me to be beside him at the head of Leviathan.

But it wouldn't be just the two of us. What I didn't know was that he had conceived another child. Not long after I was born, a woman my mother rescued from an abusive marriage and was helping to rebuild her life gave birth to a baby boy. She looked strikingly like my mother, and she fell for Jonah's charms. It didn't save her. She would never be Mariya Griffin. But she was given the same fate. She died in a pool of her own blood on the floor of her home.

The image of that woman's death was burned into my mind from the time I was sixteen. It got convoluted and twisted in my memories until I thought I'd walked through my mother's blood. When I realized my mother died years before that would have happened, when I was eleven, it threw my entire worldview into question. I questioned if my mother's death. Or if the image of the woman dead on the floor was imagined.

It took until I was an adult to know what really happened. The woman was not my mother. But she was Dean's. In another life, she could have been my aunt. We could have shared laughter and jokes with each other. I could have grown up playing games and teasing my cousin. We would have been a happy family.

But that's not the life I ended up having.

Jonah had never stopped thinking about his son and his quest became to have both of his children. His focus on both of us, especially me and my career with the Bureau, slowed his criminal pursuits enough to drive a wedge between him and Anson. He split away, eager to prove he could outthink, outsmart, and outmaneuver me. That he could be greater than Lotan.

He might not be loyal to Jonah any longer, and it's obvious Leviathan wants no part of him, but just like he said, the grip of the organization is strong. It never really lets go.

"Anson doesn't ever say anything by accident," I say. "That's something he shares with Jonah. They are as methodical and purposeful in their speech as they are with everything else in their lives. He knew exactly what he was saying when he said once a person was marked by Leviathan, they were marked for life."

Xavier pokes the balloon again.

"The tattoos," Dean nods. "But you've interviewed everyone in the prison with the tattoo or signs of one being removed. You didn't find out anything."

Poke.

"There has to be something else in them that I'm not thinking about. There are so many different ones and I'm wondering if some of the people who have them don't have anything to do with Jonah at all. They just happen to have sea monster-themed tattoos, so I'm wasting my time even trying to find connections or see if they might have helped him."

"I thought you said that the tattoos were different depending on the person in the organization," Dean says.

Poke. The popping sound is starting to get to me.

"They get more elaborate and detailed, but they are similar. There are a few at this prison, though, that look completely different. Different styles. Different colors. Added symbols and words. One had the monster eating a boat. One looked like the monster was swimming with a mermaid. Those aren't things Greg ever described or that I've seen on any of the other followers."

Poke.

"So, you focus on the other ones. I know the interviews didn't give you much, but you didn't really expect them to. Keep looking at what they were doing, where they were, what programs they participated in. If there's a pattern there, you'll find it."

Poke.

"I hope so. The longer this takes, the farther away Jonah can get. This is humiliating. For me and for the Bureau. And law enforcement in general. Cutler finally did a press conference about the escape, so now people are talking about how lax the prison system has gotten and that everyone is at risk because dangerous terrorists can just get out and roam free."

"Just one," Xavier chimes in, then pokes the balloon again.

"What?"

"Just one." Poke. "He's just one dangerous terrorist out roaming free. Unless, of course, you want to count all the people he influences, but I don't really think that's fair if you're talking about the impact of his escape. Since he is the only one who escaped, the public can really only decry the law enforcement system for the failure of having one dangerous criminal getting out and roaming free. The others are just potential at this point."

Poke.

"Thank you, Xavier," I say. I look back at Dean. "And the thing is, there's nothing I can do about it. That's what's driving me insane. I can't call him. I can't reach out to him in any way. I don't know where he is or what he might be doing. I'm in a position of wanting someone to just disappear from the face of the planet while also putting all of my energy into trying to figure out a way to get in touch with that person." Poke. "Xavier!"

"Hmmm?"

"Why do you keep poking the balloon?"

"Because it comes back," he says. He pokes it again. "I push it away, but it comes right back. No matter what…" he pushes the balloon harder so it bounces almost down to the floor, then waits until it drifts back up and floats over to cover his face, "it comes back. It always comes back."

I look over at Dean. He shrugs. "Maybe you just need to poke him."

CHAPTER TWENTY

March

"THERE ARE FAR MORE CASES TO BE HANDLED AND MORE PEOPLE to be helped. I am confident in the capabilities and skills of my fellow agents and have no hesitation in entrusting them with this situation. As of now, I am turning the investigation over to the task force and know they will work diligently to bring it to a close. I do want to assure the public that we have not received any threats from the fugitive or any of his associates. The prison has been thoroughly evaluated and any and all risks have been addressed. The identified security breaches were rectified swiftly and forcefully, and we do not believe there is any further compromise that may allow for another escape."

Cameras flash in front of my eyes and I sweep my eyes over the crowd of reporters in front of me. I ignore most of the waving hands and the questions being shouted at me.

"Agent Griffin, is it true that you have recently gotten married?"

I smile in the direction of the question and nod.

"Yes. I married my long-time partner Sam Johnson in December. He is an incredible man and we share a dedication to law enforcement. He is the sheriff of Sherwood County, Virginia, where we live and where I am very much looking forward to spending a lot of time in the coming months." I make a show of checking my watch, then wave at the crowd. "That will have to be all. Thank you."

I hurry off the platform and am quickly flanked by Sam on one side and Noah on the other. We make our way away from the press conference and back into the building. I'm ushered into an office where Bellamy and Eric are waiting. A few moments later, the door opens and Dean and Xavier come in. Dean looks breathless and is shaking his head while Xavier nearly glows.

"I nearly lost him out there," Dean says. "He got sucked into the reporters trying to chase down Cutler as he headed for the car."

"But you found him," Sam says. "It's fine."

"And he got the question in. That's what we were going for," I say.

"Don't you think at some point people are going to start to recognize Xavier?" Bellamy asks. "If you keep putting him in these little roles, somebody is going to figure it out."

"No, they won't," Xavier protests. "I'm undercover. No one recognizes me. See, right now, I'm just Xavier. But wait." He tugs the sweater he's holding down over his head, pushes up his sleeves, and dramatically puts on the hat Dean was holding. "Now, I'm Mr. X. Investigative reporter."

"You literally look the exact same," Sam chuckles. "Though I have to give it to you—cool code name."

"Listen," I say, holding out my hands between them before they can get into a snit. Nobody needs to see Xavier in a snit. "It doesn't matter if someone thinks they recognize him or not. The point is, he got the question out, I got to answer it, and it's being broadcast all over the place and will probably get some sort of funky video-sharing remix with like, Godzilla behind me or something. That's what we wanted."

"And you don't think anyone is going to find it strange that was the one question you took from a reporter? You're announcing your supposed withdrawal from a manhunt that should be one of the most important of your career because you want to go home and spend time with your new husband?" Bellamy asks.

"Of course, not. I'm a woman. Everybody will eat that up. After that whole minor incident where Sam and I stopped a passenger train from being blown into a million pieces while stopping everyone on board from finding out about the several dead bodies? At the press conference after that, they asked Creagan the damage potential of the bomb, his insights into concealed-carry policies on mass transit for off-duty law enforcement officers, and what measures were being taken to improve on-ride safety for those eager to continue riding the rails. At the one interview I did, they asked me if I would recommend Zumba to help all the ladies out there stay in shape and what book I read last. It came out under the title 'FBI: Fitness, Beauty, Intelligence.'"

"Well, that does describe you," Sam offers, an amused twinkle in his eye.

"Awwww," I plaster on a fake smile, leaning over to kiss him and pat him on the chest. "Thank you, honey. It's misogynistic as hell, but trust me, it's exactly what a lot of people want to hear."

"And the perfect poking strategy," Dean adds. "Tell Jonah you're not looking for him anymore and that you're nesting down in Sherwood."

I let out a sigh. "Come and get me, Jonah."

"I want to try Zumba."

Everybody looks at Xavier. He's wrestling himself out of his sweater, so it's one of those moments when I'm not sure if he was actually talking to me or if it was meant to be a thought and he just forgot to keep it inside.

"Alright, so now we wait. I'm working through the list of vendors and volunteers at the prison, trying to see if there are any familiar names or if any of them could have possibly worked with Jonah to create an escape plan. There weren't as many volunteers or programs over the couple of weeks before he escaped, and there weren't any visitors, so that narrows things down. But there are still some I'm looking into," I say. "I'll also keep working on Greg's notes. Dad has given the task force all of the information he has from when he went undercover to try to crack Leviathan. We'll just keep searching."

"Sounds good," Bellamy nods.

We all get up to leave.

"Noah," I ask after him as the others are walking out. "Have you found anything yet?"

He shakes his head. "No. We're still looking, though. The 911 call couldn't be tracked, but we put out a bulletin asking for the public's help getting us any information about what they might have seen in the area during that time. If they heard anything, saw anything, had some-one tell them a drunken rumor down at Kelsey's bar. Anything they have, we want to know about it. There's a tip line, so hopefully, we'll get something soon."

"Okay," I say. "Thank you."

Noah glances over his shoulder toward where Dean and Xavier have just walked out of the room. They'll leave in a different direction so we're not all seen together. Despite the impressive clandestine skills of Mr. X, I think it's better if we keep a low profile.

"How is he doing?" he asks.

"Better," I say. "Some of the deeper injuries are still healing, but he's had worse. He's frustrated."

"I'm sure he is," Noah says. He glances back again. "But that's why I figured he would be more forthcoming and cooperative about the investigation."

"What do you mean?" I ask.

"He hasn't really talked to me about what happened or offered any-thing that might help find out who did this to him. He just says he can't remember anything after calling his client," he explains.

"That's because he can't," I say. "There's nothing for him to be forthcoming about, and he's cooperating as much as he's able to. He genuinely can't remember. Dean has blackouts. Whole chunks of time, sometimes just a few minutes, sometimes days, that he can't remember. It's happened to him since he was a teenager. I told you that."

"I know," Noah nods. "But it seems strange to me that there's nothing he can tell me at all. Even why he was calling his client or who he would get in a car with."

"He can't tell you why he was calling his client," I point out. "That's confidential information. He's a private investigator. He can't just talk about his cases, especially when they are ongoing and as sensitive as this one is. If he says he needed to talk to his client about the case, then that's what he was doing, and that's going to have to be enough. And why does it matter who he would get in a car with? Dean isn't a child. He doesn't need to have permission to ride with someone."

"But he does, in fact, need to ride with someone to end up as far away from home as he did in the timeframe that he did. As you said, he is not a small man. He's big and he's powerful. He's also military-trained—and reputation has it, he is sometimes not the nicest person."

"We're sliding quickly from listing off traits to insulting the victim of a violent crime," I state.

"That's not what I mean to be doing. I'm just saying I can't imagine someone forcing him into a car without there being some sort of scuffle that others could hear. Xavier inside. The neighbors. Someone would notice if people were trying to take Dean against his will. Which leads me to believe he got into someone's car voluntarily. So, who does he know that he would get into the car with?" Noah asks.

"I don't know," I shrug. "He's not very social."

"See if you can find out. I'll let you know if anything comes up," he says.

"Thank you."

As Noah walks away, I notice Eric is still lingering just inside the door. Bellamy and the baby aren't with him and the others have already left, so it is just the two of us in the small room.

"Emma, you've got to talk to me," he says. "We've never gone this long without talking."

"We've talked," I reply.

"About the case during meetings. That doesn't count. Didn't Bellamy tell you I'm sorry for what I said?"

"Yes," I say.

"Then what? Is it because I didn't say it to you myself? I'm sorry. I shouldn't have said that to you."

"Alright," I say. "I appreciate the apology."

I start for the door, and he lets out an exasperated sound.

"That's it? Are you seriously that mad at me?" he asks.

"I don't have anything else to say to you. I'm not mad at you, Eric. I just… don't have anything to say to you."

He doesn't stop me as I walk out of the office and find Sam.

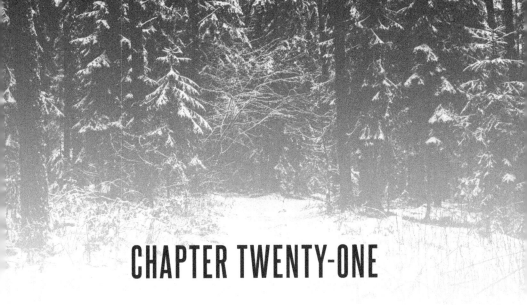

CHAPTER TWENTY-ONE

April

"I DON'T REALLY THINK THIS IS FAIR," SAM SAYS. "SHOULDN'T SHE be looking for the eggs?"

"She can't walk, babe," I say, moving the half-eaten coconut cake in the middle of the table away from me so I don't go for another slice.

Xavier scurries past with Bebe strapped into a forward-facing carrier on his chest and a basket in his hand. She has a plastic egg gripped in one chubby hand and a pair of bunny ears on her head.

"But he probably knows where all of them are already."

"He didn't watch you hide them," I say, sticking my finger into the icing left on my plate and licking it off.

"It's Xavier. He knows things."

His phone chimes and he looks down at it. A concerned look crosses his face.

"What's wrong?"

"It's an alert from the Breyer precinct. They're asking all departments to go through their missing persons cases again," he tells me.

"They still haven't identified that woman?" I raise an eyebrow.

He shakes his head. "Apparently not."

"Are there any missing persons cases in Sherwood?" I ask.

He chuckles. "Do you think she's from around here and we just haven't noticed?"

"No," I say. "I don't think anyone could actually go missing from around here and it not be spread all over everywhere within a day or two. If that woman was from here, Pearl would have already called Breyer to ask if they found her favorite diner order in her stomach during autopsy."

"True," he laughs. "Disturbing, but true."

"Bebe found the golden egg!" Xavier calls from across the yard.

⌒

May
Detective Simon

The flowers were piling up in a thick carpet on the spot where the woman's body was found. The ones at the bottom were starting to bruise and dissolve down into the ground. She leaned down and used two fingers to pluck a piece of plastic that had surrounded one of the bouquets out of the new grass.

The wooden markers they'd set down to create a grid around the area during the beginning of her investigation were still plunged down into the earth. No one had ever bothered to take them up when there was nothing left to search for.

Maybe that responsibility was hers. But she left them there. Too many times she'd come back out to this patch of grass and stared down at it, wondering if the site would ever really not be a crime scene. The snow had been gone for months. The sun had heated up the soil and brought in a new growth of green grass that broke through the tangle of faded brown from last year.

But she could still see the woman's skirt pulled up around her thighs and her dark hair spread across her pale skin.

"Who are you?" she whispered. A breeze that started with the cool of winter and ended with the breath of summer rippled her hair. "Who were you?"

∽

June

"You've gone through that list a hundred times," Sam says, setting a glass of iced tea on the wicker table in front of me.

I uncross my ankles and drop my bare feet down to the planks of the front porch so I can lean forward and pick up the glass. The tea is the perfect sweetness and the lemon wedge at the bottom is just tart enough. No one has ever asked me for relationship advice, but if they ever do, I will tell them there's no secret to happiness. It's not actually so difficult. Just marry someone who you'll fill a freezer full of emergency cinnamon rolls for and who knows to put a lemon wedge in your tea.

"I know, but this time I'm comparing it to the ones from the last couple of months," I tell him.

"Why?"

"I want to see if there are any vendors, volunteers, or programming that were used right before and during the time when Jonah escaped, but aren't around now. Or ones who might be around less. If there is, it could mean they had something to do with the escape."

"And? Have you found anything?"

"Nothing concrete. The vendors have all stayed the same. Apparently, they are the same ones the facility has used for years. There's an approved vendors list that all federal facilities in the state use. It ensures quality, security, all those things. So, there is the possibility that he was able to influence one of the vendors over a long stretch of time and they helped him. That's one option. The volunteers and programming are less consistent. Not surprisingly, they don't allow many volunteers."

"At a maximum-security prison? Would never have thought it," Sam cracks.

"Sass aside, the point is, they do allow some. Mostly religious leaders and nurses. I can see Jonah beguiling a nurse, but a holy man would be more of a stretch, I think. I'm trying to get more information about the nurses, but I can't just request their personnel files and personal records without cause. And, unfortunately, 'someone escaped six months ago' doesn't seem like enough of a reason."

"What about the programming?" Sam asks.

"They offer a pretty decent number of activities and classes for the inmates. Some of them are structured, like the GED program and vocational courses. But then others come on a shorter basis and sometimes rotate throughout the year. Yoga, creative writing, theater, even sewing. They have a crochet group that makes blankets and scarves and things for people in need. Of course, there's a library, but there's also a book mobile type group that comes in with new titles, magazines."

"But those are larger group activities, right? It would be next to impossible for him to form a close enough relationship with one of those instructors to have them be willing to help his escape, much less have the opportunity to make a plan that stayed private," Sam offers.

"Exactly."

"So, where are you now?"

"Nowhere," I sigh. "I'm nowhere."

"That's not true," he says, sliding closer and reaching out to take my hand. "You're right here."

♾

July
Wheeler

The bright flashes of color exploding in the sky reflected off the flask he raised up toward them with every burst. Hot air around him carried the smell of smoke from the fireworks and a cookout somewhere in the neighborhood. It was as nostalgic a smell as opening a cardboard box sealed around Christmas ornaments still clinging to the needles from last year.

He closed his eyes and breathed it in. There was another flash of light, a blast of heat across his face, and the smell of smoke. He opened his eyes to dissipate the smell of remembered gunpowder. He scrambled to bring the flask to his lips and wash down the scream.

The last drop slipped across his tongue and he already needed more.

It took concerted effort to get the bottoms of his feet to push into the ground and straighten his legs. For an instant, he couldn't tell if the grass was rising up to him or if he was falling down toward it. The flask slipped from his fingers as he made contact.

He rolled onto his back and felt like his body was sinking down into the earth. Staring up into the sky, he watched the last of the fireworks fill the darkness, then fade toward nothingness. He wondered what it would feel like if the dying sparks raining down became snow.

⌒

The sun and I get up at about the same time on July 23.

It's been a tradition of ours all my life. I'll admit I didn't show up for it for a few years there. But now that the third member of our special early morning club is back, we're on again.

Which is why I am ready and waiting in the kitchen with my biggest mixing bowl, a bag of flour, and a brand-new bottle of real maple syrup when the door opens and my father comes in. He has a grin on his face and a bottle of multicolored sprinkles in his hand.

"Happy birthday, sweetheart," he says, coming over to kiss my cheek. He pulls me in for a hug and whispers in my ear. "We both know it's the real one."

It makes me laugh the same way it has every time he's said it. The warmth of his embrace fills in a little bit more of the empty space that was left in me for all the years he didn't.

To everyone else, including the doctor who delivered me and my birth certificate, I was born on July 24th. But my father insists that my head was all the way out before midnight, which means I was here. He couldn't get anyone else on board, so celebrating that day as my birthday became something for just the two of us.

"Alright," he says. "You start making the pancakes…"

"With sprinkles."

"With sprinkles, and I'll work on the eggs."

I grin as I start gathering the rest of the ingredients for my favorite birthday breakfast. I will eat my weight in pancakes any day of the year, but adding sprinkles is only for my birthday. I dig through the pantry and suddenly can't find the flour. I realize I got a new bag when I went to the store yesterday. I must have left it in the car.

"Be right back," I tell Dad. "I just have to run out to the car. I must have missed one of the bags of groceries yesterday."

Grabbing my keys from the hooks by the door, I slip on a pair of flip-flops and head out to the driveway. I notice something sitting on the top step and leave it there until I get the wayward bag from the trunk and scoop it up on my way inside. Looking down at it, I see a card attached to the top with my name on it.

I go back into the kitchen and set the flour down before picking up the card and taking it out of the envelope. It's typed, like a note from a florist or delivery service.

"What's that?" Dad asks, glancing over his shoulder at me.

"It was on the front porch," I tell him. I read the note, then grin at him. "You were really serious about getting the jump on me this year, weren't you?"

"What do you mean?" he asks.

I show him the note. "I wanted to be the first to wish you a happy birthday. With love."

He shakes his head as I finish reading the note. "Let me see that." He crosses the kitchen to take the note from me and reads it with a frown. "Emma, I didn't send this."

"No one else celebrates my birthday on the twenty-third," I say. "Everyone else celebrates on the twenty-fourth. And only my closest friends even know about our date."

"Not just them," he says.

For an instant, I'm confused. Then a flash goes through my mind of being on the train racing toward Feathered Nest and the grisly puzzles I had to figure out to save the lives of everyone on board two trains. One of them involved finding the combination to a padlock. The clue that eventually revealed the combination was using "23" as my birthday and not "24". This was the work of Anson. One of the most twisted and horrific games he played with me. But there is only one person who could have told him the family joke about my birthday.

"Jonah."

"I don't think you should open the package," he says. "You don't know what could be in there."

"I really don't think he would do anything to hurt me," I tell him. "Not physically, anyway."

Before he can argue with me, I push my finger under the piece of tape holding two edges of paper on the bottom of the package. It releases and reveals a box that looks like a smaller version of the one I opened at my wedding reception. I look at it carefully, turning it around in my hands to examine every angle. I wanted to notice if there was anything strange or suspicious about the box beyond just its existence.

"What's going on?" Sam asks, coming into the kitchen bare-chested in the cotton sleep pants he slept in. He yawns and rubs his hand through his hair as he kisses me on top of the head. "Morning."

"Jonah sent her a birthday gift," Dad says.

That wakes Sam up. The sleep disappears from his eyes and he whips around to look at me from the coffeemaker. He crosses over to me.

"What are you talking about?"

I show him the box. "It was on the front porch when I went out to get the groceries I forgot in the car yesterday. The card just said he wanted to be the first one to wish me a happy birthday."

"No signature?"

"No."

"You shouldn't have opened it," Sam sighs. "You know how dangerous that could be."

"I already told her that," Dad tells him. "But she insists she doesn't think Jonah would hurt her."

"Emma," Sam says in a tone that says he's disappointed I'm not being more cautious.

But I'm not being an agent right now. I'm not looking at this through the eyes of a law enforcement professional. I'm just me and I want to know what the hell is going on.

"What is it that you think this is?" I ask, holding the box up a little higher. "A bomb? This box is, what, three inches by three inches? I highly doubt there's too much potential in it, even if there is something explosive inside. And since I see no white powders or crystalline substances, I'm going to go ahead and take my chances."

Taking the lid off the box reveals folded tissue paper. He planned these gifts, wanting them to look exactly alike so there would be no question he sent them to me.

I unfold the tissue paper and find a necklace nestled on padding.

"A manatee?" Sam frowns, looking down at the box. "I didn't know you like manatees."

"I don't, particularly," I tell him, the same confusion reflected off my own face. "I mean, they are cute in their floating pudge kind of way. I like seeing them when I'm in Florida, but it's not like I've ever felt especially connected to them or had them as a personal symbol or anything." I look over at my father. "Dad? Does this mean anything to you?"

He shakes his head. "No. I don't know why he would pick that for you."

"It means something," I say. "He doesn't do anything without thought. I haven't heard from him in seven months. He wouldn't just wander into a store and pick something random to send me after all that time."

"Or he did," Sam offers. "For that specific reason. He knows you are waiting to hear from him and will be sensitive to anything he says or does. Maybe he's trying to make you think he means something with that necklace. He's trying to give you a fake clue that will send you on a wild goose chase so you stay away from him."

"Good point," I acknowledge. "But what could it mean?"

"How about this," Dad says. "Let's at least get through your special birthday breakfast before we start following the clues?"

"That's probably wise," I say. "I am not missing out on my sprinkles this year."

The last of the cobwebs finally clear from Sam's face and his eyes widen. "Oh! Happy birthday, sweetie." Even as he says it, the last word is stretched in a yawn.

"You can go back to bed," I laugh. "I'll let you know when breakfast's ready."

⌒

August

It's been almost a year since I've climbed the stairs into the attic and walked through everything into the small room on the far side. This room is one of the pieces of my early life my mind blotted out of my memory. The therapist I was once tasked with talking to regularly once told me the mind does that to protect you from things that are too hard to handle.

I know that's the generally accepted view of why swathes of time disappear from memory, but I struggle with the idea. There are definitely things I forgot that may have been better left in the darkness of oblivion, but there are others that could have helped me or given me so much comfort. And some things were left vibrant and very visible in my mind when I wish they would go away. If the mind really does make some memories disappear as a means of protection, it feels like mine must have run out of space in whatever closet or dungeon they're stored in. Or my mind is especially vindictive and figures I don't really need all the protection.

When I first came back to Sherwood and reclaimed the house where my grandparents lived, I had plenty of memories of the home. I spent some of my happiest times here when I was young. Holidays. Summer vacations. Stretches of school years that meant I got to spend time with Sam.

But one thing I didn't remember was this room.

To anyone who might have come inside, it seemed like the house had

135

forgotten it, too. The wall was smooth with no sign of the door. I didn't discover this room until I was trying to hunt down a woman who no one else believed existed and discovered the anomaly with the blueprints of houses in the rest of the neighborhood.

Breaking into it was like opening a time capsule that should have remained buried. This is where my grandmother kept all the mementos of the son they had to cut from their lives and who everyone thought was dead. She couldn't bear to completely remove him and pretend he never existed. So she put everything that had to do with him in that room and sealed it up. She likely thought it would never be found.

The signs of Jonah are gone from it now. They're boxed up in a storage unit, tucked completely out of sight. I haven't been able to make myself throw it all away. My grandmother kept it. Those things mattered to her. He mattered to her. And one day Dean might wonder. I don't think he can put his mind in that place yet, but I won't be the one to make the choice to destroy the tangible remnants of a life before all of this.

At least, that was what I told myself about the boxes when I put them away and what I still tell myself every time I think of them since. I didn't have to worry about them. I didn't have to look into them or ever have anything to do with them.

And now I do. I sit in the room, holding the box with the strange necklace, and look around at what I made out of the space. It's a peaceful respite now, though I rarely come up here. Shelves filled with books. Comfortable furniture. It's a small, cozy space where I took back control over my home and stopped him from taking up space in it.

I'm not going to bring anything back here. I don't really want any of it in my house. But I have to go through it all. I'm down to next to nothing in my hunt for Jonah. We've pieced together everything we can from Greg's notes. There's still more work to do to reconstruct all of those thoughts and figure out what he was trying to lead us to, but for now, we've exhausted every lead we found and don't know where to go next.

It hasn't all been wasted effort. We've located several Leviathan dens and identified more members. Plans have been uncovered and stopped, which I am convinced means lives, money, and property have been saved. But I haven't found Jonah.

No one is talking. No one knows anything. No one will give us even a hint of where he is if they do know. The insights into the organization I've gotten from Anson and Greg tell me that not all of the people we've encountered actually have any clue where he is or how we would find him. The hierarchy of the organization is stringent, and only those closest to the center have real access to Jonah. They are the only ones who would be familiar enough with him and have enough of the closest thing he has to trust to know about his movements.

Because Jonah rarely actually trusts. It's more accurate to determine how much he doesn't trust a person than how much he does. On the very rare occasion he is willing to bring someone close, they still walk an extremely thin tightrope. If they betray him—if Jonah even sniffs the barest whiff of potential betrayal—there is little that can save them. Getting shot and captured was the best thing that has ever happened in Anson's life. It took him further out of Jonah's reach.

Not completely, just further. With his resources and the deep, complex network of followers he's been able to cultivate, I have no doubt if he really got in his mind to punish Anson for his transgressions, there are no walls or bars or prison guards who could stop it.

That day may come. I will probably always wait for it.

For now, I've come to the point of believing there is only one person who will give me any help at finding Jonah, and that is Jonah himself. I'll go back to the beginning, back before I was alive and before he had lost bits of himself to his obsession. By discovering who he is, I may have a chance to finally step into his mind and use the way he thinks to get me closer.

CHAPTER TWENTY-TWO

September

Detective Simon

"CAN YOU REPEAT THAT?"

She couldn't wrap her head around what the caller just said. The muffled voice, sounding like it came through a modifier, wasn't helping. She didn't think a call like this one was ever going to come through, so her brain wasn't ready to receive the message. She needed to hear it again, to make sure that any of the words she thought she heard were actually said.

"A woman in her thirties with dark brown hair has been missing from her home since December."

"Yes," the detective said.

She didn't want to give anything away with the tone of her voice. She didn't want to sound too excited or make it seem like she was feeding into the caller. There were a lot of women in the area. Most with brown hair. There was no guarantee there weren't others who went missing around the same time as the woman in the clearing as found, but who just hadn't been reported.

She needed to allow the caller to offer the information and go from there.

"I believe there is a Jane Doe by her description," the warped voice said.

"What information do you have?" she asked.

"9928 Gracey Square."

The line clicked.

"Sir?" Detective Simon said, assuming the voice she was hearing was a man. The modifier meant it could have been a woman. She had no guess about age. Couldn't detect an accent.

But she didn't really care. The person hung up before telling her what made them call, who they were, or what they might know about the woman. All they gave was a vague description and the address. She didn't even know what the address was to.

It could have been nothing. It might not have even been the right woman. The caller didn't give any actual identifying information for her, just that she was a woman with dark brown hair. That could have been anyone. And yet it was something. It was the only thing they'd gotten. Even a shred of connection was worth attention.

She grabbed up the notepad where she had written the address and brought it over to Wheeler. He looked up at her with eyes sunken deep in reddened sockets. They were sinking deeper. It seemed eventually they would disappear completely. But maybe then he'd better be able to see.

∽

Wheeler

"What is it?" he asked when the young detective came up to the side of his desk.

She bounded like a puppy and gave him as much of a headache. She didn't seem as young as she used to. The months that passed aged her. The days melted away with the snow and blew away in the warm breeze, burned away in the searing heat, and etched themselves in the corners of her eyes.

"A tip," she said.

"Alright," he said, barely affected by her words.

"About Jane Doe," she said. Her voice steeped the words in weight and emphasis, like there was tremendous magnitude in what she said.

He hated how she said it. Not just the importance she put in it, but the familiarity. She made the woman singular. She'd forgotten a word that drew a fine but distinct line in the stand. It was a line that very often distanced law enforcement agents from each other during investigations, even if they didn't fully realize it. "The".

It differentiated between a name and a label.

Jane Doe was not a name. It was not a single person. The detective did not know this woman. She didn't know anything about her. They weren't friends. They didn't have a connection. But she referred to her as Jane Doe, as if that was her name, rather than "the Jane Doe", signifying she was a missing person being labeled as such.

Forgetting that one word could be dangerous. It blurred lines and created the sense that this was all that woman was. If an officer thought of her as Jane Doe, as that being her name and her identifier, they started to chip away at the things that did make her an individual once. It started to wash away her life and focus only on her death and the time after. Giving her that name made her death the birth of a new person, one that could be manipulated and framed into a different light, given a personality and imagined existence that was likely wildly different from the one that was actually there. That twisted and knotted with reality, choking out the truth in favor of what the officer wanted to believe.

By creating a new person in their mind, they stopped themselves from being able to fully recognize who they really were, which could stall or even ruin an investigation.

He always kept that "the" firmly in place. Especially this time. So much time had passed and they'd gotten no further than they were the night she was found.

"Which Jane Doe?" he asked.

There were more missing women in the area. Two more had been reported in the time since she was found. Different appearances. Different ages. Different circumstances. Different lives. All Jane Does.

But not to Detective Simon. It was obvious looking at her that she believed there was only one. Only one who she could be talking about. She'd investigated the others. She'd kept their files in the back of her mind. But she hadn't sunken into them.

"From the clearing," she specified.

"What is it?" he sighed.

"A person called, described a woman with dark hair who has been missing since December, and gave me an address," she said.

"An address? To what?"

"I don't know. The caller didn't say."

"Did you get the caller's name or contact information?"

"No. They were using a voice modifier so I couldn't even determine if it was a man or a woman. They didn't leave their name and they hung up before they gave any other information."

"So, all you have is an address? And you assume it has to do with the woman from the clearing."

"It fits her description. We need to check out this address," Detective Simon said.

"First we need to find out what it is. People call tip lines just for kicks all the time. They want to see if they can get a bunch of cars racing off to an abandoned lot, or have a team draw guns on one of their friends."

Simon rolled her eyes and nodded. "I'm very aware of the concept of swatting. But I don't think that's what this is. The caller didn't make it sound like there was something urgent happening or that anyone was in danger. Nothing that would warrant an extreme response."

"Which means whoever it is might just fancy themselves a sophisticated swatter, or mouth breather who wants to sit back with his can of lite beer an' bowl of corn nuts and watch ya show up to an empty lot full o' old tires and trash," Wheeler huffed.

"I really don't think so. That isn't what the call sounded like." He didn't have anything to say to her. She stepped back away from him like she was waiting for him to say something. "Fine. I'll go myself."

He wanted to let her. He wanted to go back to the coffee that had gone cold in the corner of his desk and scroll through faces on the screen of his computer. He wanted to keep counting down the minutes until the date on the dry erase board propped against the wall of his cubicle.

But there was a part of him that still remembered what it was like to have the drive and energy that she did, even if there wasn't as much of it there as there once was. He remembered the beginning of his career as a detective. He remembered feeling like he'd accomplished so much because he wasn't just a uniform anymore. That he was going to make a difference.

She was impulsive and unpredictable when it came to this case. Too intense. That could be admirable. It could also be dangerous.

He went to her desk and found her hunched over her computer, furiously reading about the address.

"What did you find?"

"It's a house," she said. "A little more than an hour from here."

"Who lives there?" he asked.

"I'm trying to find that out. The owners are listed as Holly and Myles Stanford. They've owned it for decades, but I can't confirm they actually live there," she said.

"They have children?"

"I'm trying to get as much information about them as possible before I go out there."

"You need to slow down," he said.

"Slow down? We've been trying to find out anything we can about this woman for almost nine months. That seems slow enough for me. This tip was completely unexpected and we need to act on it before something happens and any information that might have been useful to us disappears."

"You don't know what this tip means. And if you lose your head and jump into somethin' without all the information, you could miss details. You could overlook what you should actually be lookin' for. And you could piss the wrong people off. I don't wanna make this case more of a pain in my ass than it already is.

"Find out who these people are. Get the info you need about that house and why someone gave us a tip that a missin' woman was living there. Then we talk about what to do next."

～

Detective Simon felt the urge to reach for the gun at her hip as she walked up to the front door of the house. There was no real reason. The house sat peacefully in the row of houses dotting a quiet suburban street. The bright green grass looked even and smooth, separated from the other lawns of the neighborhood with only shady oaks or neatly planted beds she could imagine would burst with bright blooms come spring. It looked pristine.

It also looked occupied. Which set her on edge. If the woman who lived here had really been missing for almost a year, it shouldn't look so comfortable, so cozy. It wasn't just the perfect lawn. It was easy enough for a professional to come mow the lawn and keep the ornamental plants at bay.

But there was a pair of shoes on the front porch. A newspaper at the end of the driveway. The latch on the gate leading into the backyard was slightly lifted, like someone had gone through it recently and hadn't put the latch firmly back into place.

As they stepped up onto the porch, a light in the back of the house flipped on. Her heart jumped up into her throat and something between excitement and nervousness sheared off in thin sheets in her stomach, sinking to her feet.

She reached up and knocked on the door. When nothing happened, she knocked again, announcing herself. There was no movement inside.

"Looks like nobody's home," Wheeler observed.

She was close. Simon knew it. She could feel it. Even as Wheeler was making his way back toward the car, she stayed. She knocked again. Determination and drive replaced the nerves. Her hand fell away from her thigh where it had rested.

"This is Detective Simon. We need to speak with you. Please come to the door."

There was no response, but she wouldn't give up. She walked down off the steps and stalked down the sidewalk, brushing past Wheeler without caring about the look on his face or what he might have to say. She walked down to the next house and knocked on the door. It opened quickly. Almost as though someone had been waiting for her to come. She wouldn't be surprised to find out that they were. The arrival of their cars likely caught the attention of the neighbors. They could be standing at their windows, watching, wondering what was happening.

Simon was hoping for that. If they were that nosey about their arrival, there was more chance of them being aware of what was happening around them. Which meant they might know the woman.

And why none of them noticed that she disappeared.

"Hello," she said to the woman who looked out at her with suspicion in her eyes. "I'm Detective Wendy Simon. Can I ask you a few questions?"

"Is there something wrong?"

"I'm just working on a case and am trying to locate a few people who might have information for me."

"You don't look like you're from around here. I don't recognize your badge."

"No, ma'am. I'm from Breyer. I'm in the crimes against persons division. We're working on a missing persons case. Can you tell me about your neighbor?" she asked.

The woman shook her head. "Don't know any of the neighbors. We keep to ourselves around here. Better that way."

She didn't expect that response. The neighborhood seemed like one that had block parties and exchanged cups of sugar. Not one that hovered behind closed doors and waited for others to go inside from checking the mail so they could water their grass.

"So, you've never met the woman who lives next door?"

"I spoke to her once when she locked herself out and needed to use my phone to call a locksmith," she offered.

"She didn't have her cell phone?" Simon asked.

"I suppose if she did, she would have used it."

"Yes. And when was this?"

"A good bit back."

"Before last December?"

"Yes. It was still warm enough out that she only needed a sweater. I remember thinking the color was a strange choice for her. All that red hair and she was wearing coral."

Detective Simon felt a rock sink into her stomach. Maybe Wheeler was right. They were on the wrong path.

"Red hair?" she repeated, making sure she heard correctly. "Your neighbor had red hair?"

"Yes. That kind of orangey color. She looked like that cartoon. With the red dress. Coral is definitely not her color."

"Have you seen her recently?"

"No," she said. "As I told you, we don't socialize much around here. I don't notice the coming and going of the people around me. What they do is their business."

"But you noticed that my partner and I came," she pointed out. "You were all but waiting at the door when I knocked."

"I keep to myself," the older woman shrugged. "I don't make a fuss and I don't get into other people's lives."

She stepped back and closed the door.

Simon went to three houses across the street and had similar conversations. By now Wheeler was in the car, the windows rolled down and his head leaned back. He was checked out. He'd barely been in it, to begin with.

The man in the fourth house told her much the same, but this time, he mentioned dark hair. It gave Simon a bit of hope. Maybe she hadn't completely fallen off the edge. Maybe she wasn't really wasting this time. She was just missing something. A roommate?

When the man told her he hadn't seen the woman living in the house across the street in a long time and couldn't really remember the last time, she asked the same thing she had five times before. Who was living there now? Had he seen anyone there?

He knew there had been a car in the driveway not too long before and the newspaper always got picked up, but he wasn't friendly with them. He didn't know who it was. It seemed to him whoever was there had a job with unusual hours, because the lights were always coming on late at night or in the very early morning. And the car would come and go at strange times.

She was just starting to thank him when she heard an explosive sound come from the house across the street.

Without saying another word, she jumped off the porch and ran across the street, passing the car where Wheeler was scrambling out. Her hand was on her gun and by the time she was on the porch, her boot planted in the center of the door, she held it in front of her.

"Simon, what are you doing?" he shouted behind her.

"That was a gunshot," she said.

The door cracked open under her boot, and she stormed into the house.

CHAPTER TWENTY-THREE

THE EDGE OF SUMMER IS JUST STARTING TO COME OFF DURING THE day. It's still hot enough during the day some days for sweat to bead on my neck and roll down my back. But the change of seasons is noticeable in the evening.

When the sun is going down and the quiet of the summer insects no longer filling up the twilight settles in, it's cool enough on the front porch to drape a blanket over my lap and hold a cup of coffee close to my chest so I can feel the heat rising up onto my face. It carries with it the smells of pumpkin spice and I don't care who knows it.

At this moment, there isn't anyone out with me to know it. I'm staring across the yard at the little yellow cubes of windows in the houses on the other side of the street, but not really seeing them. I almost don't notice when the door opens and Sam comes out to sit beside me.

He's already in his sweatpants and a long-sleeve t-shirt and he smells like soap and shaving cream. I snuggle into the well of his chest for a moment just to breathe him in.

"I got out of the shower and was having a whole conversation with you before I realized you weren't in the house," he says. "What are you doing out here?"

"Waiting," I say.

"Waiting for what?" Sam asks.

I take a breath. I don't really want to answer him. But I figure he probably already knows the thoughts going through my head.

"For Jonah. For him to show up or to do something. It's too quiet. It's been too quiet for too long. The fact that I haven't heard from him or seen him. I haven't heard about anything happening that seems like he would have planned it. It doesn't make me feel any better. If anything, it worries me more. I hate to be that cliched person and say it feels like the calm before the storm, but that's the only thing I can think of."

"I know."

"It's been nine months, Sam. And except for that weird necklace on my birthday, there's been nothing. And all I can think is that's because he's putting all of his energy and attention into something huge. Something bigger and more destructive than anything we've known he's done before. And what keeps going through my mind is that it's my fault."

"How could it possibly be your fault?"

"Just like Eric said. Jonah is the way he is because of me."

"No. Jonah is the way he is because of Jonah. Because there's something wrong in his head. It's not because of you. Just because he focuses on you it doesn't mean you are to blame for any of this. He would have been this way no matter what. Even if he didn't think you were his child, he would be the same person."

"Whether that's true or not, it doesn't stop it. Whatever he's doing, whatever he's planning, I don't know how to stop it. If I can't even figure out where he's been this whole time, I can't do anything about how much devastation he might be setting up for even as we speak. I don't know how to protect the people who are in danger."

"You don't know that anyone actually is," he says.

"Of course I do," I say. "As long as Jonah is breathing, someone is in danger. And, honestly, they still will be even when he's not. The reverberations from the damage he's caused will carry on for longer than I think any of us know. Definitely longer than I care to think about."

"Have you thought that maybe he's learned his lesson? Or maybe

THE GIRL IN THE WOODS

that he hasn't learned his lesson, but that he was burned by ending up in prison and has decided he would rather live a life of freedom out in the world even if it meant he didn't have the wealth and power he used to?" he asks.

"No," I say. "That's not him. It's not like being a fugitive is an easy, carefree life, and he's already done it. He already went for years with people thinking he was dead and only getting by on the fact that he could borrow my father's life. When Dad went undercover, that made life a lot harder for Jonah. And when everyone realized he was alive and responsible for so many things, it became even harder.

"Trying to navigate life outside of prison now would mean being out in a world where everyone knows his face and what he's done. I really don't think it would be worth it to him to be out here if there wasn't something he was trying to do."

He nods. "So, what now?"

"Now, I wait."

⌒

My phone ringing the next morning wakes me up. I reach for it under my pillow and squint at the unfamiliar number on the screen. My heart jumps in my chest. I pushed the blanket back as I sit up.

"Hello?"

"Emma Griffin?"

"Yes," I say, my brain taking a second to process that it's not Jonah's voice coming through the phone.

"This is Detective Wendy Simon from Breyer. I got your number from Eric Hernandez at the Bureau."

"Breyer?" I ask. The name sounds familiar, but the fog of sleep is still stopping it from getting all the way through to the logical thoughts.

Xavier would say all the cars are there, but if they aren't hooked up, the coal will only get the train so far.

I'm pretty sure this is what that means.

"What's going on?" Sam asks groggily as he moves beside me and rubs his eyes with the heel of his hand.

"Yes. I am investigating a case and I need to speak to you about it. Would it be possible for you to meet with me?"

"You need me to come to Breyer?" I ask.

"No," the young-sounding detective replies. "Actually, I'm currently about half an hour outside of Richmond. If you would meet me at the hotel where I'm staying, I would appreciate it."

"I need to ask what this is about."

"I'd prefer to speak to you in person. I assure you, it's urgent."

"Alright," I say. "I'm at home in Sherwood now, so I won't be able to get there until later this afternoon."

"That's fine. This is my personal number. Call when you are close."

She hangs up before I can say anything else. I wipe the sleep from my eyes and get out of bed.

"Babe, what is going on?" Sam asks. "Did you say something about Breyer?"

"Yeah," I say. "That was a detective from that area. She says she needs to speak to me about a case she's investigating."

"That's the precinct that sent out the alert about the missing woman," he muses.

I nod. "It's also the one closest to the prison."

"I know."

I stop in the middle of getting dressed and look at him. A few beats of silence pass between us.

"Do you think they found him?"

"I think you would have heard already," he says, climbing out of bed.

"Unless that was me hearing," I say. "She wouldn't tell me what she wanted to talk to me about. Just a case that she's investigating."

"You're going to go down there?" he asks.

"No," I say, shoving a few things into the duffel bag that at this point feels like I should just keep packed and in my trunk. "She's not in

Breyer. She's about half an hour outside of Richmond. I'm supposed to meet her at her hotel."

We go into the kitchen and he starts the coffeemaker. He pulls my biggest travel carafe out of the cabinet and I start packing food for the road. It's one of our rhythms now. We've gotten used to all kinds of mornings. Lazy mornings where we stay in bed until it starts to feel indecent and then just a little bit longer. Easy mornings where we both have to go to work, but there's nothing urgent. Hurried mornings where we both have intense things ahead of us. Mornings where one of us leaves and the other stays.

And mornings that come as a shock and throw us into something unknown. But even the unexpected is expected in some ways. I'll need coffee. I'll need food for the road. I'll miss my husband while he stays in Sherwood to do his job. I don't regret getting in the car and driving away.

It takes a few hours to drive to the address the detective sent me, but I call her when I'm close and when I pull up, a woman I can only assume is Detective Simon is standing outside. I roll down my window.

"Detective Simon?"

She takes a step closer to me. "Yes."

"I'm Agent Griffin."

"I know who you are. Thank you for coming."

"I'm going to park. I'll meet you inside."

Getting my bags, I cross the parking lot and walk into the hotel. The detective is standing off to the side, her back to me as she talks to someone. I don't know what's going on, but I can't imagine this will be done quickly enough to justify the drive back to Sherwood tonight. I go to the front desk to check in and the clerk tells me there's already a room reserved for me.

"Breyer PD is covering your room," Detective Simon says, coming up beside me. "It's the least we could do asking you to come out here."

"That really wasn't necessary," I tell her.

"Don't say that until you've heard what's goin' on."

151

The accent is familiar. I turn around to see a stare so surrounded by ghosts and the very edges of images that will never disappear the eyes are almost black.

"John," I say. "It's good to see you."

"That's debatable, but I know I'm sure glad to see you."

He steps forward and wraps me in a hug. It's not a completely natural movement for him. It never has been as long as I've known him. But the gesture means something.

"I thought it was strange to hear from a detective I've never met."

That isn't a light statement. I feel like I've met every detective and investigator working in all the precincts throughout Virginia. Especially those close to Richmond, Feathered Nest, and just outside of DC. I know I haven't, but I've encountered so many of them and worked on so many cases in conjunction with them it's odd to encounter one whose name I've never even heard.

Particularly this close to the prison that lost track of Jonah. That department has heard plenty from me.

But perhaps not this division. If John Wheeler is here, it means I've been called out by the crimes against persons division. Missing persons, homicides.

"I didn't realize the two of you knew each other so well," Detective Simon notes.

There's something in her voice that reminds me of high school.

"We've worked together several times before," I tell her.

"I was wondering why you were so quick to suggest we contact her," Detective Simon says.

I don't hear the same note of jealousy now, but it's been replaced by bitterness.

"She's the only person you should be askin' for help," John says. "She's the only one who might save this case."

"Is someone going to tell me what we're even talking about? I've driven all this way and still don't know why."

"C'mon in," John says plainly. "We're up in the conference room."

They lead me to a room that looks like it's been set up as a make-shift war room. Files are stacked up on the table and a large white board on the wall has evidence of notes scribbled in dry erase marker and then rubbed away many times. On one side is what looks like was once a list of names, each scribbled off one by one. I vaguely recognize some of the names from the prison records I've been scanning over and over again for months.

There is only one name left, written up at the top and circled in red.

Jonah Griffin.

CHAPTER TWENTY-FOUR

"**Y**OU HEARD THE GUNSHOT AND CAME INSIDE, RIGHT?" I ASK, stepping past the police line into the modest home on Gracey Square.

"Yes," Detective Simon says. "I was at the house across the street speaking to the neighbors about the tip that came in and I heard the gunshot. It sounded like it was coming from over here, so I came inside."

"But you didn't actually see a person with a gun, see smoke, smell anything?"

"No. I just heard it."

"And you're sure it was a gunshot?"

I don't bother to look at the young woman. I know she's glaring at me. And I can understand it. I would probably feel just as aggravated as she does if I was in her position. But I can't be bothered by that right now. I need every piece of information that's available, and that includes understanding her perspective and motivations.

"Yes," she confirms.

"How can you be sure?"

"I'm familiar with gunshots."

She shifts her weight slightly, her hand brushing over her thigh the way I've seen it do that motion a few times since I got to the hotel.

"You were injured in the line of duty," I say, nodding toward her thigh.

"I was," she says. "Why does that matter?"

"Your reaction to the sound. Immediately assuming it was a gunshot and there was danger," I say. She stiffens and I lift the edge of my shirt to show her just one of my scars. "I'm familiar."

"So, you think I heard a car backfire or something and freaked out?" she asks. "That I burst in here without cause?"

"No," I say. "That's not what I'm saying. What I'm saying is you clearly didn't hear a gunshot coming from inside this house because there was no one in here when you came in. And no one outside. No broken windows. No bullet damage anywhere. What's important is you heard something loud enough to get your attention from across the street. We just need to know what."

"How could that possibly be the most important thing about this?" she asks.

"Because if there was a sound, something made it. And there's a strong possibility someone intended it. Which means they knew you would react the way you did. They wanted to get you into this house."

I look at the framed pictures displayed around the living room, then walk down the hallway the way John directed me to the small bedroom converted into an office. My stomach turns and it feels like my heart stops in my chest when I see the papers spread out across the desk.

"Who would do that?" Detective Simon asks. "Who would go to so much trouble to get me inside?"

"I'm guessing the same person who gave you the address in the first place. Someone who wanted you to keep looking at this woman." I walk around the desk to put myself in the proper orientation to look at the blueprint. "Someone who wanted you to know Jonah is responsible for her murder." I run my hand along the drawing of the prison, seeing the image of the actual building in my head. "What was her name?"

"Miley Stanford," Simon says. "Named for her parents Myles and Holly."

I cringe, then feel guilty for the response. "So, you've spoken to her parents?"

"Yes. They live abroad. They bought this house when they were first married and they gave it to her when they moved. There's an account that pays for the utilities and other expenses, a lawn care company. Everything."

"Trust fund?" I ask.

"Something like that. They told me they knew their daughter would need help, but they couldn't be there to give it to her personally. They wanted her to have some sort of independence. So they set up the account and arranged for everything."

"And that's their idea of independence?" I raise an eyebrow.

"Apparently everything was always provided and done for her growing up and she never had to handle anything on her own. She lived with them until they moved a few years ago. So, to her, this was being more independent than she had ever been."

I nod. It isn't my place to judge. I just need to know about her and what was going on in her life leading up to the day she died. Including when Jonah got his claws into her.

"What else can you tell me about her? Or about her parents?" I ask.

As the detective talks, I continue to look through the cascade of horrifying evidence on the desk and throughout the office. I have no idea how she would have gotten her hands on the blueprints and plans of the prison, but here they are, detailing every corridor, every cell, every office, every mechanical system, and every entrance. It still doesn't fully explain how Jonah actually got out of the prison without anyone noticing, but we're getting closer.

Detective Simon tells me about the comfortable, if not quite lavishly wealthy second-generation parents and their only child, the daughter they named after themselves and indulged as much as possible. Which included her owning her own horse and competing in shows, lavish vacations, and attending private schools.

I look through journals and notepads filled with what I can only describe as coded messages. It's unlikely they are actually coded. That would take too much effort for someone to do with materials they were keeping in their own home. After all, if she was so concerned about them being seen or understood by someone else, she wouldn't have them just out in her office. Instead, it's more like a personal version of shorthand with the possibility of a few code words thrown in.

Even with the papers out in full display, there are some things people don't even want to put out into the world openly for themselves. The types of thoughts that you hold tight within you and don't even let yourself think all the way through. Images and replacement words form the thoughts so they aren't even completely heard in your own head.

I've had plenty of those thoughts. But they've never involved learning the inner workings of a prison to break someone out.

But that is clearly what Miley was planning.

"If her parents were so invested in her and were continuing to support her all this time, how did they not notice she was missing for almost a year?" I ask.

"When I spoke to her mother, she said they'd had a falling out with her last fall. They'd been planning to come back to celebrate the holidays with her, but then things came up and they weren't going to be able to make the trip back. She was really upset and they felt like it was their fault, so they wanted to give her some space."

"Nine months is a lot of space," I note. "More than that, if they hadn't spoken to her since fall."

The detective shrugs. "They figured she would call when she was ready. Everything was still being used at the house, the fund was being drawn on for the expenses, and they hadn't heard anything was amiss with her, so they just thought she was angry and would come around."

"Has everything here been photographed and documented?" I ask.

"Yes," she nods. "We didn't move anything, but it's all logged."

I nod and open the top drawer of the desk. Inside is a date book. I snap a picture of it where it's sitting, then pull it out and set it on a small empty section of the desk. Unsurprisingly, there are several months of blank pages, but as I get closer to the beginning of the year, a smattering of days with comments start to show up on the pages. By the pages dedicated to February, there are few blank days.

"It looks like she'd planned on being busy," I say. "Strange that none of these people in her contacts reported her missing, or noticed that she matched the description of a missing person. You would think someone with this many appointments and plans would have at least one person who would have noticed her disappearance to let someone know."

"That was my impression," the detective says. "It doesn't make sense that she just fell through the cracks."

"What does John say?" I ask.

She draws in a breath loudly enough for me to look up from reading through the notes on the calendar. They're written in similar shorthand to the notes on the notepads and journals, making it impossible to understand exactly what the victim was supposed to be doing on those days. Her jaw is set and she looks like she's trying to convince herself not to show some sort of emotion.

"Wheeler dismissed this case almost from the beginning. When she was first found and we didn't know exactly what happened to her, he focused heavily on the campers who found her. It was like he couldn't shake being suspicious of them, even though there was absolutely no evidence they had anything to do with her death. Then when nothing came from the investigation and no one came forward to claim her or give any hint of who she was, he stopped caring.

"He decided she was someone who wasn't worth investigating. That was only exacerbated when we found out she had LSD in her system. He says she had a bad trip, headed out into the woods, and ended up dying of exposure. In essence, she killed herself. He says he's seen it a thousand times and it's never worth wasting time and resources on it because it's just going to come right back to her."

"And when you found all this?" I ask. "What does he think about this?"

"He believes Miley got involved with Jonah somehow and he manipulated her into wanting to help him escape. He got what he wanted when he escaped, then he didn't need her anymore and he abandoned her. She took drugs to deal with the betrayal and it killed her."

"The sound of your voice tells me you don't believe that," I note.

"The fact that you're here tells me you don't, either."

CHAPTER TWENTY-FIVE

"**I** HAVE A LONG HISTORY WITH JONAH," I say carefully.

The detective nods. "I know you do."

I look down at the desk again.

"I'm going to need all of this collected for evidence. I need to go through every piece of paper and try to understand as much of it as possible. I'll need unrestricted access to it during the investigation."

"I'll have it collected by the CSU and booked into evidence, then transferred to the investigation room so you can get to it whenever you'd like."

"Thank you. Did you look around the rest of the house?"

"Only enough to clear it and confirm no one else was here."

"Did you have someone check through it for false walls, hidden exits? Something that would allow a person to remain out of sight during a check, or even get out of the house without someone noticing?"

She shakes her head, looking slightly bewildered by the question.

"No," she says. "We haven't had the time."

"Did you think of it?"

"No," she admits.

I take out my phone and send a quick message. "That will be taken care of tomorrow."

"The investigators could examine the house," she offers. "There's no need to waste Bureau resources."

"It's not a waste. If you want something done properly, you make sure you have the right tools. I'm bringing in a specialist with a very specific set of skills. If there is something other people aren't seeing that needs to be seen, or something that doesn't make sense and it needs to, he'll be the one to figure it out. His name is Xavier Renton."

I walk out into the rest of the house. There has to be something here that they didn't notice when they were first going through the house. And that's not a shot against them—a quick search to clear the house would have been cursory at best when it came to the details. They would have moved rapidly through every room, closet, and crawl space of the house to find anyone who could have been lying in wait, or even someone who could have been hurt.

The primary goal of a clearing search is to quickly ensure there are no threats in the area, not to try to understand more about the person who lived in the house. They wouldn't have had time to take in the finer points, to find out what was missing that should have been there. But that's what I'm doing now. There are too many questions still hanging over this house and Miley Stanford's death. So many pieces of it don't make sense. Especially our mystery tip line contributor who wanted to make sure the police came into the house and found all the information about the escape.

"Tell me again exactly what happened from the time you got the tip about this address until you called me," I say as I walk into the bedroom.

The detective repeats the story about the tip and I take particular note that she couldn't tell if it was a man or a woman calling. That was interesting to me. Tips called in to police can always be anonymous. Of course, it's preferable for a caller to give their name and contact information so that it's easy to get in touch with them again and get more details, or to have them accessible if they need to be a bigger part of the investigation or the case. But it's easy to understand why some people would be unwilling to be that candid.

There's a general consensus among law enforcement that it's more important to get the tip first, even without the caller's information, than it is to know all the details right off the bat. A lot of times we can work our way through the case using that information and eventually find the person who gave the tip. Even if we can't, what really matters is that tip can give us leverage and lead us on a path that gets us through the investigation.

In this case, I really want to know who called in that tip. It has to be someone who knew Miley but didn't report her missing. Someone who knew what she was doing in that office, but didn't say anything about it sooner. Whoever that person is, they have vital details about what happened to Miley. Maybe they even know how Jonah got out and where he is now. I want to know those details.

I open the door to the bedroom closet and sift through the dense assortment of clothes hanging in there.

"Eclectic tastes," I mutter, mostly to myself.

"What?"

I look over my shoulder at her. "Oh. I was just noticing her clothes. Most people have a pretty consistent style. Color palette. A silhouette they like. Something that kind of ties their wardrobe together. But there's a lot more variety in here than I'd expect."

"Her parents did say that she was involved in a lot of activities and did a lot of things," she points out. "Maybe she was that restless kind of person who was always searching for herself. Always trying to find her place in this world or what spoke to her soul. Maybe it was part of her becoming independent for the first time in her life."

It's obvious this case has had a tremendous impact on Detective Simon. This goes beyond just the death of this woman. She's attached and I'm curious as to why. I don't dwell on the details of the bedroom anymore. I need to keep her mind here, focused on the actual investigation and trying to understand what happened. So I move her back to telling me the sequence of events that eventually brought me here.

"After you received the tip, what did you do?"

"I wanted to come out here immediately, but Wheeler said we needed to look into it first and make sure it wasn't a prank."

I nod. "That's a good place to start."

She scoffs. "I'd think you would have more of a sense of urgency and drive than that."

I look at her for a few seconds, trying to figure her out.

"Have you ever hiked to the top of a waterfall?"

"Yes."

"Did you climb up a tree to get there because it was closer to the water? Go up the rocks that were actually in the water because you figured it would get you to the top faster?"

"No," she says.

"Didn't you have more of a sense of urgency and drive than that?" I ask. Her mouth opens like she's going to respond, but she doesn't have anything to say. "The point is, you can't always go straight to the end. You take the steps. You find the path, you heed warnings, you make sure you know where you are going and what you might need to overcome in order to get there. It might seem like you are delaying what you should be doing, but if you skip all of that, you're going to end up wasting time and compromising what you should have been doing to begin with. And you could end up getting hurt. When you've been around long enough and done enough investigations, you'll see it differently."

"Don't condescend to me. I'm not some kid still in the police academy. I might not be in the FBI, but I'm a detective and I earned my way here," Simon replies.

"I'm not condescending to you and I wouldn't give a damn if you were still a kid in the police academy, or if you were right beside me in the field at the Bureau. I'd tell you the same thing. I've got years on you, Simon. And a lot more experience. And I know that not everyone takes this as seriously as we do. Not everyone understands what we're doing. People make jokes, they pull pranks, and they try to throw us off our path. It's annoying as hell and it costs millions of dollars in wasted energy, effort, resources, and hours. Things that should be focused on what is actually being done.

"If you had come right to this house and it ended up being nothing, or a little old woman living alone, or some jackass teenager with a camera streaming live to make his buddies laugh, it would have damaged the investigation and compromised your reputation and trustworthiness. It also would have been splashed all over the news and alerted Jonah and anyone else who might be involved in this shit how far the investigation has gotten.

"You give up those cards, you're inviting the criminals to dance on you. They're always going to be a step ahead of you, Simon. Always. Whether you like it or not. Whether you want to believe it or not. Even if you want to think you are coiled up deep in their minds and are smarter than they are about everything, they are always going to be ahead of you. They are the ones you are chasing. They are the ones who did what you are still trying to understand. You will never get ahead of someone who has already offended. The only hope you have is to eventually catch up to them and run fast enough beside them that they don't get ahead of you again.

"You don't want to be chasing a criminal who you can get ahead of because that means they are going to do it again. You are anticipating their moves. I will always do everything I can to stay a step ahead of Jonah because I know as long as he is alive, he will never stop. It's up to me to stand in his way. That's what I'm trying to do right now. I'm trying to chase him and to stand in his way at the same time.

"But I need you to stop standing in mine. Tell me what you found out about this house and the people who owned it when you look into the tip."

The detective looks bristled, like the last thing she wants to do is cooperate with me. I really don't care. She would be far from the first person who has been resistant to me stepping in and joining a case they are investigating. All that matters to me is that I get the information I need and can keep pushing ahead.

She tells me the same information about Holly and Myles Stanford she did before.

"Alright," I nod when she's finished. "So after you found all that out, you came here. What did you see?"

"The house looks lived-in. There was a newspaper in the driveway, the gate latch was a little bit open. There was a pair of shoes on the porch. It looked like every other house, like at any second the woman who lived here was just going to walk out. But the caller had very clearly told me the woman was missing from her life. He described the dead woman."

"You said the caller said a woman with dark hair," I point out.

"Yes," confirms.

"Alright. So, you think that the woman this caller described is the woman you saw dead, and yet you also think someone is inside the house."

"Yes. A light turned on toward the back of the house. I thought maybe it could be the person responsible for her death."

"But you didn't know anyone was responsible for her death. At the time, you had no reason to believe that anything happened to her except she dropped acid and died of exposure. What made you so determined to get into this house?" I ask.

"The caller said she was missing. She was the only person living in the house. Or at least the only person who was supposed to be living in the house. And if there was someone else living here with her, that meant they knew for nine months that she was missing and didn't say anything about it. I needed to know what happened."

"But no one answered the door," I say.

"Right. I knocked, announced myself, everything, but no one answered. I saw that light come on. But no one came to the door. That was when Wheeler checked out. He decided it wasn't worth continuing to pursue and went back to the car. I went to talk to neighbors and found out none of them know each other. They keep to themselves and don't socialize, which means none of them really recognized that she was gone and none knew who was staying at her house."

"What else?" I ask. "Did any of the neighbors say anything interesting, that might make any kind of difference?"

"The only thing that stood out at all was the woman next door. She said she didn't know Miley and didn't pay attention to anything that was going on over here. She said the only time she interacted with her neighbor was one time she came over because she locked herself out of the house and needed to use the neighbor's phone to get a locksmith. She said the thing that stood out to her about Miley was the color sweater she was wearing."

"The color sweater?" I ask.

"Yes. She was bothered that she was wearing a coral-colored sweater with all that red hair."

I pause. "Red hair? I thought the victim had dark hair."

"She did. The tip caller even described her that way. But the neighbor said she had a lot of orangey hair like the cartoon character in the dress."

I think about this for a second, trying to figure out what the woman meant by it. It pops into my head.

"Jessica Rabbit?" I raise an eyebrow. "The neighbor said she looked like Jessica Rabbit?"

The detective nods. "That was all the information she would give me, so I talked to four others."

"And what did they say?"

"All essentially the same thing. The neighbors don't mingle. They don't get involved in each other's lives. One of them mentioned that she had dark hair, not red, which made me think maybe there had been a roommate? Or she'd dyed her hair? One remembered seeing a car there a couple of days before, but didn't know for sure if it belonged to Miley. That's when I heard the gunshot."

"What you thought was a gunshot," I say.

She glares at me. "It was a gunshot. I know that sound."

"There is no bullet damage inside this house. There is no bullet damage outside the house. No one was injured. There was no one in the house. You did not hear an actual gunshot. But it was enough to get you into the house. Which means someone knew you would react that way."

"Anyone would react that way," she defends herself.

I shake my head. "Not anyone. Most people go the other way when they hear a gunshot. Or they stay in place and call for help. They knew you were going to come to that house and that you would respond to the sound of a gunshot by running into the house. Someone wanted you to come in here and find these things."

"Do you think they were planted?" she asks.

I shake my head. "No. I think they're genuine. Where she was found, going into those convenience stores and talking about the prison when she was already under the influence of the drugs… It all adds up. It makes sense that she was there talking about going to the prison to see Jonah."

"But there was no visitation. The prison was locked down," Simon points out.

"And she wasn't there to visit. She was there to break Jonah out of prison. Being under the influence of the drug would make her disoriented and cause hallucinations. It would also diminish her inhibitions so she would be more likely to discuss something she should be keeping quiet, like going to break someone out of prison. I believe all of this was hers. She used it to help Jonah plan his escape, and someone knew about it. They wanted you to find out about it."

"There was someone here," she insists. "I watched the light turn on and I heard the sound."

"Where was the light?" I ask.

"In the back corner of the house."

I go to the room with the window she said she saw light up. It's a sitting room leading off the kitchen.

"Here?"

"Yes," she nods. "This window lit up like someone just walked in and flipped the switch."

"And the sound of the gunshot came from here, too?" I ask.

"I don't know for sure, but it sounded like it was coming from there."

I look around to find all of the light sources. There is an overhead light and two lamps. The overhead light is operated by a switch on the wall and the first lamp has to be touched on the base to turn on and off.

The second lamp is closest to the window. Unlike the other lamp, it has a switch. I turn it and the lamp lights up. It's plenty bright enough to be very visible from outside the window.

"You just showed how every one of these lights needs a person to manually turn it on," the detective says.

I crouch down and look under the table where the lamp is sitting. There's a pile of magazines blocking the electrical outlet, and when I move them, I find a small white box plugged into it. I touch the button on the side and the lamp turns off. I touch it again and the lamp turns on. Pulling it out of the wall and removing the lamp cord from it, I turn around and toss the box over to Detective Simon.

"Here's your intruder," I say.

She flips the box around in her hands. "What is this?"

"A smart device adapter. The lamp is plugged into it and then it can be operated remotely. You were right. Someone did turn the light on while you were standing outside the house. But they weren't in the room. They have a phone or a computer attached to that device and can control it from wherever they have internet. If I don't miss my guess, there's another one of those somewhere that is connected to a recording of a gunshot."

"It was all set up," the detective whispers.

"But by whom?"

CHAPTER TWENTY-SIX

"**W**HERE DID THEY FIND IT?"

I rush out of the house, ensuring the uniform officers stationed outside know not to let anyone inside unless I give authorization.

"The old train station up off the interstate," says John on the other end of the line.

"Send me the address. I'm on my way."

I end the call and turn around to Detective Simon.

"They found Miley's car. John is there. I'm going to go search it. I need you to get me Miley's autopsy records and the statements from the two witnesses at the convenience stores."

I get in my car and check my messages, starting the engine and pulling out of my spot before I've even finished putting in the address into the GPS. Fortunately for me, it's not a very far drive. There are two police cars already at the edge of a parking area that was once covered in gravel but is now mostly sand and patches of grass. Several abandoned cars clutter the space, but the officers are gathered around one at the back.

I park beside them and head in long strides toward the car. I pull out my badge and hold it up as officers turn toward me with the look that says they are eager to tell rubberneckers to leave.

"FBI," I start. "Where is John Wheeler?"

"Emma, over here."

I walk around the officers to a nondescript champagne sedan. It's coated in a fine layer of dust, but the license plate is perfectly readable.

"This is it?" I ask.

"Yes. We had a BOLO out for the plates. Patrol identified it a couple hours ago. We see a lot o' abandoned or stolen cars out this way, an' squatters or junkies'll come through, so we've upped the police presence. We can't always cover it every day, but a beat goes by at least a few times a week."

"So the car hasn't been here for long," I say.

He shakes his head. "No more'n a day or two. Respondin' officer said that's what got his attention. This one wasn't there last time he drove by. When that happens, he runs the license plate if it's still on. It flagged the BOLO an' he called it in."

"Have you looked in it yet?" I ask.

"Just a glance. CSU barely got done. Doesn't seem to be much o' note inside. They might've got some fingerprints, but there weren't any hairs, blood, weapons, anythin' like that."

"Well, I'm not surprised there wasn't any blood or weapons. There really wouldn't be a reason for there to be. The fingerprints might be useful if they are in the database. Mind if I take a look?"

He steps back and holds out his hand in a gesture toward the car. "Be my guest."

"Thanks."

I open the trunk to search through it.

"Imagine the great Emma Griffin, FBI, askin' me for permission to investigate a lead."

I close the trunk and roll my eyes at Wheeler.

"Enough of that."

I get in behind the wheel and look around the cabin. There are traces of fingerprint dust, but other than that, the car is neat and clean. Same for the seats and under the floor mats. I open the glove compartment and find only the manual and a small travel first aid kit. The driver's side sun visor is empty and the passenger side has only a business card tucked into the elastic band across it.

I take it down and look at it.

"What's that?" John asks.

"A business card for a makeup artist," I tell him. I flip it over. "Nothing on the back."

I take out my phone and snap a picture of the card before putting it back into place where it was. As I get out, the tow truck that will bring the car to the police impound lot arrives.

"Sorry there wasn't more," John says.

I shake my head. "It's alright. It would have been nice to find something that might show who's been driving the car and staying at the house, but I guess they did take the time and put in the effort to dispose of the car. It would have been a massive oversight if they had left something like a collection of selfies with Miley or a sticky note with their forwarding address."

John lets out a short laugh. "But it woulda been nice."

He starts back toward his car and I notice the heaviness that seems to press down on him. It didn't used to be there.

"John?" He turns toward me and makes an acknowledging sound. "Why don't we go grab a cup of coffee? I'd like to run things by you and see what you can tell me."

He nods and I get in my car, waiting for him to pull out so I can follow behind him.

∽

"How are you doing, John?"

I take a sip of my coffee. It's pumpkin spice, but not as good as when Sam makes it for me at home.

He nods as he forces down a deep sip of his own drink. I pretend I didn't notice him tip the flask from his inside pocket into the cup before I sat down. It's not enough to impair his driving, but still concerning. I'll suggest he takes the rest of the day off when we finish.

"You're just gonna jump right in, ain't ya?" he asks. "I thought we were goin' over the case."

"We can," I nod. "Tell me your thoughts on everything."

"Everything?" he asks, emphasizing the 'g' in the word. He doesn't often.

I take another sip. "Everything. Start with the night the body was found and go from there. I've already heard Detective Simon's perspective. I'd like to hear what you have to say about it."

He gives me a bemused half-laugh. "I'm sure you've heard plenty from her."

"Why do you say that?"

"She's young, Emma. She only has a couple years under her belt. You could count the major cases she's handled on one hand. More homicides, o' course, but they've all been straightforward. Shootin's. Domestics. Vehicular incidents. This situation's really gotten under her skin. She's gotten herself completely wrapped up in it."

"She says you checked out at the beginning," I say.

The tips of his fingers twist his cup around as he watches it. "That sounds about accurate."

"Did you?"

His eyes meet mine. I remember when they didn't look the way they do now. When there was still life in them. They were brighter the last time I saw him. The light is collapsing from the outside, like a star slowly dying.

"It was the holidays. I was home. I wasn't exactly in a condition to be handlin' a death notification."

"You were on call," I say.

"I know."

I think about what he said. "Wait. The holidays? Not early December?"

"No," he shakes his head. "Just before Christmas."

"Jonah escaped from prison several days before my wedding," I point out.

John nods. " ME said she was out there for a while before the campers

172

found her. There was that nasty cold snap through that whole month. She was frozen solid. Kept the critters from spreadin' her around."

I cringe. "Thanks for that. What did you think when you first saw her?"

"I was suspicious of the campers. I thought it was too convenient they were out in the freezing cold, pitch black, in the middle of the holidays, an' happened to stumble on a body. I didn't know how long she'd been out there." He takes another sip. "I wanted to find out what happened to her. I wanted to catch the son-of-a-bitch who hurt her. But the longer that went on, the more it seemed like no one hurt her. She ended up out there on her own, because of her own decisions.

"No one came forward to identify her. No one acknowledged she was gone. There was nothin' left to avenge for her. She'd made her choice."

"But what if she didn't?"

"She was on LSD, Emma. She wandered into stores miles away from where she was found, babblin' about going to a prison on lockdown. Then she went out into the woods in nowhere near enough clothin' and died. There were no injuries on her. The blood comin' from her mouth was from bitin' her lip when she fell."

"She helped Jonah escape. These things aren't a coincidence. Do you think she was just fascinated by the prison and somehow found a blueprint? That she has all those pages of notes and sketches because she was fantasizing about helping him and that manifested it into being real?"

"How could they have planned an escape? He's been locked up for a long time. It's not like this woman could sit with him an' do layouts of his escape plan right there in visitation."

"Have you checked his visitor logs?"

"Emma," he sighs, rolling his eyes and leaning back in his chair.

"I just want to know if she's on them. If she ever visited him in prison, her name would be on his list and there would be a record of her visits. Did you check that?"

"Not yet," he says. "All of this just happened. We haven't had a chance."

"We need to find that out," I say.

"You sound almost as wrapped up as Simon is," he remarks.

"Because I care?"

"Because you're tryin' to make something exist. Simon is acting like that woman is a member of her family, or kindred spirits, or some such. She's buildin' her into an image of somethin' we don't know she ever was. Givin' her a personality we have no way of knowin' she really had. All I've done is stay realistic. She was never reported missin'. Not by her parents, not by any friends, not by a boyfriend. And the descriptions of her and even the artist's sketch of her didn't do a thing. That means something. But she doesn't want to see it."

"Someone has been in her house, John. Over and over again. Maybe this entire time. They've been using her car, staying in the house. Now I don't know if I believe that she left those notes on her desk or if I think whoever took over her house found them and put them on display to be found. And if they did that, why? Why either way? Why wait all this time to alert the police of her involvement? Someone wants people to know what Jonah did. Why not gather up all the information and bring it in? Why do it like this? But the thing that bothers me the most is this person knew Miley well enough to be familiar with her house. They had access to her car. They want the truth about her death to come forward. And yet, they didn't report her missing."

"Maybe they don't want anyone to know they couldn't save her."

Silence settles between us.

"Really, John, how are you?"

"I'm fine."

"You're drinking."

"I'm fine."

"We haven't stopped looking, John. We're going to find him. There are agents out there every day trying to find a way in so we can identify him and take him down."

"And I haven't stopped waitin' for my son to come home."

174

CHAPTER TWENTY-SEVEN

I'M HOLDING THE PHONE BETWEEN MY SHOULDER AND MY EAR AS I pull off my shoes and toss them into the corner of the hotel room. I unbutton and unzip my jeans, taking hold of the phone again with one hand and using the other to wriggle them down.

"Did you find anything?" Sam asks.

"Not really. I read the autopsy report and looked at the pictures. It's just like Wheeler told me. There were no signs of trauma on her body. No significant injuries or defensive wounds on her hands. No ligature marks. She had a cut on her lip from biting it when she hit the ground, but that's about it. She had the beginning of some frostbite, but not a lot, which means she died pretty quickly. She only had one tattoo, no body piercings, no major scars from surgery or abuse. That doesn't necessarily mean there weren't fainter scars or more subtle signs that were covered up by the discoloration of her skin being frozen. But nothing that really stood out. I was actually surprised."

"How do they think she was murdered?" Sam asks.

"She helped him escape. There's still a lot to be figured out about that part. But for right now, we know she somehow gained access to the plans for the prison, so she had intimate knowledge of the entire building. I have a lot of notes and journals to go through to try to find the details of the plan. It doesn't really matter, though. She was on his approved visitor list. There's a record of her visiting him pretty soon after he went in.

"It isn't hard to see how it could take a while to come up with and prepare a plan to escape a maximum-security prison, so the amount of time that passed isn't much of a concern for me. Our guess is she helped him escape from the prison and he knew she would be a liability if she were alive.

"As soon as they were far enough from the prison that he could move on to the next stage of his plan, he dosed her with LSD. It isn't injected, so there would be no needle marks in the skin or bruising to show he was holding her firmly to give the dose. Instead, he would just need to get the tab in her mouth. That could be as easy as having it integrated into a fake note or document that he said needed to be kept concealed.

"I also never underestimate Jonah and his ability to convince people to do things that might sound out of the norm or even a little outrageous. After all, she had just helped him escape from prison. It might not be that big of a leap to think that all he would need to say is 'open your mouth' and she would do it. The tabs aren't very big and depending on the concentration of the drug on it, the effect can be extremely intense within about half an hour.

"He gave it to her, possibly encouraged her to change out of her warm clothes and into something he knew would cause exposure quickly, then left her. The trip hit, she started wandering, and she ended up dying in the woods," I say.

"Why do you sound like you aren't completely convinced of that?" Sam asks.

I go into the bathroom and set fresh towels close to the shower. Reaching in, I turn on the water so it can get warm. One thing I've learned about this shower over the last couple of days is that it needs some encouragement to get hot enough for a decent shower. Or at least hot enough for a shower for me. Sam likes to affectionately refer to the preferred temperature of my showers as 'Satan's front porch', so user results may vary.

"It's not that I have a problem thinking he killed her. In fact, that makes perfect sense to me. Jonah sees people as disposable. They are just resources, tools he can use up and then dispose of when they aren't useful anymore. It just seems like a strange approach. That's not his usual style.

"But being in prison for a while can change a person's perspective. It also changes what he has access to. It's entirely possible he wanted a different method but didn't have access to what he would need. Getting out of prison is difficult enough. I highly doubt he would add the extra challenge and risk of stealing a gun on his way out.

"He might have used other tools to get out, but we still don't know how he actually accomplished it, so what he used might not have been an efficient means of murdering her. It wouldn't surprise me to find out she was supposed to bring him a weapon. He might have requested that she bring a gun and she didn't, so he had to go with what was available to him.

"The point is, he wanted to get rid of her. He wanted to make sure she wouldn't be able to tell anyone what happened. The only person who can be trusted with a secret is a dead person."

"Except this dead person had someone tell her secrets for her," Sam points out. "The anonymous caller."

"That's one of the things I still don't know. Right now, this whole situation is looking like a big puzzle with a bunch of the pieces missing. I don't know how this girl managed to get tangled up with Jonah, or how they planned the escape while he was in prison. I don't know how he actually escaped. And I don't know what he did or where he went after. Or who found out about all of it and took almost a year to come forward with it."

"What about her parents? Are they coming back?" Sam asks. "I'd assume they'd want to be here to make final arrangements for her."

"I haven't had any communication with them. Detective Simon is the one who spoke with them over the phone and got the information about Miley that we have. She hasn't mentioned any plans for them to come back. But that doesn't mean that they won't. Just means they didn't share them with her."

"Did she ask them if they have any idea who might have been staying in the house? Or who their daughter would trust enough to give them access?" Sam asks.

"She did. They told her they hadn't heard anything about someone staying with her, and didn't know of any of her close friends or if she was dating anyone. The last time they spoke with her, she hadn't mentioned anyone new in her life, and there hadn't been anyone of note in a while before that. But you have to remember they haven't heard from her in over a year."

"Yeah, but she's been dead for most of that. She can't exactly start forming close bonds with people now."

"According to Xavier she could," I say.

"According to Xavier, a lot of things," he says.

It's not a whole sentence, but no truer words have ever been spoken.

"Speaking of Xavier, how is he? How's Dean?" I ask.

"They're fine. Dean spoke with Noah yesterday about a lead they thought might have come up about his assault, but it didn't pan out."

"Has the recording of the 911 call come back from the Bureau audio forensics lab yet?" I ask.

"No," he says. "Apparently there's a major backlog from a specific case and they've done some cursory work with it, but haven't been able to identify the voice or figure out where she was when she made the call."

I let out a sigh. "Alright. Well, I'm going to hop in the shower and try to get some sleep. Getting started early again tomorrow."

"What are you doing?"

"I'm going to interview the witnesses. The convenience store owners. I've read through their statements and watched the small amount of surveillance footage available, but I feel like I need to talk to them myself. Some things didn't come up in the initial interviews and investigation that I want to ask. I'm curious about how she was getting around."

"What do you mean?" Sam asks.

"These stores were a few miles apart, and then she was found miles away from them. It was so cold outside that she froze to death. She couldn't have walked that whole distance. Someone would have noticed her. And it would have taken too long for her to make it in the timeframe that she did without the cold getting to her. Yet, neither of the store owners said they noticed her getting out of or into a car. No car matches the description of hers in the surveillance footage. And there was no car anywhere around where she died."

"Maybe it got towed?" Sam offers.

"No," I say. "If it got towed, they would impound it and only the registered owner would be able to get it back out. I don't see Jonah driving her around to various places when she was already under the influence of the drug that would lead to her death. That would defeat the purpose of distancing himself from the murder. And if he did take her car, why did he bring it back to her house? And what would he have done with the keys so that whoever has been driving it around could use it?

"I don't think she had her car with her. It had to be another car. It's just a matter of figuring out which one and what happened to it."

"I'm sure you will," he tells me.

"Your faith in me never ceases to amaze me," I say.

"You never let it down," he says. I let out a sigh. "What is it?"

"I just don't understand how something like this happens. How could she be manipulated that way? It's hard to understand for anybody, but especially for someone like her."

"Why someone like her?" he asks.

"She had everything," I explain. "What could he have possibly offered her that would have been so appealing she could be manipulated into doing something so dangerous and illegal that ended up costing her life? She was given everything in life."

"Not everything," Sam says.

"What do you mean?" I ask.

"Her parents left her here and moved to another country. They refused to come home to spend the holiday season with her. They didn't blink when they didn't speak with her or hear anything about her for a year. They might have given her a lot, but in her eyes, not everything. Not love."

I realize he's right. She obviously doesn't know it, but her parents haven't even shown up or shared any plans to come back even now that they know she's dead. Being given all the tangible things and opportunities in the world doesn't cover up the need for validation.

"She thought he loved her."

"It's very possible. Go on and enjoy your shower. Get some rest and figure this out so you can come home. I miss you."

"I miss you, too. I love you."

"Love you. Goodnight."

CHAPTER TWENTY-EIGHT

SET MY PHONE DOWN ON THE BATHROOM COUNTER AND STEP INTO the shower. It creates a blissful sting on my shoulders and back, and I turn around so the pulsating water can work out the tension in the muscles along my spine for a few seconds.

I've just gotten through washing my hair when my phone rings. Figuring it must be Sam remembering something he was supposed to tell me, I reach out of the shower, dry my hand, and scoop up my phone.

"Hey," I say. "Give me two seconds to rinse off and I'll be right back."

"Emma."

I stop still.

"Jonah."

I scramble to get out of the shower and grab a towel to dry off.

"Emma, I need you to listen to me."

I go out into the room holding the towel against me and dig pajamas out of the dresser.

"Where are you?" I demand. "You need to turn yourself in."

"No," he says. "That's not going to happen. Especially not now. I saw the news report."

"You're wanted for murder," I say, pulling the phone away from my ear only long enough to drop the shirt down over my head.

"I know. That's why I'm not going to tell you where I am."

"Then why are you calling me?"

"I didn't kill that woman," he insists. "I didn't have anything to do with her death. I need you to believe me."

I scoff. "Why would I believe you?"

"I've taken responsibility for everything you've ever asked me, Emma," he says. "I've told you the truth."

I can't stop the bitter, mirthless laugh that bursts out of me at that statement.

"Are you serious right now, Jonah? You've told me the truth? My entire life is built on lies that you told."

"I've told you who I am and I've admitted to what I've done. I've been honest with you. And I need you to believe me now."

"Even if I was going to, why would it be important that I believe you?" I ask. "I'm not the one with the warrant out for you. I'm not the one bringing you up on charges. I'll do everything in my power to investigate and prove beyond the shadow of a doubt that you did this, but it's not up to me. Why does it really matter if I believe you?"

"Because I need to know you know the truth," Jonah says.

"Never base any of your hope or perceptions of self-worth on my opinion of you," I say. "It will never be anything more than that you are a cold, vicious, selfish monster who cheats, lies, steals, brutalizes, and kills for whatever purpose suits you that day. That's never going to change. Adding or taking away one murder isn't going to make a difference."

"I need you to solve it, Emma."

"Excuse me?"

"I need you to figure it out. To solve the murder."

"You want me to clear your name?" I sputter, not believing what I'm hearing. "Don't waste my time, Jonah. You escaped from prison and murdered the woman who helped you, but you want me to figure out a way to get you out of it. Unbelievable."

"I escaped from prison, but I didn't kill that woman. You need to prove that."

"This is ridiculous. I'm not talking to you about this anymore. Goodbye, Jonah."

"Do it for her," he says before I can hang up.

"What?" I ask.

"Don't do it to clear my name. Do it for her. She deserves people to know what actually happened to her and who is responsible. Blaming me won't do any good. It will give the police and the Bureau another reason to hunt me, but what difference does that make? What good would it do to attach my name to a murder I didn't commit and leave the person who may actually have done it out in the world with no accountability and no consequences?"

"I saw her plans, Jonah. I went to her house. I know that she was in touch with you. That her name was on your visitor list. She visited you."

"A woman named Miley Stanford visited me years ago," he says.

"Yes," I confirm.

"Does anyone even know who she is, Emma?" He pauses, but the question has struck me silent. "I need you to do this. Think about what I said. Decide what you should do."

"How do I get in touch with you?" I ask. "I'm guessing if I try to call this number back it won't connect."

"If you decide you want to talk to me, go to the news report on my escape out of Breyer. The one that was released when it first broke. It doesn't matter what username you want to use, just post the comment 'Emma is looking for you'. I'll see it."

"Why can't you let me call you?" I ask.

"You know better than that, Emma."

The call drops and I sit on the end of the bed, stunned. When I feel like I can think clearly again, I call Detective Simon.

"Agent Griffin," she says. "What can I do for you?"

"I need you to give me all the information you have about Miley Stanford. Birth records, school records, her parents' contact information. Anything."

"What's going on?" she asks.

"I just need to look further into her life," I tell her.

"Maybe I can help. What are you looking for?" I ask.

"Her."

"I don't understand," she says.

"I know. Neither do I. Not yet. But if I get that information, I might," I say.

"I'm still at the office. I'll send what I have through to you."

"Thank you."

I end the call and go back into the bathroom to brush out my hair and twist it into a thick braid to keep it out of my face. It's how I usually sleep, but that's no longer on my mind. Jonah's words are sharp and heavy in my mind.

A woman named Miley Stanford visited me.

Do people even know who she is?

It takes longer than I want it to for the message from the detective to arrive, but when it does I pull it up on my computer and start digging through.

⁓

The next afternoon, I stalk into the police station and go directly to Wheeler's desk.

"How did you not know?" I ask.

He looks up at me and I wonder how much of the residue at the bottom of his cold mug from the morning was coffee.

"Mornin', Emma," he says flatly.

"It's two-thirty in the afternoon," I say. "How did you not notice this?"

"Notice what?" he asks.

"This," I say, dropping papers on the desk in front of him. "Any of this. Detective Simon is so absorbed in this case and has looked into Miley Stanford's life so extensively, yet neither of you noticed what I would consider a fairly important detail."

"What detail?" he asks.

"It's not her."

"What are you talking about?"

I turn around to see Detective Simon coming toward us.

"You said you looked into her life," I say. "That you found out about everything her parents did for her. The private schools. The horse. The vacations. All of it."

"I did," she nods.

"Then how did you not notice it's not her?"

"What do you mean it's not her?" she frowns.

Aggravation has my teeth grinding against each other and my jaw set hard. I'm fighting to keep myself under control. It wouldn't do any good to unleash everything I'm actually feeling.

"Your corpse. It's not Miley Stanford."

Simon's face drops. She recovers and shakes her head. "Of course it is. The tip led us to her house. Her parents confirmed she was living there. All those notes about the escape and the prison blueprint..."

"That was Miley's house. Those were Miley's parents. It's just not Miley's body. I researched everything you sent me. The stories are true. Miley was given absolutely everything her parents could afford. She had a fantastic life. All of that did happen. It just didn't happen to the woman found dead in the woods." I sift through the papers I put down on the desk and pull up one of the autopsy images. "This is the dead woman." I find another picture and set it down beside the image of the corpse. "This is Miley Stanford."

"Look the same to me," John observes.

"They look similar," I clarify. "Dark hair. Pale skin. Maybe the same color eyes, but that's harder to tell with the Jane Doe. Ice crystals over the eyes will do that. But Miley is two inches shorter and at least twenty pounds heavier."

"Weight can change," Simon points out.

"Sure," I say. "But scars are a bit harder. Especially ones from an appendix removal. Miley had one when she was fifteen. Emergency surgery. It left a huge scar. She also has no known tattoos and that one on the body is not new. If I'm not wrong, and I sincerely doubt that I am, it has been there for far more than five years."

"Five years? Why would that matter?" John asks.

"Which brings me to the next bit of information that slipped past you," I say. "Five years is significant, because that's when Miley went missing."

"What?" Simon asks.

I take another document out of the stack and set it on top.

"The missing persons report her mother filled out just over five years ago. Filed with the department near her home. Miley Stanford. Five feet five inches. Surgical scar on her stomach. No known tattoos." I take out another document. "And the official withdrawal of the report. Filled out again by her mother, four months after the report was filed. Saying she was recovered alive and well, and everything was good."

"But it's not her," John says.

"But her house is full of pictures of the woman the campers found. The ID that was found in her house has that name," Simon says.

"Which begs the question…"

"Who is she?" John asks.

"And where the hell is Miley," I say. I lean closer to John, pressing my hand down onto the desk to support my weight as I lower my voice. "You need to get your shit together, John. You're drinking again. And you're losing sight of what's right in front of you. I know you, John. You're better than this. Put the damn flask away. You're not going to find Miley at the bottom of it. Or the man who shot up your son. It's time to be alive again."

I push away from the desk, gather up the papers, and start away from the desk.

"What do we do now?" Simon asks.

I stop and turn to look at her. "I suggest you let go of whatever fantasy is in your head right now and start figuring out who that woman actually was."

I walk away again.

"Where are you going?" she asks.

"I'm going back to the hotel to read the news."

CHAPTER TWENTY-NINE

To say I'm conflicted as I stare at the comments section under the article about Jonah's escape would be a massive understatement. Finding out the woman I've been referring to as Miley Stanford is someone else, and that the whereabouts of the actual Miley Stanford is a mystery, has my mind twisting around. I'm not sure where my thoughts about Jonah lie anymore.

Miley Stanford was a real person. Her parents were real people. They lived a life together. Now I've seen pictures and videos, award certificates, transcripts. This was not a crafted life. Miley existed. She just isn't the woman who was using her name and ended up dead beyond the tree stand miles from the prison.

Her parents reported her missing, but then withdrew it saying she'd been recovered. And this new information throws even more confusion into her parents' actions. It makes no sense that they'd respond this way to the woman they thought was their daughter going missing. Why would they report her missing when she went missing once, but then the next time she does say they wanted to give her space and allow her to work it out for herself?

When they withdrew the missing persons report, was it actually their daughter who had resurfaced? And if not—why would they claim another woman as their daughter? Either way, I needed to know what happened to both of them: the real Miley, and the woman who claimed her identity.

Which brings me back to Jonah. This development makes me question the plausibility of Jonah being responsible for her death. The more I considered the circumstances of the woman's death, the more I wondered what the point of him murdering her that way would be.

I'm not suddenly seeing Jonah as compassionate and gentle. I have no doubt he would have someone help him and then dispose of them without a second thought. It wouldn't be any different in his mind than using a rope to climb down from a window and then throwing it away.

He's been known to enjoy the ritual of killing. I might even venture so far as to say at the very least arranging murders is one of his favorite things. But he also uses murder as a means to an end. As elaborate and intricate as his ritualistic murders could be, others were straightforward and utilitarian.

Killing the woman who helped him escape from prison wouldn't be a murder to bring him pleasure. If he wanted to enjoy the process, he would have chosen a far more complex and personal approach. His ritual killings carried messages. They were for a purpose. And he wanted them found. From the two henchmen he tortured and slaughtered in the abandoned hotel, to the men skinned alive and dropped in ditches by busy roads, to Greg wrapped in plastic with photographs and cash and left on my yard, Jonah's murders were like his gruesome version of art. He wanted them seen and admired.

This woman's death fell in between the two styles, too far unlike either one of them to fit with Jonah's ways. It would have been so simple for him to strangle her and toss her aside. To run her down. To beat her. To stab her. It just doesn't fit Jonah's style to dose her with a drug and let nature and her own impulses take their course.

And I can't help but wonder who this woman was to him. Both the true Miley and the one masquerading as her. How did he encounter either one of them, and what did they mean to him?

I've spiraled myself to the point of changing my mind and thinking he didn't do this. Blaming him would just be a convenient way to find an answer to who killed her. It's always easy to believe someone who has already killed has killed again. It means less work for the investigators and faster justice for the family. But it isn't right. Like Jonah said, she deserves to have the person actually responsible for her death to be held accountable for it.

I can't help but recognize how likely it is that the person who killed her was also the person living in her house and using her car. And who called in the tip. Directing investigators toward Jonah could get the heat off of themselves.

But as soon as I feel settled on that, my thoughts go back to everything I've experienced with Jonah. Maybe he's manipulating me. This could all be another one of his games, something to amuse himself and to keep me off balance so he can always feel like he has his grip tightly on me.

I don't want to believe him. I don't want to defend him or put any effort into clearing his name. I don't want to use any of my time and energy to make his life any easier.

But I also don't want to think I'm allowing a murderer to go free. That I'm giving in to the manipulation designed to conceal the truth. I don't want to allow my own pain and scars to keep me from doing what I've devoted my life to doing. Upholding the law and defending justice.

And then there is the little voice at the furthest back corner of my mind that asks... what if she wasn't murdered at all? What if she did take that tab herself on purpose? She could have been a junkie aching for her next trip after all. Maybe she just got the dose wrong or put herself in a bad situation she wasn't prepared to handle. Or she could have been a desperate woman who raced downhill until she stumbled and couldn't take it anymore, so she decided to chase away the madness and end on her own terms.

I don't know. And that's what brought me to this article and to the comments section beneath it. A long string of comments shines a light on every corner of the human mind and every reaction possible to the news of Jonah's escape. I've read many of them, but after a while, I had to stop.

I scroll down to the bottom and watch the cursor blink for a few seconds before adding my own.

"Emma is looking for you."

It doesn't take long for my phone to ring.

"You're going to help me," Jonah says without any greeting.

"I haven't fully decided what I'm going to do," I start. "But let's be very clear about this. If I do investigate this, it won't be to help you. It will be to help her and to make sure whoever is responsible—if there is anyone responsible—is given justice."

"What do you mean, 'if there is anyone responsible'?" he asks.

"This doesn't look like a murder," I say. "I'll admit I did what I've lectured about a thousand times before and jumped to conclusions. I latched onto a story because it was sensational."

"That she was murdered," Jonah says.

"That you murdered her. But there's so much that doesn't make sense about it."

"I didn't kill her," he replies. "I need you to understand that. I need you to know that's the truth."

"You said you've been honest with me," I say. "That you've told me the truth."

"I have."

"Then you need to tell me the truth now."

"I will."

"Who was she? I've been calling her Miley. Everyone has been calling her Miley. But that's not who she was."

"You figured that out," he nods. There's a hint of pride in his voice that makes my stomach start to turn.

"Who was she?"

"The name she gave me was Serena."

"Serena what?"

"I didn't ask. I didn't need to know."

"What did she do to Miley? She was living Miley's life. A woman who had been declared missing and then supposedly returned. She was living in her house. Driving her car. Using her name," I say.

"There are some things I just can't give you an answer to, Emma. You have to understand that I'm still trying to figure some of this out. But I know Serena didn't hurt Miley."

"How do you know that?"

"You'll have to trust me."

"I'll never trust you."

A tense silence falls on the line. My instinct is to push him to tell me how he escaped and where he is, but I know he won't tell me. I don't think he'll lie. As strange as it sounds, I feel like he really is trying to tell me the truth. But I'm afraid that if I venture too far from the path he's leading me on, he'll disappear again. Then I'll be left with a mountain of questions and even further from finding him and getting him back behind bars. For now, I have to stay in my lane.

"Did Serena help you plan your escape?"

"Yes," he answers without hesitation. "She helped me with the planning and the preparation. And she was meant to help me with the escape itself. She was supposed to be waiting for me, but when I got to the pre-determined spot, she wasn't there. I waited for her for as long as I could, then I left. I didn't know what happened to her or where she was. I thought maybe she'd decided she couldn't do it."

"You knew she was using Miley's name, so you knew she was living in her house. Did you go there to look for her?" I ask.

"No. If she wanted to change her mind about helping me, I wasn't going to put either of us at risk by going to her home. I left the area without knowing where she was or what happened to her. I didn't even consider something might have happened to her until I checked the news and saw the report about the unidentified body found a few miles from the prison.

"Even then, I wasn't sure it was her. The news didn't give all the identifying details about her and some of what they said didn't make sense. I had to look into it to be sure. I know it took me a long time to give the tip, but I had to make sure it was her, and then I had to take steps to put plenty of space between me and the investigation before I did it."

"Wait," I say. "You called in that tip?"

"Yes," he confirms. "After so long and no other information coming out about her, I knew I had to do something. I figured when I gave her address, they would search the house and find something that linked her to the escape. So they would call you."

"Why did you escape? Why now?"

It's not a question I really intended to ask, but it came out of my mouth before I had a chance to think it through and stop it.

"I didn't want to miss your wedding. I missed you and Dean. I needed to try to reconnect with you both. And there was some… unfinished business I needed to handle," he says.

"Unfinished business…"

"Emma, I did not kill Serena. And I don't believe for a moment that she killed herself. That's why it's so important that you look into this."

"You really believe someone killed her," I say.

"Yes. And I'm afraid she's not the only one."

"You think this person has killed before?"

"I think he's a serial killer."

CHAPTER THIRTY

"A SERIAL KILLER?" I FINALLY ASK.

I don't know how long it's been since he said it, but it feels like the question has broken through silence.

"Yes. I believe Serena is just one victim of a prolific serial killer who hasn't even been recognized yet, but who I believe has been operating for several years. Now he's escalating."

"If he is already a serial killer, how is he escalating?" I ask.

"The rate of his killing," Jonah explains. "If I am right in what I believe has happened, he only had three victims a year for a few years. I've attributed at least six to him this year."

"If you know who is doing this, why don't you do something about it? Turn him in. Give the information to the police. Send it straight to the Bureau if you want to. If you think there's a serial killer out there, why haven't you stopped him?" I ask.

"Because I can't prove it."

"What?" I ask.

"I can't prove he is who I think he is. The cases seem unrelated. A couple of the victims went unidentified for quite some time, and are still considered accidental deaths."

"You're telling me that you believe there is a serial killer, but there is no evidence to actually support that. And that Serena was killed by him."

"Not that there is no evidence," he clarifies. "Just that the evidence has to be found."

"How do I know this isn't one of your games? That you're not doing this just to keep me from trying to find you?" I ask.

"I know you don't think I have the right to ask you this, but I need you to trust me."

"Trust you?" I sputter, the words coming out of me in a burst of air that is somewhere between a laugh and a shout.

"Emma, you are the only hope. You are the only one who can do this. I truly believe that."

"Why me?"

"Because you are just like your father."

"Jonah," I say in warning.

"A brilliant and dedicated law enforcement agent," he continues, even as his name is still hanging in the air. My heart feels like it has stopped in my chest. "But with the stubbornness and determination of your uncle."

There's quiet between us as we both navigate the moment.

"Send me what you think I need to know."

"Thank you, Emma."

I hang up and wait until my breath settles in my lungs and the tears recede into the backs of my eyes before I pick up the phone again and dial. It clicks after two rings.

"Emma?"

"I love you, Dad."

"Is everything okay?"

I nod even though he can't see me. "Yes. I just wanted to say I love you."

"I love you, too."

The email from Jonah comes in right as I'm hanging up with my father. In it is a list of names and a few details of each death. The sparse information shows me exactly what he meant. These deaths don't seem to have anything to do with each other. They don't even seem like murders. I draw in a breath and set the computer aside. Changing into lounge clothes, I call for delivery for dinner, get the coffeemaker cranking up, and settle in for what I can already see is going to be a long night.

～

With only a brief post-sunrise stretch of sleep behind me, I head back to Miley's house. Fall has come on fully today, and I wrap my sweater tight around myself to ward off the chill as I hurry up the sidewalk to the door. It's strange having to separate the name from the woman now. I'd only known the ice-sparkling face of the woman with the name Miley attached to it. Now I have to remember they aren't the same person. The woman who lived here as a child is not the woman who lived here just a year ago.

The uniformed officers standing guard over the house have been replaced by a lockbox holding the key to the replaced lock on the front door. I input the code and use the key to open the door. The house feels different this time through. Like the air isn't holding so much potential and intensity. It's the atmospheric equivalent of letting out a deep breath.

Now it's just waiting. It's calm, if still bristling on the edges. That's going to happen anywhere there's so many questions and so much possibility of tragedy.

I don't know exactly what I'm looking for. All of the documents, the blueprints, the journals, and the datebooks have all been moved out of the house to the investigation room so they can be examined thoroughly. But I still feel like there's something here.

I spent all last night researching the deaths Jonah sent over. I'm trying to find anything that might link them together, but I haven't had much luck. There are some similarities. Some things that could be thought of as the same between them. But in reality, they are no more similar than any two random cases at any given time.

All of the women, with the exception of Serena, had signs that suggested sexual assault. Some were more severe than others. Some were more of a presumption than an actual determination. All of the men had signs of injury consistent with altercations, but that could also be attributed to their causes of death. All their documented causes of death widely varied: from a hit and run accident to getting crushed by a falling tree. Or freezing to death in the snow while high on LSD.

Of course, if I'm going to follow Jonah's theory, those are not actual causes of death. Unless this serial killer ran one of the men down with a car and pushed a tree over on another, those were staged accidents.

Some of the victims had drugs in their systems when they were found. At least one was too severely decomposed to have accurate toxicology, while others were found to be clean.

I've tried to look at the cases from as many different angles as possible. I've tried to find something that stands out about all of them. But I haven't been able to. I'm hoping being back in the house will give me something.

The office is all but empty except for the actual pieces of furniture. It's already offered up everything it might have. That brings me back to the sitting room where I found the smart device operating the light. There's no real way to tell how long that device was in place. It's possible it was on a timer and turned on automatically at the same time every day, though I think it would be too much of a coincidence that it would come on right at the time the detectives came.

And Sam continues to tell me what he always has: there are no coincidences.

I step up to the window and look out. It gives me a direct view of the house next door, the one where the woman Detective Simon spoke to described Serena as having red hair. I stand there for several seconds, waiting to see what might happen. All the neighbors said the same thing. They don't socialize. They don't interact. They keep to themselves.

It sounds like all of them are trying not to have any responsibility toward any of the others. I understand that, but I find it strange. This is an established neighborhood. Some of the people living here have been here for decades. It's hard to believe after all that time there isn't more of a connection among the neighbors.

But even as I stand there looking around, I don't see anyone come out of their homes or looking out windows.

I leave the sitting room and go to the bedroom. Back in her closet, I look through all of the clothes hanging on the heavily burdened rod. A faint hint of perfume still clings to some of them, a reminder of the human who once wore them.

I've run out of drawers to dig through and the lack of sleep is starting to drag on me when I hear what sounds like someone at the front of the house. My hand rests briefly on my gun as I make my way down the hall toward the sound.

As I come around the corner, the door opens. My gun is in my hand directed at the door before the man takes his first step fully inside. He stops short when he sees me, but he doesn't put up his hands like most people do or shout out with surprise. Instead, a slight smile seems to come to his lips.

"Who are you?" I ask.

"I'm sorry to startle you, miss. But I assure you, there's no need for the weapon."

"It's Agent," I say. "And Ma'am."

"I apologize again."

I lower my gun. "Who are you?"

The levity disappears from his face, replaced by sadness.

"I was sent by Miley's parents," he says. "To ensure her final arrangements are seen to."

He looks like he's working on mustering up tears. Something about this man strikes me as strange. His eyes are a pale, piercing blue, standing out against prematurely silvery hair streaked with black above his ears. His tailored charcoal pants and fitted lightweight sweater topped with a full-length trench coat create a monochromatic image that's out of place in the comfortable, but older and more modest neighborhood.

"They aren't planning on coming?" I ask.

"Unfortunately, they haven't been able to make plans to return yet. But they don't want to feel as though their little girl is here alone and has no one watching over her. I promised them I would make sure to follow her final wishes."

"And those are?"

"She'll be cremated. I'm here to choose clothing for her."

"I don't mean to be insensitive here, but you do realize that she has been dead for nearly a year? Her body was kept in cold storage by the police rather than being directly cremated, but it hasn't been released yet. And when it does, again, I apologize for this, it won't be in a condition to have a viewing."

"I know," he nods. "But after so long waiting to be reclaimed, it's important to her parents that Miley have as much that's really hers as possible. Even if that's just clothing to wear during her cremation. When her body is released, it will go to a funeral home, right?"

"Yes," I say.

"And they will prepare her for cremation, which means they can put her in her own clothing."

I'm not going to pretend I fully understand his motivation, but I'm also not going to argue with it. There's no need to push back against grief.

"Do you have a key to the house?"

"No," he admits.

"How were you planning on getting inside?" I ask.

The hint of a smile comes back to his lips briefly, then falls away.

"I guess I'm not thinking clearly. It's such a devastating situation."

"Yes," I say. "And what's your name?"

"Salvador Marini," he says.

"Mr. Marini, I can appreciate you wanting to help the family, but this house has not been released yet. It's still considered a secure location for the investigation, only accessible by authorized individuals. I apologize, but you will need to leave. If you'd like, you can describe clothing to me and I can get it for you out of her bedroom."

I'm careful not to say a name. I'm watching his reaction and listening to every word he says.

"Thank you. That is very kind of you. There is a blue dress with white stars on it. If you can find that."

"Please wait outside."

I wait until he's outside to go into the bedroom and go through her clothes to try to find that dress. I can't find it and I go outside, locking the door firmly behind me. He nods when I tell him about the missing dress.

"I'll find something. Thank you, again, for your help."

CHAPTER THIRTY-ONE

Victim 1 - found dead near a deer stand. Possible accidental shooting. Possible sexual assault.

Victim 2 - drug overdose in azalea gardens of a public park. Evidence of sexual assault.

Victim 3 - found dead behind an abandoned academic building. Stabbing. Evidence of sexual assault. Traces of drugs in her system.

Victim 4 - found dead in house under construction. Drugs in her system. Determined to be a suicide. Possible sexual assault.

Victim 5 - partial skeletal remains found in lingerie with several sexual items.

Victim 6 - found hanging in a barn. Drugs in her system. Determined to be a suicide. Evidence of repeated sexual assault.

Victim 7 - found submerged, caught in net. Drugs in her system. Possible sexual assault.

"EMMA?"

The combination of my name and a light knock on the door stops my progress on the chart I'm making. I look up and see John standing in the doorway.

"Hi," I say.

"Can I talk to you for a sec?"

"Sure," I nod.

He comes in and I push the chair beside me with my foot to move it away from the table so he can sit down, but he stays standing beside the table.

"You were right," he starts.

"About what?" I ask.

"How I've handled this case. My drinkin'. All of it."

I nod. "I'm sorry for how I said it. I could have had more tact."

"No," John replies with a shake of his head. "We're beyond tact, Emma. You needed to say those things an' I needed to hear them." He hesitates for a beat. "Thank you."

"You're welcome."

I can tell he feels uncomfortable once the words have passed between us. He's never been a particularly effervescent man. It's hard for him to admit to any kind of emotion. Or that he's wrong. He wants to move past the conversation and I'm not going to stop him.

"What are you workin' on?" he asks.

I nod toward the chair. "Have a seat."

He sits and I gesture at the large piece of paper on the table in front of me.

"I'm making a chart. These are women found dead over the course of the last few years. Throughout Virginia, Maryland, and South Carolina."

"What's the connection?" he asks.

"That's what I'm trying to figure out." I drum the tip of the pen against the paper. "I need to tell you something."

"Go ahead."

He listens in silence as I tell him about Jonah and my new investigation.

"Emma, are you sure about this?" he asks.

"No," I answer without hesitation. "But I don't feel like I have much choice. I don't think Jonah killed her. And if there is any chance what he's saying is true, there's a killer out there who has already killed nearly two dozen people and is not only not stopping, he's getting faster. I can't just pretend I don't have that in my mind."

"And if he's not tellin' you the truth? If he's just doin' exactly what you said? Keepin' you at bay by lettin' you chase around some phantom serial killer?"

"Then I look like a fool and he has another few days of freedom. I'm willing to do that. It's worth that risk, if there's even the slightest possibility that lives could be saved. And when this is over, I will bring him in. I've already done it once. I'll do it again."

I wait for John to argue more, but he doesn't. He just nods.

"What you got so far?"

"Where is Detective Simon?" I ask.

"She's followin' up on the actual Miley Stanford case again to try to figure out what happened."

"So you have some time?" I ask.

"Go ahead."

I smile and turn back to my chart. "These are the female victims. There are a couple of others for me to add, but this is most of them, not including Serena. Do you notice anything about them that links them?"

"No," he says.

"Exactly. That's the brick wall I'm running into. And considering this is the only thing I have to go on, it's a fairly significant brick wall."

"You said the female victims," John points out. "Does that mean there are males, too?"

I nod. "Yes. They aren't any easier. There are drugs present and they all have injuries. But since most of them have causes of death that are listed as pretty horrific accidents, those injuries make sense."

"Do they make sense, or do the reports say they make sense?" John presses.

I let out a breath. "Right."

"That's the thing. There are similarities. It's not like they're on different planets. But if that was the way it was, it would actually seem more suspicious. There ain't but so many circumstances that can end up with bodies. Lots o' different ways to kill a person, but when it happens, most of them tend to involve the same basic elements. There's all these different possible causes of death. Then there's all these contributin' circumstances. You just mix and match. The old school Chinese food menu philosophy," he smiles. A little bit of the old light returns to his face.

"That's certainly one way to look at it," I admit. "The point is, there are these ways that the deaths are alike, but there are so many differences it's hard to really make tangible links."

"You'll figure it out," he says. "If there's somethin' to find, you'll find it."

⌒

I'm still searching two days later when Sam arranges his schedule to take a couple of days and come visit me. It feels so good to hug him I want to just spend the rest of my day standing there in his arms. But he's drawn to the charts I've made and taped up on the wall of the hotel room. There are duplicates in the investigation room so I can continuously update and visualize.

Sam is less than happy I've decided to help Jonah. Even when I explained that I don't really see it as helping him, but helping Serena and the other victims of the serial killer if one actually exists, he still wasn't particularly enthused. I don't blame him, though. He's watched every step of the suffering Jonah put me through. He doesn't want to see me go through any of that again. And he doesn't want me in any kind of danger.

But I have to do this. And he understands that.

I explain the two charts, the female victims and the male victims, outlining any similarities I've found. There's still nothing that really links them together, but I faithfully write down everything that any of them share, even if it is just the color of their hair, whether they have earrings or not, and if I can find any kind of social media for them. Things like that don't seem like much, but I can't make that assumption. I don't know what is going to be the piece that finally falls into place and makes everything make sense.

He examines the chart for the male victims as I outline some of the scant connections I have made to him. I can see his brain working as he goes over the details of each of the men.

"One thing I realized is that in the earlier years—assuming this is actually when he started killing and not just when Jonah started noticing them—there were more male victims than female. Jonah said there were three victims each year, but that's not exactly accurate. A couple of years there were four. And the male victims tend to happen closer together. But this year, there have been more women."

"Mmmm-hmmm," Sam says, acknowledging what I said without looking away from the chart.

"What is it?" I ask.

"The injuries on some of these guys and the way they were found. Did you notice anything in particular about them?" he asks.

"You mean that they sound shockingly like what happened to Dean?" I nod, turning back to the chart. "Yeah. I did notice that."

"But Dean is alive," Sam says.

"Last I checked," I nod.

"And he definitely didn't have any hallucinogens in his system."

"He did not. And someone called 911 for him. I'm guessing you're going to tell me it can't be a coincidence."

"You know me so well."

CHAPTER THIRTY-TWO

"**Y**OU'VE NOTICED SO MANY OF THE SAME THINGS I DID," JONAH says a few days later when he contacts me next. "You have so much knowledge about social media, which is funny since you don't have any of your own."

"None of this is funny, Jonah. Not that it happened, and not that I'm having to investigate it. I feel like you built this up to keep me distracted from other things, like hunting you down. It's like when a teacher gives a room a whole bunch of busy work just to make them do something and not annoy her."

"That's not what this is," Jonah protests. "I'm genuinely happy and so proud of you for your work. I've never had the opportunity to watch you work this way. You're incredible. I've always known that. But it's still amazing to actually watch it. This is exactly why I said you're the only person who could do this, Emma. You're the only one who would see the same things I do, and more. You're the only one who would continue to chase the truth even when it seems hopeless. You are so close already. I know you're going to figure it out. You're going to identify him and be able to prove what I've suspected all along."

This makes my skin crawl and anger creep up my spine. "Jonah, if you know who this person is already, why haven't you told me? Why don't you just tell me who you think committed these murders and why so this can be over?"

"It isn't that easy, Emma. Just like I told you at the beginning, and like you're figuring out now, there aren't easy connections between the cases. The forensic evidence that will usually be used to build and prosecute a case in this situation doesn't exist. Either they didn't look for it at all, or it wasn't there when they did. There aren't any fingerprints or DNA. I haven't been able to identify a paper trail or create any social link that would put them in the same place at the same time."

"And yet, for some reason, you are absolutely sure your killer is the one who killed all of them? Even people who the experts determined killed themselves or were killed by complete fluke accidents?"

"Fluke accidents don't happen like that with that much frequency," he says.

"Neither do serial killings that have nothing to do with each other," I fire back.

"They do. They have to," he insists. "Those people were murdered and all by the same person. You just need to figure out how."

"This is ridiculous. You know enough that you have a specific suspect in mind, and yet you won't tell me. You must have some kind of idea of the motivation for the killings, or how they are committed, or you wouldn't have that suspect. But you won't even give me the name so I can look into it."

"I can't, Emma."

"Dean came close to being a victim exactly like them," I shout.

"I know," he says simply.

I haven't talked to him about Dean's attack before now. I didn't even realize he knew about it. But he answers me with calm steadiness, like there's nothing I'm saying to him that comes as a surprise.

"You do?" I ask.

"Of course," he says. "Dean is my son. He's my child. I can't be near him or speak with him, but I do everything I can to stay close by keeping up with him. You don't have children, Emma, so you don't understand. You don't know what it's like to feel so distanced and so desperate. He's an adult, I understand. I also understand that I lost the right to have anything to do with him right now. But that isn't going to stop me from wanting to know that my child is thriving—and if he's not, to do everything in my power to find out why and rectify it.

"I know about his attack. I've known about it since it happened. It hurt more than I can possibly tell you that I wasn't able to go to the hospital to comfort him. But you know as well as I do that isn't a possibility right now."

"And you know as well as I do that even if the entire world wasn't trying to hunt you down, he still wouldn't want anything to do with you. You did nothing for him as a child. You've never been a beneficial part of his life." My breath catches in my throat. "You killed his mother, Jonah. You destroyed Dean long before you had a chance to play the doting father."

"He is my son," he repeats grimly. "You can't see what I do. But I see everything through your eyes. And I know that what happened to Dean is not a coincidence. It's also not a singular incident."

"Even if any of that is true, you're still withholding critical information that could be instrumental in unlocking this case and possibly saving other people. You promised to be truthful with me and now you're dangling this in front of me. I'm sick of playing your games, Jonah. You've dragged me through enough of them and I'm not doing it anymore. I'm not feeding into your bullshit again."

"It isn't a game," he counters. "And, yes, I did promise to be truthful. I also told you I will only tell you what I can, and I can't tell you his name."

"Why not?"

"Because you have to be the one to solve it, Emma. You have to be the one to figure it out. If I was just to tell you who I think is responsible for it and you went backward to piece it together, there would be no case. The word of an escaped felon isn't exactly considered reliable, and it would call your reputation and professional ethics into question as well."

"Are you threatening me?" I ask.

"No. I'm telling you that I have every faith you will solve this. But it has to be your case. You have to have enough understanding of what happened and enough evidence to lead you to the person, and then enough to build the case that will put him behind bars. It has to be meticulous. He's gotten away with all of this for so long and if there is even the slightest misstep, it could put him right back on the streets and he won't stop this time. Do you understand what I'm saying to you?" he asks.

I hate that I do.

"Yes."

"I need you to listen to me carefully. Hear what I'm telling you. What happened to Dean was not a coincidence. Your husband is right. There's no such thing. Everything happens in conjunction with the world around it. His attack was not a coincidence and it was not a singular event."

He keeps using the same words. It's very intentional and I know he won't elaborate. That is what he's giving me and it's up to me to use it to find out the rest.

"Eight of them," I say, laying out the printouts of faces on the table in front of me. "Cases that have been completely overlooked and considered dead-ends because nothing could connect them to a specific person and even the victims don't have any information to offer. Eight men found brutalized, but alive. All of them without any memory of what happened to them, or at least a complete unwillingness to talk about anything they might remember. Just like Dean.

"Their injuries aren't exactly the same. Some are far more severe. They seem to be inflicted by different things. Some have signs of healing and others don't. Just like the murders, there are more differences than there are similarities, but when they are put right there, side by side, it's difficult not to recognize how alike they are and make the assumption they had to have something to do with each other. But what? And what do these men have to do with the women? Why would the same killer go after both sexes, with apparently different motivations and styles of murder?"

"It's definitely unusual," Sam says over the video chat. "That's not how serial killers generally operate."

"It's not," I acknowledge. "Most have very specific types of victims.

They go after them for the same reasons, kill them in much the same ways. Leaving any alive is not only rare, but often seen as a massive mistake rather than an intentional move. This is bizarre, to say the least."

"You said you thought you'd found a connection," he says. "What did you find?"

"It's not necessarily a connection. It might be nothing. But it's there and right now, that's something. Do you remember when I was investigating my friend Julie's disappearance and I read her diary?"

"I'm never going to forget that case."

"Me neither. And one of the things that stood out about it was using that day planner to trace her movements and make connections between different people involved. You'll also remember the timer."

"The calendar." His voice is powdery with the unpleasant memory of that situation. It feels so recent even though it was nearly two years ago.

"Right," I nod. "I had specific intervals, dates on which the killer was going to act again. When I was looking through Serena's date book, I noticed entries at fairly regular intervals around many of the deaths. So, I compared them with the timelines I had available for some of the other victims. I don't have much information on all of them, but I was able to use social media and some other things for a couple of the other women.

"I was able to find similar notations or posts around dates that coordinate with other victims on those timelines as well. But they don't reference each other. They don't contact each other. There are just instances of them being active around the same times. But that still doesn't really mean much. I mean, maybe it could be some sort of a link. But what? And what would it have to do with any of the men?"

"Speaking of men, have you heard any more from that guy who showed up at Serena's house?" Sam asks.

"Well, that was actually something else I wanted to mention to you. I reached out to Miley's parents. We all made the decision not to let them know what's actually going on quite yet. They're going to have to be involved at a later stage, but until we know what happened to Serena, it could actually be counterproductive to get them too involved. Without them here it would be an unnecessary complication.

"But I did want to talk to them about Salvador Marini. I'm not sure what involvement Miley's parents have in any of this. I want to keep working on the assumption that they think Serena was their child, which means they very well could be making preparations for her funeral, even after they aren't here."

"Why does the way you say that make me think they aren't?" Sam asks.

"It's not that they aren't. It's just not exactly the way he said it. When I spoke to Miley's mother, I mentioned she and her husband sending Salvador to Miley's house to get clothing for her viewing, and to see to her final arrangements. She seemed a little confused at first, like she didn't know what I was talking about. But then she explained that she and her husband didn't contact him. Salvador reached out to them. He said he was a friend of Miley's and wanted to offer his condolences and any help he might be able to offer.

"When they told him that they weren't able to get back here, he offered to handle everything for them. She said she thought it was a very sweet and kind gesture, but maybe a little bit odd because she didn't know him. She didn't know who he was and hadn't heard Miley talking about him. She thought she might remember her daughter saying something about a male friend, and then they might have started with an S, but that's it."

"That doesn't exactly sound like a strong enough relationship for him to be taking on her final arrangements," Sam notes.

"No, it doesn't. But he was adamant about making sure everything was arranged properly. He plans on having her cremated as soon as her body is released from cold storage."

"And they don't have any idea who he is?" Sam asks.

I shake my head. "No. But I might have reason to believe Miley knew him quite well."

"Why is that?"

"I looked into those notes in her date book. Some of them I couldn't figure out. She didn't write everything in full words. Sometimes it was just letters. Sometimes shortened words. Sometimes she just drew little symbols. But some of the notes mentioned specific places or events. So, I looked into them to figure out what they were and if the other women might have had any connection to them. I haven't found any of the other women yet, but I did find Salvador."

"He was at the same places?" Sam asks.

"Yep. And in some of the events, his company was a corporate sponsor. There are pictures of him at these events, interviews with him in different articles and publications. He just keeps popping up in places where she was," I explain.

"Have you talked to him about that?"

"I'm going to today. I set up an appointment with his secretary to go to his office and meet with him."

CHAPTER THIRTY-THREE

ALVADOR MARINI'S SECRETARY USHERS ME TO A SMALL WAITING area when I arrive at his office. It's early in the day, so I don't expect to have to wait long. But I end up there for almost an hour, continuing to scroll through social media on my phone to try to put together links between the various victims of this supposed serial killer. Finally, I hear his voice speaking to his secretary and I get to my feet.

"Mr. Marini," I start.

He looks surprised when he turns and sees me. "Agent. To what do I owe this pleasure?"

"I need to speak with you," I tell him.

"I'm sorry, but I have a very busy day scheduled. It will have to wait for another time. I'm backed up with my appointments as it is."

"I'm very aware of that. I've been waiting for the appointment I made with you for almost an hour."

He looks at his secretary for confirmation. She nods and he turns a skillfully cultivated smile in my direction.

"Perfect. Come into my office." I walk in behind him and he closes the door. "Can I get you a coffee, Agent…"

"Griffin," I say. "And no, thank you. I just need to ask you some questions about what you were telling me at the house the other day."

He goes to an elaborate espresso machine on an imposing built-in bookshelf at the side of the office and makes himself a cup. He nods as he walks back across the room and releases the button on his jacket before sitting down at the desk. He gestures at the chair across from him.

"Please, sit." He sips his coffee, makes a little sound like he's enjoying it, and sets the cup on the desk. "I was at the house to get clothes for Miley."

I nod. "Yes. That's what you told me. You also told me you were sent by her parents. But I spoke with her parents and they said that you were the one who reached out to them, not the other way around. You knew they weren't going to be able to make it back to this country, so you wanted to handle things for them."

"That is true. I admit, I probably should have worded that better. I am the one who reached out to them to offer my support and services. She always spoke so highly of her parents; I can't imagine the kind of pain they're going through right now. Especially considering they aren't able to be here to handle these issues. I wanted to do whatever I could to provide comfort and make it easier for them."

"And how do you know her?"

"She worked for my company for a time."

"She wasn't working for you anymore when she died?" I ask.

"No. She had decided she wanted to pursue other opportunities. She was a very talented and ambitious woman. I had no doubt she would be able to accomplish anything she set her mind to."

I give a tense smile and a single nod.

"Right. And do you make it a habit of getting this invested and involved in the lives of former employees?"

"This is the first situation like this I've encountered. I've been fortunate not to have experienced other losses like this," he says.

"How often did you see each other?"

He twists his head back and forth subtly in a gesture that says he wants me to think he's thinking hard but just can't place the information. He is going to start rattling off more meaningless statements, so I stop him before he does.

"Let me just cut to the chase. I've been doing extensive research into the deceased's life to try to understand what brought her to the end of that life. Her date book showed her schedule was pretty much always full. She notated where she was going and what she was doing, though sometimes in a way I couldn't decipher. Those that I could understand, I looked into, and I noticed something that stood out to me. Do you think you could take a guess about what that is?"

He takes another sip of his coffee, then opens his hands up on the table in a noncommittal gesture.

"I really don't know," he replies.

"You," I say. "I noticed you. Your name, company, and picture show up at a high number of the events and activities she attended. Now, if she was employed here, that would make sense. But if it was, as you said, brief, I don't understand why those overlaps in your schedules seemed to carry on for a considerable length of time."

His head drops forward and he holds his fingers on the desk in front of him as he smiles in that way that admits he's been caught.

"You are very good at your job, Agent Griffin."

"You have no idea, Mr. Marini."

"Well, in this situation I can tell you are very thorough. and you're right. I haven't been completely honest with you. Miley was more than an employee to me. Much more. We had been seeing each other for quite some time. This is very embarrassing for me, and I hope this doesn't have to go beyond this office."

"I can't promise that. I'm still investigating a suspicious death."

"I understand. The thing is, I'm married. My wife and I were going through a rough patch when I first met Miley and I fell for her. She was beautiful and charming and gave me a kind of attention I didn't feel I was getting anymore. I'm not trying to justify my behavior. It was wrong and I don't want to hurt my wife."

"You don't want to hurt her so much you continued to see another woman for years and after you found out she was dead, you took it upon yourself to make her final arrangements for her?" I raise an eyebrow. "Forgive me for saying this, but you are not very good at being discreet."

I actually don't give a damn if he forgives me or not. This man puts my spine on edge and I hate even being in the same space as him. The strange, unpleasant quality I noticed when he was at the house is still there, only stronger now. My hackles are on full alert.

"You're right. I could have tried much harder not to be so obvious with my affections. But it was very hard. She was a compelling woman. I only wish I could have helped her when she was alive."

My head tilts slightly to the side. "Helped her? What do you mean?"

"With her drug problem. I didn't realize it was so severe until she went missing."

⌀

"He didn't realize it was so severe until she went missing?" Bellamy asks dryly.

The pitch of her voice says she gets the same suspicious, slimy feeling from the interaction I did.

"Yeah," I say. "He said last year right around the holidays he and his wife reconciled. They decided it was important to them to work on their marriage and really try to make it work. So, he told Serena and she was very upset. When she went missing, he at first assumed she had just gone off to soothe her wounded pride, but then she just didn't show back up. He decided she must have gone deeper into the drugs. He said he was devastated to have his worries validated when her body was identified."

"So devastated he didn't recognize her description?" Bellamy asks.

"He played that off that he doesn't watch the news very often and though he knew of a body that was found, he didn't let himself think it was her. But it's the comment about his worries being validated that stood out to me. That makes it sound like he was upset to find out that she had drugs in her system."

"She did," Bellamy says.

"Yes. But that wasn't released to the media. It's one of the details about her that has been kept confidential."

"Maybe her parents told him. Did the parents get that notification?" she asks.

"Yes," I say. "So that is possible. It's just another thing that isn't sitting right with me about that man."

"You're really suspicious of him," she observes.

"It doesn't feel right. Any of it."

"Did he have any connections with the other victims?" she asks.

"Nothing concrete," I admit with a sigh. "I went over everything with a fine-tooth comb trying to find any communication between him and other victims, links between them and his company, anything, but nothing panned out. The only thing that came up was that he was in the general areas where some of the bodies were found within a few weeks of the discoveries. But that doesn't really mean much. It's definitely not enough to prove he had anything to do with their deaths. But that's still more than I have connecting him to the male victims."

"What do you have for them?"

I can hear Bebe burbling and chatting away in the background and get a little squeeze in my heart. I miss my family. Especially as fall carries on, I feel like I should be with them. This is the time of year when the cookouts we usually have together over the summer turn into warm, cozy dinners inside. We go apple picking and make apple butter. Xavier probably has several new sourdough starters to name.

I tell myself this won't last forever. I'll be home soon. But this is where I need to be now.

"There are some basic similarities, but the only thing that's really significant that I found is most of the men were either out of work or had been posting about looking for work in the weeks leading up to their deaths or attacks. Not all of them. And I couldn't find information like that about some of them. Dean definitely wasn't looking for work before he was attacked."

"Well, Dean is kind of always looking for work. He's a private investigator. Looking for his own work is the only way he's going to ever have any."

"It's not quite the same thing. These men had been out of work for a while. Some of them seemed pretty desperate. And other ones were posting about looking for something new or wanting a different kind of career.

And the thing is, a lot of them seemed to have found work fairly close to when they were attacked or when they died."

"What kind of work?"

"I couldn't really find any details. Just some posts saying they had a lead or had gotten the job. I've been able to access bank records for a couple of them and they had new deposits like they'd been paid by somebody. But if that's the link among all of them, who is it that's hiring them? They're all in different areas and do different things, so I can't imagine it's the same person giving all of them jobs. And there's no link to Salvador Marini and his company."

"That's a good lead, though. Do you remember that case with the guy and his nephew who pretended they had a horse farm and needed a live-in ranch hand? They put out an ad and hired guys who were really down on their luck. They brought all their possessions out into the middle of nowhere and ended up shot and robbed," Bellamy says. "It happens."

"I know," I nod. "But there isn't anything like that here. I've been reading through their social media accounts trying to find comments or messages from the same person or company, but there isn't anything. Some of them had profiles on job finding sites, but, again, no similar connections, or if they did share some it was big-name companies that are connected to just about everybody."

"And there aren't any welcome aboard messages or anything?" she asks.

"No. There are a lot of comments saying 'congratulations' or 'good job', but those are all from their friends or family members. And it's normal to congratulate someone who has just gotten a new job."

"That's true."

"It's times like this I wish I was a man," I sigh.

There's silence on the other end of the line.

"Emma, I love and support you no matter what, you know that. Is there something we need to talk about?"

"No, but I appreciate it," I say. "I just mean this is the kind of situation where I would want to go undercover."

"As what?" she asks.

"A young guy going through a hard time, looking for a job. Offer my-self up and see what happens."

My phone beeps to tell me I have another call coming in. I tell Bellamy I'll call her back and switch over.

"Hey, babe," Sam says.

"Hey, honey. I was hoping I'd get to talk to you before bedtime to-night. Do you think I'll get to see you again this weekend?"

"That's actually what I'm calling about," he says.

"The less than happy sound in your voice indicates to me this isn't you calling to tell me how excited you are to come see me."

He laughs. "I wish I was. I'm actually going to have to go out of town."

"Out of town? Why?" I ask.

"My Aunt Rose just called me. She hasn't been able to get in touch with my cousin Marie for almost a week and she's really worried about her."

"Marie is a grown woman," I point out.

"I know," Sam says. "But apparently she didn't call on Rose's birthday and she has never missed her mother's birthday. She said Marie has been going through something recently, but she doesn't know exactly what it is. I'm going head up to Michigan and see if I can help."

"Alright. I'll miss you."

"Does that mean I can't convince you to come with me?"

I sigh. "You know I can't. I wish I could. But this investigation just keeps getting more complicated and I can't leave it."

"I know," he says. "But I can always try."

Someone knocks on the door to the conference room and I look over my shoulder. Salvador is standing there and gives me a small wave.

"Babe, I'm going to have to go. Are you leaving today?"

"No, I need to get some things in place. Probably tomorrow or the next day."

"Okay. Call me later. I love you."

"Love you. Bye."

I hang up and turn around to face Salvador.

"Your boyfriend?" he asks.

"My husband," I correct him.

He nods as he comes further into the room without invitation.

"That's right. You're a ma'am. I apologize. He's a lucky man."

I cringe inwardly and choose to ignore him.

"What can I do for you, Mr. Marini?"

"I hope I'm not intruding on your work. I contacted the precinct to ask to get in touch with you and they said the easiest thing to do would be to find you here. I wanted to apologize again for being a little bit shady."

Hearing the word 'shady' come out of this man's mouth sounds off.

"Thank you," I say. "I appreciate you eventually being honest with me."

"On that token, I'd like to offer my assistance in any way I can for the investigation. If you have questions about her or there's something I might know, please don't hesitate to ask."

"Thank you, Mr. Marini."

CHAPTER THIRTY-FOUR

I FLIP THE BUSINESS CARD MARINI GAVE ME BACK AND FORTH IN MY fingers. Something about the way he interjected himself back into the investigation pisses me off. It feels purposeful. Less someone who feels bad for lying and genuinely wants to be helpful, and more an animal circling, wanting to stay close and check on its prey.

I look down at the card for what must be the hundredth time, trying to soothe the tickling in the back of my mind.

Salvador Marini

Coliseum Events

Something finally clicks. I set the card aside and take out one of the journals found with the prison blueprint in Miley's house. I've been trying to decipher the notes in it hoping to get more insight into how Jonah actually escaped. But now I focus more on the entries at the back of the book.

While everything at the front of the journal references the prison or Jonah himself either directly or indirectly, these pages are more like personal contemplations. It's like Serena used the journal both for her planning and to record her thoughts, making sure to tuck those away where they would be even harder to find.

Some of the entries are straightforward and easy to read, containing little more than a record of what she did on any given day. They remind me of the gratitude journal entries my therapist once recommended I keep on a daily basis. But others sound more like poems. Short sentences and words with veiled meanings that make it harder to understand exactly what she's trying to get across.

I read through them, jotting down the lines that stand out to me on a yellow legal pad.

For the pleasure of the Emperor

To grow the Empire

Soon, my page is filled with references to the Emperor or the Empire. There's also a name, one that isn't linked to any of the victims. Charon. It appears several times in the journal and when I check to confirm my suspicions, I find it written across a few days in her date book.

I go back to the pictures of the events that Serena referenced, trying to find images of Salvador and Serena together. I find plenty of him, but none of them together. As I go through them again, I start to notice what seems like women lingering in the background or the very edges of many of the pictures. None of their faces are clearly visible—they're turning their heads or holding up champagne glasses at just the right angle to cover their features. In a few, the woman has turned to show off the deep cutout of the back of her gown, leaning against the arm of a man, presumably her date. I see this pattern in several photos at several events.

Something about them keeps bringing my attention back. I look through them over and over, comparing them to the victims and not finding anything. Then I notice one of them in the background of a picture tagged with one of the female victims. Again, her face is turned away so it's not a full-frontal image of her features, but there's a silhouette of the side of her face and it looks very similar. There's a name beneath it. Diana.

Bolstered, I pull up more images and start searching for even the slightest hint of these women crossing over into the lives of the victims. I find several and write down the names. I stop when one of the pictures makes an image burst in my head. I can still feel my fingertips running across sequins and feeling the cool satin underneath. I grab my phone.

"Simon."

"Detective, it's Agent Griffin. I need to ask you about the day you went to Miley Stanford's house for the first time."

"Alright," she says with a note of aggravation in her voice. Not that I can blame her. We've been through this several times before. I just need to hear it again. "The woman you talked to, the older neighbor next door. She said that she didn't pay attention to her neighbors, right?"

"Yes."

"And that the thing that stood out to her most about the woman living next door to her was her red hair and bad sweater colors."

"Yes," Detective Simon confirms.

"She said she reminded her of someone."

"Jessica Rabbit."

I pull up a different gallery on my computer and scroll through until I find the pictures I took of the full bedroom closet. I pause on the image of a bright red sequin dress with a low cut-out back.

"Jessica Rabbit. Thank you." I hang up and pull up comparison pictures on my phone. "She doesn't want her neighbors, but somehow she was able to describe Serena in a wig and this dress with uncanny accuracy," I murmur.

I scroll through the images and start finding more articles that look familiar. With a little more focus, I start matching them to the pictures of the women in the background—no, the specific woman in the background. After a few more minutes of looking at the pictures, I go to the news article and type in my usual comment. Jonah calls within seconds.

"Everything alright?" he asks.

"What does the name Emperor mean to you?" I ask.

"Where did you find that?" he asks.

"It's in Serena's journal. I've been looking into a man who has been triggering every instinct and red flag since I first saw him, but I haven't been able to connect him to anyone but Serena. Until now."

"What's going on?" he asks.

"I found quite a few pictures of him with what I thought were different women who didn't want to show their faces. That didn't surprise me all that much considering he admitted to having an affair with Serena, who he still calls Miley. I figure if he can have an affair with her, why not have several other women on the side?

"But then I started looking at the social media and news clippings and pictures provided by the families of the other victims and noticed the women were showing up in those pictures as well. The captions have a bunch of different names, but I recognized the clothes."

"The clothes?"

"Yes. When I first investigated the house, I noticed the closet in the bedroom is full of clothes. Almost overwhelmingly full. And there didn't seem to be much rhyme or reason about the style. There were a bunch of different types of clothes in there. I thought it might just be because she was indulged and ended up wanting everything. But now I'm thinking it's more along the line of she wanted to look like several other people.

"When Xavier came and went through the house, he didn't find any hidden compartments or false walls. Nothing that looked like a way to sneak in and out of the house, or to hide anyone. But he did go into the small storage space in the office and said it was nothing but storage. Just boxes of holiday decorations and Halloween costumes. I bet if I went back there and looked, what he thought was Halloween costumes would turn out to be wigs."

"What are you thinking, Emma?" he asks.

There's tension in his voice. I feel like I have the end of a fine string and I'm gradually pulling him in.

"I don't know. I don't understand. I keep looking for a way to connect him with the victims, but I can't find it. The only link I've found now is Serena and it doesn't make sense. Why would she dress differently and use fake names? What does she have to do with any of those women?"

"I think you know, Emma. Deep down, you already know. I gave you a clue a long time ago. Let me know when you want to talk again."

∽

The next morning when Sam arrives to say goodbye before heading out, I don't feel any closer to understanding what Jonah was trying to tell me.

I've gone over the pictures a dozen more times. I went back to the house and compared all the clothing. I know I am right on the edge, but something is stopping me.

"I don't know what he means," I sigh. "He says he gave me a clue, but that's exactly what he hasn't been giving me. He's been doing everything he can to avoid offering any kind of help."

"What else has he given you?" Sam asks.

"Indigestion?" I say. "Early wrinkles and a seriously non-ornamental family tree?"

Sam offers a commiserating laugh and pulls me in close for a hug.

"I'm sorry, babe. I wish I could stay and help you."

"I know. But your family needs you right now. Go find Marie and I'll see you when you get home."

"I'll call you when I get there. I love you."

"I love you."

I kiss my husband goodbye and close the door behind him. Walking back through my hotel room, his words hit me. What else has he given you?

"The necklace," I whisper.

It's shoved into the back corner of one of the drawers, stuffed there with the intention of throwing it back in his face when I finally confront him. Now I pull it out and rip open the box. I shake the tissue paper, cotton padding, and necklace out onto the table in the sitting area and examine each piece along with the box. I turn them over, pull them apart. There's nothing hidden in or around it. Eventually, all I'm left with is the manatee pendant.

I hold the pendant in my palm and examine it. Why a manatee? What's the point?

I open my computer and start researching. I'm reading an article about the cultural impact of manatees when I stop and re-read the same sentence several times.

"A prevailing theory is that sailors at sea for long stretches would see manatees and mistake them for particularly buxom women with tails, giving an origin story to the myth of mermaids."

I grab my key and dart down to the conference room, barely able to control myself enough to type the code into the security pad to access the room. When the door finally opens, I go to the file containing Serena's autopsy pictures. There's one that focuses on her back.

And the large mermaid tattoo that takes up a good portion of it.

Back in my room, I look through the pictures of Serena dressed up again. Even in the lowest dresses, there's no sign of the tattoo. I scroll through the pictures on my phone and find the one of the business card left in Miley's car. The one for the makeup artist.

I dial the number and take a breath to settle my voice before he answers.

"Gavin St. James," he answers.

"Mr. St. James, this is Agent Emma Griffin. I'm with the FBI. I need to ask you a couple of questions."

"Is there something wrong? Did I do something?" he asks.

"I just need to ask a couple of questions," I tell him. "Do you have a client named Miley?"

"No," he says.

"Alright. How about Serena?"

"I used to," he says. "But she ghosted me about a year ago."

"Why did she used to come to you? Did you do her makeup for events?" I ask.

"Yes, but not in the way you're probably thinking," he says. "She didn't need me to do her face. She had me cover up a tattoo on her back. Full-on waterproof stage makeup. Seamless to her skin tone. She always said it was crucial there wasn't a single hint of the piece showing and the makeup needed to stay through anything until she removed it. She would bring in these spectacular dresses and I had to make sure she looked perfect.

"But I could never understand why she wanted to cover it up. It was gorgeous. A really elaborate mermaid. And the thing is, it just kept getting more complicated over time. She kept adding to it. There would be more details or more colors. Of course, that made it more difficult to cover up. But why but I really wondered was why bother going through all that to keep making the tattoo bigger and more detailed when she was just going to cover it up?"

My heart is in my throat but I manage to thank him. He asks if there's anything else he can do to help, but I reassure him that he's done enough. I don't even know if I say goodbye before ending the call. My mind goes back to the earliest days of investigating Jonah's escape and the search for identifiable tattoos on the inmates. And the one that stood out. A mermaid swimming with a sea monster on the back of an inmate kept in protective custody.

All these years I only ever thought of men.

Greg never said it. Anson never said it. Jonah never said it.

But I just assumed. I probably heard different and just never processed it. I had the image so firmly stuck in my mind.

None of them ever only said "he".

It was always "they".

And now… "she".

CHAPTER THIRTY-FIVE

"YOU HAVE ME WORKING MY ASS OFF TO DEFEND A MEMBER OF Leviathan."

Jonah's breath crackles through the phone line.

"Yes. Serena was a part of Leviathan. One of the closest to me."

"You did this. You planted the evidence in Miley's house. You put the blueprints of the prison and the journals. You're the one who's been staying there," I say through gritted teeth.

"No. No, Emma. I didn't plant anything. All of that was truly hers."

"You killed her. She betrayed you, so you killed her."

"No. I cared about her. I didn't kill her. I told you the truth. She was supposed to help me escape, but she wasn't at the meeting place when I got there. But I did go to her house. I wanted to check on her, but she wasn't there."

"You said you wouldn't lie to me."

"And I haven't. I didn't go to the house immediately. I stayed hidden. but when I didn't hear from her, I started to worry."

"You were so worried it took you almost a year to call in the tip so people would know... what, her alias? Is Serena even her name, or is that just what you named her?"

"That is her name," he insists. "And I've explained to you why I waited. I was worried about her and the more I found out about what was going on, the more concerned about the Emperor I became. But no matter what else is going on, the reality is I am on the run. I had to make sure my tracks were covered and I could stay out of the grip of the police. Out of your grip."

"I can't believe you manipulated me like this."

"Listen, Emma. When I called in that tip, I knew suspicion would fall on me. But I know the truth. And you do, too. You know who he is. You're so close, Emma. This is exactly why I came to you. I knew you were the only one I could trust to prove who killed her."

"Not anymore," I snap. "I'm done with this."

"You can't be."

"Yes, I can!" I shout. "I can do anything the fuck I want to. Remember, I think like my uncle. And that's all you've ever done. You lied to me. Yet again. I was stupid enough to think that I could believe you, and you lied to me."

"Not really. Not about what was important," Jonah says.

"I thought I was helping a victim."

"She is a victim," he cuts back sharply. "She was murdered, just like all those other girls."

"I went against everything in my gut and in my head to listen to you. You convinced me I was doing the right thing, that I was helping someone who needed it. I left my home to come here and do this. My husband just left to go out of town to help his family and I'm not with him because I'm doing this. But not anymore. I'm not wasting any more of my time or energy. Not for you. And not for someone like her. I knew something was wrong. I knew there had to be more, but not this. Nothing like this. I'm done."

"When did you lose your humanity, Emma?" he asks.

"What?"

The question shocked me so much the response comes out more like a gasp of air.

"Where did you lose your soul? Your conscience? When did you decide you could play god?"

"That's not what I'm doing."

"It's exactly what you're doing. You say that you joined the Bureau to protect people. To defend the victimized. To punish the ones who have done wrong. You walked away from the man you loved. You gave up your art, your dreams. You put me in prison. You have killed. All to uphold what you said were your strongest beliefs. That no one deserves to be a victim."

"I still believe that."

"Then where is the line? Where do you get to decide that a person is no longer a person? Where do you get to be the judge and decide a life is no longer worthy? That a human being is deserving of another crushing it?"

"You've never had a problem drawing that line," I say, the words growling in my throat.

"But you always have."

"He's right, Emma," Xavier says.

I'm still shaking so hard I can't stop pacing. I've been pacing since I got off the phone with Jonah. As soon as I called Dean to tell him what I'd just found out, he and Xavier got in the car and headed here. Now that they're here, I'm glad to have them near me, but I'm still so angry I can't stop moving.

"What do you mean he's right?" I demand.

"Every person whoever comes into this world, no matter for how long, takes up space in it. That is theirs, given to them as a pure gift at their birth. They don't earn it. They don't deserve it. None of us do. If we had to prove enough worth and goodness and value to be allowed to be on this earth, none of us would be. Because being here, being human, having the chance to experience everything that means, is far too precious for anyone to actually deserve. The space that every person is given belongs to them and is theirs always. No one has the right to take their space from them, or to take them from their space. You have never questioned that."

It's about the last thing I want to hear right now, but maybe what I need the most.

Serena was murdered. And so were the others. Regardless of who she really was, what does your heart tell you?"

I stop and stare at Xavier for a few seconds. I don't understand how he can be this person. After everything that he has been put through and all that he experiences daily, just trying to get through a life he doesn't understand and that wasn't made for him, it would make sense for him to be withdrawn and jaded. And yet there's a peace within him the world can't touch.

I let the silence linger for a while. I know what I have to say, but I really don't want to.

"I have to keep going," I mutter, feeling like the words are being drawn out of me through a hole in my chest. "For all of them."

"Good," Xavier says.

I sit down beside him, and he reaches over to take my hand, turning it over so he can trace his fingertip along my fingers into my palm. When he has stroked each gently, he folds my fingers in toward my palm and sets it back down.

"Thank you, Xavier."

"Where do we start?" Dean asks.

"Jonah referred to the killer as the Emperor. He won't say his name, but he called him the Emperor. Serena used that phrase, too. Does that mean anything to you?"

Dean shakes his head. "No."

"You still can't remember anything?"

"Not after calling Xavier."

"Alright. Then we go to her. She interacted with each of the female victims before they died. I'm sure she did for the men, too, but I can't prove that. Not yet. I'll find the link, but for right now, I have the women. She tried hard not to be photographed so she was recognizable, but you can match up her clothes in the pictures. The shape of her body, the silhouette of her face. They all match. It's the same person in each of those pictures, but there are different names."

"Different names?" Dean asks.

"In the captions or written on the pictures," I explain. "She pretended to be a different person with each of the victims. Diana. Ceres. Flora. Minerva. Salacia." I pause. Now that I'm seeing the names written out and saying them all together, they're falling into place in my mind. "These names. I know them. The Emperor. The Coliseum." I look at each of the men. "These are Roman goddesses."

I look through my notes again and shake my head.

"What is it?" Dean asks.

"There's another one. Serena mentioned it in her journals, but I didn't understand what the entries were about. She wrote them like poems or in code, so they didn't mean a lot to anyone but her. But this name pops up a lot." I turn the paper so they can see it, pointing to the name. "Charon. Who is that?"

Dean shakes his head, but Xavier speaks up immediately.

"It's not a who," he says. "It's a what."

"A what?"

"Charon. It's not a name."

"Who is it?" I ask.

"Some think of it as a demon, others call it a psychopomp, a spirit. Sometimes called the ferryman. He was responsible for bringing the souls of the recently deceased into the next life across the River Styx. But with that spelling, it's primarily seen in Greek mythology."

"A deliverer of souls," Dean muses. "That sounds right."

I shake my head. "No. He just said that's Greek. Everything's Roman. Does this spelling show up in Roman mythology?"

"Not in mythology as often," he says.

"Shit," I say, rubbing my head.

"But it did in regular life."

I stop and look at him, my hand dropping from my face. "Regular life? What do you mean regular life?"

"The Charon was seen at the games in addition to the arbiters. He accompanied the dead from the arena, or ushered the nearly dead into the next world to end their suffering."

"How did he do that?" Dean asks.

"A hammer to the head," Xavier says.

"Holy shit," Dean says.

"Wait," I say, what Xavier is telling us sinking in. "The games. You mean… gladiators?"

∽

I'm scrambling to pull up a map that I can use to mark where each of the bodies was found so I can see what's in the area when Bellamy finally answers her phone.

"B, where's Eric? I've been trying to call him and he's not answering. Doesn't matter. Listen to me. I need you to get in touch with Noah White. He also isn't answering. Apparently, no one is answering me today. You need to head to Harlan as soon as you can. We need to find where Dean was held after his attack."

"I'll call Eric," Bellamy says. "But I don't know when I'll be able to get him. He went undercover."

"He did what?"

"He's on an undercover job," she says. "He said it was for you. Don't you know about it?"

"What are you talking about? Eric doesn't do undercover."

"He said that's why it was perfect for him to do it. No one will recognize him," she says.

"Where did he go?" I ask, trying to keep the terror down. "Is he alone?"

"I thought he was around where you are. He didn't give me an exact place but said you would be nearby. He's not alone. Some guy contacted him with details about the job."

"What guy?" I ask. "What's his name?"

"I don't know if it's his real name or not. He called him Mars."

Xavier draws in a sharp breath and his eyes widen. I look at him and he whispers to me.

"The God of War."

CHAPTER THIRTY-SIX

Eric

T HE PAIN WASN'T AS BAD AS THE CONFUSION.

Eric tried to open his eyes but found that one of them wouldn't cooperate. It felt swollen and throbbed from the top eyelid around the orbital bone and onto his cheek. He reached up and touched it with his fingertips and the tender skin reacted by sending waves of pain to his brain.

It was the least of his worries, though.

He strained through the groggy mist of his mind, still trying to process where he was. How he'd gotten there was still a mystery. Yet, as out of it as he was, he knew he needed to take in every detail he could see, hear, and smell. Anything that might help him survive. Anything that might help him get out.

The room was small and dank, like a basement. He could smell sweat and blood, though that might have been his own. His nose felt like it might have taken a shot of the same caliber his eye did.

There was a single, dim bulb high overhead. The room was small, but it still wasn't enough to illuminate it all. All Eric could see was the spot in the center, just past his feet, which was bare and covered in a dusty linoleum floor.

He could smell mildew. It came in strong on the back of the sweat and blood smell, and it dawned on him that the room he was in appeared to be a bathroom. Or at least, it had been in the past. There was no sink, no toilet, no shower, but the pipes ran along the wall like at one time they had been there.

A door opened across from him. Bright, blinding light scoured over the surface of the room, making him shut his eyes tight for a moment and shake his head. When he looked back, he tried to look above the light at the silhouette of the man coming into the room. He was larger than Eric was and wore a full mask. His body was cast in shadows.

The man in the mask came in wordlessly and yanked him up by the arm. Eric tried to focus on him, but the man shoved him ahead, forcing him to concentrate on getting his legs working. He failed and fell, his face slamming on the floor. The man chuckled behind him and yanked him back up by the waistband of his jeans and the back of his shirt, tossing him forward.

"Down the steps," he growled, and Eric looked ahead.

There were steps leading down and steps leading up. Up was darkness and silence. Down was more of the mildew smell, more of the sweat and blood.

A push to the center of his back got Eric stumbling down the steps. His mind went to Bellamy and Bebe. Whatever was going to happen to him, he had to try to survive. He had to survive for them.

As he got to the third to last step, the room was revealed to him. He couldn't understand it. It didn't make sense.

The floor was covered in dirt. Around the room were cheap pillars, forming a circle in the center. A wall had a giant window cut out with darkened glass. Eric got the impression there was someone behind it. Watching.

Random objects and clutter were scattered around the room. A tire iron. A rope. A wooden baseball bat. A toolbox, open, with tools inside. They were on the outside of the ring of columns that rose to the ceiling. Spotlights lit up every corner, every angle. There were no dark, shadowy places there.

A man stood in the other corner of the room.

He was tall but lanky and lean. He looked like an athlete. Fresh scars and open wounds painted his chest and stomach. His eye was similarly bruised and puffy, but it looked like it had been opened up and allowed to bleed. It was an old boxer's trick. It was so he could see. They used to do it with a razor blade.

He looked scared but determined. His eyes were scanning the ground around him, noticing the same things Eric noticed. But he hadn't moved. He stood stock-still in the corner across from where Eric was coming in and shook his hands at the wrist like he was warming them up.

"Why?" Eric asked of the masked man behind him.

He snickered behind his mask.

"For the pleasure of the Emperor," he intoned. "This is what you were hired to do."

With that, he slipped back behind the door and slammed it shut. Eric heard a key turning a lock. He was locked inside.

Turning back toward the other man, Eric opened his mouth to speak. He wanted to tell him he didn't want to fight. That they should work together, to try and escape. That together, they could take the masked man.

But before any of that could come out of his mouth, it was shut by a hardened fist.

Eric stumbled back, smashing his back on one of the pillars and wheeling around for balance. The man was already hounding him, his fists clenched, looking for an opening. For a brief second, Eric saw something in the back pocket of the shirtless man's jeans.

A clawhammer.

It clicked, somewhere in Eric's still groggy brain, that there was only one way out of this. He had to survive. He had to fight. He had to win.

There was no talking to the other man, who looked crazed and wild. Like he had been through this before and knew what to do—and how to do it. He knew what was expected of him. He wanted to force Eric to the ground, then hit him with the hammer. As Eric shuffled and tried to find his footing, he could see spots on the dirt where he could envision the ending of other fights. Pools of dried, dark dirt where blood had spilled.

He planted his foot and saw an opening. The man was favoring his right side, leaving his left open. He raised a fist to smash back down on Eric, but Eric was too quick. He deftly shifted his weight and pushed forward, swinging his own fist hard into the man's ribcage.

It caught the other man off guard and he didn't get his feet under him in time. Eric followed up the right hook with a speeding elbow right into his nose. There was a crunching sound as he crumpled for a moment to one knee. Eric pressed forward, using the temporary shift in momentum to run forward and shove the man away with both hands. The man staggered back, but before he could regain his balance, Eric dashed forward and dropkicked him in the chest. It sent him rolling backward as Eric landed hard on the dirt on his back.

Scrambling to his feet, Eric scanned the room, looking for a weapon. He didn't want to do this, but he had to. He had to make it back home. He had to see Bellamy and Bebe again. There was no other choice. This man would kill him if he didn't at least incapacitate him.

Then he saw it. Near his feet was a baseball bat, the thick end pointing toward him. He reached over to grab it and was suddenly sent sprawling through the air, his breath leaving him in a loud whoosh. His fingertips just held on, and he pulled the bat toward him as he landed, rolling over it and bruising his ribs. The handle of the bat snapped on impact, leaving a jagged edge.

A sick part of his mind, a part that would never otherwise make itself known if not for the situation he was currently in, saw the jagged edge and knew it was for the better. Now the bat was two different weapons fused into one.

Grabbing the handle end that was left, Eric got to his knees, pulling the bat back and preparing to swing. The other man was close, too close to get as much of a swing as he wanted, but enough to do some damage. He connected with the man's knee, and he howled in pain. But as he pulled the bat back, the man came swinging down from above with the clawhammer.

Eric saw it just in time to move his head, sacrificing his shoulder in the meantime. It struck him just as he swung the bat again. A lightning bolt of agony shot through his entire body. Both men dropped their weapons as they crumbled to the ground. The clawhammer had fallen and flipped a little way away. Eric leaped toward it with his good arm. His other screamed in pain inside his mind, but he had to ignore it. He needed that hammer, if for no other reason but so the other man wouldn't have it.

A growl of pained frustration rumbled behind him as he got his hand on it and grasped it. Spinning to his back, he lifted it up, and in a stroke of luck, it deflected an iron bar being swung down at him. The man wheeled it back to swing again and Eric took a desperate swing at his leg with the hammer. The man fell back, trying to avoid the swing, but lost his balance. His leg was no good anymore. It couldn't hold him up. As soon as he put pressure on it, he fell.

The man fell on his ass right by the toolbox. Eric saw the opportunity and darted toward him with the hammer. He smashed it down on the man's forearm as he reached for the toolbox, crushing it and slamming down again. He screamed in a wild, primal rage and bucked himself over, reaching with his other arm for Eric's face.

He clawed at his eye, the bruised one, and tore the puffy bruise open. Eric could feel blood spurt out and run down his face as he slammed the hammer down randomly. He was missing the man and couldn't see him for the blood that was rushing down his face. Suddenly, something heavy and cold smashed the side of his head and the world went black.

Eric was probably only out for a second, but when he came to, it was to the feeling of intense pain. His eyes couldn't focus, and his body felt like steel rods were inserted into his bones. Everything hurt. There was no strength, no energy left in him. Blood poured from a wound near the top of his head on the side, joining with the stream coming from above his eye.

The other man was catching his breath nearby, huffing and puffing and groaning. One leg was near useless, and the opposite hand was in a similar state. But he knew as well as Eric did that there was only one way forward. Survive.

Eric's eyes slowly began to focus on the face of the man now crawling toward him. His eyes were cold, black, and dead inside. In his teeth, he had a screwdriver as he dragged himself toward Eric's limp body. Every part of

Eric's brain was screaming at him to get up, to fight, but he had nothing left. The last shot had taken it all out of him. He needed a minute to rest.

But in a minute, he would be dead.

The man was close, close enough that when he held himself up on one hand and tried to get his opposite knee under him, Eric could feel the sweat and blood dripping off of him onto Eric's back. The man got himself upright, screaming in pain, and took the screwdriver out of his mouth. He lifted it high above his head and Eric shifted, desperate to move, to fight, to survive.

Sound suddenly filled the room, and the man froze. One singular loud shot rang out. Eric watched, dumbfounded, as his body jerked backward violently. The screwdriver fell and landed harmlessly on the ground, and the man landed hard on the dirt floor.

"Eric!"

He knew that voice. He tried to turn toward it, but his body wouldn't let him.

A face came into his blurred vision, but he could recognize it anyway. Emma hovered over him, concern etched her face. She was holstering her gun, one hand reaching for Eric's chest to check his heartbeat. She froze, then seemed to relax, looking up at another body walking across the room to where the other fighter had fallen.

"He's alive," she said. "What about him?"

The figure bent over the man and was quiet for a moment, but then spoke.

"Alive, but barely. We have to get them out of here," Dean said, his voice distant.

"Eric," Emma said, her eyes now boring into his. He could barely see them as blue points of light surrounded by swimming shapes and colors. "Eric, can you hear me?"

"Yes," Eric forced out. He felt like his throat was made of sandpaper. It hurt to breathe.

"Where are you hurt?" Emma asked.

"My... head," Eric groaned. "Mostly my head and neck."

"Can you move your toes?"

"Huh?" Eric asked.

"Your toes, can you move your toes?" Emma demanded.

He experimented a bit inside his shoes, his brain barely remaining tethered to consciousness. "What?"

Emma said something to him about making sure he wasn't paralyzed, but he didn't quite catch it. The blackness was starting to close in around the corners of his vision.

"Ow!" he yelped, his vision suddenly returning. He barely lifted his head to look down. Emma had removed his shoe and pinched his foot. "That hurt."

"Good," Emma said. She huffed a laugh and seemed to relax on her haunches. "You will seriously do anything to get my attention, won't you?"

It hurt, but Eric laughed. Emma shook her head.

CHAPTER THIRTY-SEVEN

"JUST HOW IN THE LIVIN' HELL DID YOU FIND THAT BOY?" JOHN ASKS. I look over at Xavier where he's standing at the hospital window with Bebe in his arms. They're scheming about something, as usual. He notices me looking at him and lifts his head.

"Xavier, do you want to explain to my friend John Wheeler here how we found Eric before he got Charon-ed?" I ask.

"Before I got what?" Eric pipes up from the bed.

Bellamy runs her hand back over his forehead and leans down to kiss it. She's crying but doing her best not to seem like she is.

"Oh," Xavier says. "I tracked him."

He turns back to the window and continues his whispering. Bebe reaches up with her chubby hands and squeezes his cheeks so his lips pop out. He stands patiently looking at her.

"He did what?" Wheeler gasps.

"During an investigation a while back Xavier got it in his mind to use trackers for all of us so that we don't get lost. He has an app on his phone that can locate any of us when we have our trackers near us."

"You had yours?" John asks Eric, sounding surprised. "Even undercover?"

"I figured I was going into something completely unknown. There was a pretty good chance it was going to end badly. I needed all the help I could get. The chip is in the bottom of my watch. So as long as I was wearing that, he'd be able to find me."

"That's darn brilliant," Wheeler whistles.

"Sam won't wear his," Xavier says.

I shake my head. "He won't."

"Neither will Emma," Bellamy adds.

Xavier gasps and turns a horrified look toward me.

"I do too!" I protest. "Sometimes I just… forget it." I glare at Bellamy, who shrugs sheepishly and turns back to gushing over Eric. "So, what do we do now? It's been almost a day since we got Eric out of that place. Marini could be out of state by now."

"He won't be," Dean says. "That would make him look guilty. He knows I didn't see him."

"What about the big fella?" Wheeler asks. "He still alive?"

"Yes," I say. "Barely. But he survived. He looks like he's been through several battles and the gunshot didn't help. The doctors have him in a coma to try to stabilize him and hope he heals."

"Soon as he does, we need to find out what he knows," Wheeler says.

"We need to do something now," I say. "Marini needs to come in."

⌒

Several hours later, I stand in front of a long table with the district attorney, detailing everything I have against Salvador Marini.

"Every picture has the name of a different Roman goddess. They correspond with the way the victim died or was found. This victim was found near a deer stand. The picture with Serena is labeled 'Diana'. Goddess of the Hunt. The victim near the abandoned school: Minerva, Goddess of Wisdom. You'll see that pattern throughout. Ceres, Goddess of Agriculture, and that victim died in a cornfield. This man has a fantasy of himself as a Roman Emperor. He sees himself as powerful and admired. Wealthy. This woman took the role of the goddesses who answered his prayers by bringing him victims, and he honored that goddess in the way he disposed of the women after using them as sex slaves for as long as they amused him.

"As for the men, she found ones desperate for work and convinced them they had an amazing opportunity available. Then she brought them to his own personal arenas and used them for gladiator fights. Some to the death, others just until they were so broken down and useless they didn't entertain him anymore.

Most of them have drugs in their system. Serena had LSD, others have other hallucinogens. The ones who didn't have anything that showed up on their toxicology, I wouldn't be surprised if they were dosed with mushrooms. These drugs cause disorientation, confusion, and inability to think clearly and make decisions. This made it easy to control them, and then to toss them out and have them die of exposure or be easily staged as an accident or suicide."

I finish and look at her. She lets out a breath.

⌒

"They let him go."

"What do you mean they let him go?" Jonah demands.

"I laid out everything, but the DA said it's not enough to charge him. There's no forensic evidence. No witnesses who actually saw Marini do anything. Dean doesn't remember anything that happened to him, and as soon as they found out Eric voluntarily put himself in that position in an unauthorized undercover mission, they shut down.

"It wouldn't matter, anyway. Neither of them saw his face. For right now, according to them, we have nothing. Even Serena's journals and things don't really mean anything until we have something more concrete." I let out an exasperated sound. "There has to be something else. I still don't understand why Serena was murdered. She wasn't assaulted. She's the one who brought him his slaves. Why would he kill her? What aren't you telling me?"

"She was very proud of her tattoo," he says. "She cherished every new detail she got to add to it."

"But she covered it when she was out." I point out. Then it occurs to me. "It wasn't covered when they found her body. She wanted it there when she was with you. She only covered it when Marini might see it."

"Being a member of Leviathan is an honor," he says. "Especially to be in a position as close to me as she was. But she knew she chose a dangerous life. Every member knows the risk they may be called on to give their life for the mission. And so we set contingencies in place to preserve the mission."

"What are you saying?" I ask.

"She, like all members of Leviathan, would have access to a safe, secure place. A storage cache set up for her to pass down information in the event of her death."

"Not a safety deposit box. You'd never risk that exposure…" I murmur. "It would have to be somewhere public. Hidden in plain sight, without need of identity, so a subordinate could access it."

"Correct."

A memory flickers through my mind. Greg carrying a duffel bag through a bus station.

"The train station where you parked her car. That one is abandoned, but there's a newer one on the other side of the city. It's only been there for a couple of years. How do I know which locker is hers? Or the combination to the lock?"

"The locker will be in the center row. Her combination is recorded somewhere on her body. I never spoke to the man who started her locker for her, so I don't know."

"I'll figure it out."

CHAPTER THIRTY-EIGHT

THE TRAIN STATION IS BUSTLING, BUT I BARELY NOTICE THE OTHER people there. With Dean and Xavier hanging back enough to stay inconspicuous while also having my back, I make my way directly to the lockers. Wheeler is somewhere around here. So is Simon. I don't see them, but I don't need to. They're here to make sure the area is secure. To make sure I get to the locker and back out alive.

I go to the center row of lockers and find the ones with locks. From there, I look for ones that are newer or that have names on them. It narrows the options down to three. I examine the first lock. Nothing. The second is similarly unremarkable. But when I turn over the third one, my heart leaps into my chest. Etched into the metal on the back is a faint mermaid tail.

I take out my phone and pull up the picture of Serena's tattoo. Jonah explained the combination of the lock is shared only with the person setting up the locker and the person who owns the locker. The combination is changed after the locker is established and the combination is recorded in some way on the member's body so it can be accessed in the event of their death. This is the first time I hear of artists in the organization who maintain drawings of each of the tattoos, updating them as the tattoos are updated so they can stay accurate.

Which tells me most of the combinations are secretly incorporated into the design of the tattoos, likely numbers that are meaningful beyond just the locks. I examine the picture of Serena's tattoo over and over until

I finally see them: the collections of tiny bubbles etched to either side and above the mermaid. They look like they're randomly dotted throughout, but there's a pattern. I zoom in and make sure to count each one.

Eleven on the left. Twenty-three above. Four on the right.

I put the combination in and the lock opens. My heart jumps, but when I open the door, it looks like there's nothing inside. I'm about to close it when I notice something on the top of the locker. Running my hand along it, I take down a piece of paper taped to the metal.

Opening it, I find a note in Serena's handwriting.

"Look to the light. You'll always find me."

I stand there re-reading the note, trying to understand what it means. Dean and Xavier make their way over to me.

"What is it?" Dean asks.

I hand him the note and he reads it out loud.

"Spiritual," Xavier comments.

"Somehow, I don't think so," Dean says.

I look up and catch a glimpse of Detective Simon across the room.

"Wait," I say. "I think I know what it means. Come on."

We make it back to Miley's house in record time and I run inside, heading straight for the sitting room. The smart device is back in place in the electrical outlet and I pull it out.

"What are you doing?" Dean asks.

"This light came on when the detectives first came here to search the house. It was on when I came back. I thought it was being operated remotely, but it wasn't. It's on a timer." I turn the box over and find a seam where I can separate the panels. A piece of plastic comes away and a micro-SD card falls into my hand. I hold it up for the guys to see. "In the light, you will always find me."

Detective Simon and John are standing at the door to the sitting room and Simon holds out a tablet.

"Here. It should play it."

"Thank you," I say.

I insert the card and a list of files comes up. All of them are years old, except for one.

"That one is from December of last year," Dean points out.

"The day before Jonah's escape," I add. I glance up at him and he nods.

I click the file and a second later an image of Serena fills the screen. Simon draws in a breath and I know a surge of emotion has taken over her. She's hearing the voice of a woman she revolved her life around for almost a year, and who she had never seen alive. It's another moment of reckoning, forcing her to come to terms with the reality that she is not the person the detective crafted her to be in her mind.

"This is Serena," she says. "If I haven't deleted this message and you are seeing it, I am likely dead. If so, look at Salvador Marini, a man known as the Emperor. I think someone has leaked my true identity to him. I will try to use the information I have gathered about him and his crimes to leverage my survival. If not, I've secured all of the details of his crimes, including murders, financial crimes, and corporate corruption, as insurance.

"Tomorrow I am tasked with freeing L. Tonight I will meet with Marini once more. I hope the intel I have gathered can be used for our future needs and the glorification of our mission. Please know I am prepared for this meeting to be my end. If it is, be strong. Know I would rather lay down my life for L than return. Farewell, friends."

The image of her goes still and I look at it more carefully, noticing for the first time something that brings an unexpected tightness to my throat.

"That dress," I say, touching the edge of the screen to indicate the dark fabric and white stars. "It's the one Marini said he wanted to have her cremated in. That son of a bitch."

I take the card out and hand the tablet to Simon.

"In the recording, she says that she is tasked with freeing 'L,'" Simon says. There's a question in her voice, she just doesn't know how to word it. She's still just beginning to learn about the truths and horrors of Leviathan.

"Lotan," I explain. "As a part of the body of Leviathan, she would honor him as Lotan. I think that's the key to why she was murdered. She covered up her tattoo whenever she was going to be with Marini. In all those low-cut dresses and everything, she's wearing makeup over it. She didn't want him to know she was in Leviathan. She was blackmailing him and likely extorting him. I did some research into his background and found out he's not only very wealthy and connected himself, but he comes from a family that is even wealthier and more powerful. Everything Leviathan would want to have for their own."

"You bringin' that to the DA?" John asks as I put the card back into the device so I can show where I located it.

"Right now," I confirm.

CHAPTER THIRTY-NINE

A WEEK LATER, I'M BACK IN SHERWOOD, STILL REELING. AFTER THE second time the DA refused to hold Salvador Marini because of lack of evidence and I had to watch the smug, knowing smile cross his face as he walked out of the station, I knew there was nothing else I could do there. I needed to go home.

I can't wrap my head around them refusing to bring him up on any charges. I understand how hard it is to build a case for something as massive and difficult to comprehend as the Emperor's string of rapes, tortures, and murders. It will take a tremendous amount of evidence to prove beyond a reasonable doubt he did what he's being accused of.

The lack of forensic evidence is a staggering blow. But it's not unexpected. I would actually be surprised if any does become uncovered. Not because I put that much faith into Salvador Marini. But because I know he was, albeit unknowingly, working alongside part of Leviathan. Even if she was aiming to eventually destroy him, Serena would also ensure Marini's crimes were clean and untraceable.

In her video, she said she secured evidence of his crimes. But they weren't on the SD card. They weren't in her locker. We swept the house for the umpteenth time and still couldn't find them. We've searched exhaustively over the last few days and have come up empty.

I just wish there was something they were willing to charge him with so they could get him off the street and into a cage where he belongs. I haven't given up hope. I know this isn't the end. Complex murder and slavery cases like these can take years to build to the point of bringing up charges. They're never quick and simple.

It's critical to ensure all the evidence possible can be presented at the trial. They only have one shot. If they bring him to trial and aren't able to convince the jury he did what his victims testify he did, he'll walk free. Double jeopardy means he won't be eligible to face those same charges again.

Not that there's not enough for the DA to come up with something new to try him again, but the years dragging on are tiresome and could be traumatic. Victims are often far less willing to be a part of cases after they've gone through the process for an extended amount of time. It's even worse if a trial has been thrown out and they have to start again.

It would make me feel far better if they could dole out small amounts of charges one right after the other starting now, so that he could be held behind bars while the larger case is underway. I'm willing to try my hand at charging him with obstruction of justice and trespassing at a crime scene for coming into Miley's house when I was there. But so far the prosecutor won't go along with me on it.

Just the thought of how brazen and arrogant he was is enough to bring the fury up all over again. He wanted me to see him. He wanted me to suspect him. Capturing Dean and throwing him into the arena wasn't just for his sick entertainment. It was about Dean. I don't know yet the extent of Marini's conflict with Jonah, but I have a feeling this has only just started. I'm standing at the edge of the rabbit hole and soon I'll have no choice but to jump.

I'm up in the attic trying to sort through seasonal decorations so I can get the house ready for Thanksgiving in a few weeks when I hear my phone ringing downstairs. I must have forgotten it when I was bringing boxes down. I rush down the stairs and sweep it off the kitchen counter just as it stops ringing.

"Damn," I mutter.

I check who was calling and see John's number. I call him back immediately.

"Emma?"

"Is everything alright? What's going on?"

My mind goes to Eric, who is still in the hospital. I worry something might have happened to him or that the other fighter may not have pulled through.

"He confessed."

For a second, I can't respond. I'm not even sure I heard him correctly.

"Marini?" I ask.

John laughs. It's not from humor. Maybe not even from happiness. It's just loose, fragmented energy and emotion breaking free.

"Just now," he says. "He asked if you were still in town. He wanted to confess directly to you."

"Holy hell, I wish I had been," I say. "But I don't understand. What happened? He was almost crowing when he was released after the last interrogation. He kept insisting there was no way we could prove anything we were saying about him. There was no forensic evidence and all we had was hearsay from a dead woman who has been recently proven to be an identity thief who aided a notorious terrorist in escaping from prison. He even fought the recordings and the pictures. Until we find the rest of the evidence she collected, we didn't actually have all that much."

"I know," John says.

"Then what happened?"

"He just said he couldn't take the guilt anymore. He really took some time to think about what he did and how many lives he destroyed, an' he decided he needed to unburden himself by tellin' the truth."

"I can't believe it," I say. "That's... I can't believe it. What happens now?"

"Well, we still ain't got a shred of evidence. So that's a dry well. But he is willin' to take charges on some smaller offenses to get him off the streets. He was given a temporary release in order to get some things arranged with his company, and he's due to surrender himself at the end of the week."

"I'll be there," I say.

෴

The morning of Marini's planned surrender, just hours before he's scheduled to turn himself in, I'm at the hospital with Eric. He looks so much better than he did the last time I saw him and I'm glad the air between us is cleared.

I still don't like what he said. But in the greater scheme of things, it is such a small thing. It's not worth losing a friendship I've held dear for more than half my life.

"Are you going to make peanut butter pie again this year?" he asks.

"Oh, gracious, that thing is so rich," Bellamy smiles, almost squirming in her seat at the thought of it.

"I can't imagine why you would say that," I say. "It only has a jar of peanut butter, two bricks of cream cheese, and three cups of powdered sugar in it. And some ganache. On a chocolate cookie and melted butter crust. But those are just little details."

She shakes her head and Eric laughs.

"It's Thanksgiving. We're supposed to be enjoying the bounty."

"Exactly," I say. "And honoring the great harvest of peanut butter and chocolate ganache savored by our forefathers."

I get up and go over to the door to the room, opening it and peering out both ways.

"What are you doing?" Eric asks.

"Checking to make sure Xavier didn't somehow hear me and is swooping in as the superhero version of Mr. X to admonish my sins against American history," I say.

They laugh, even though there's a little part of me that thinks somehow Xavier does know what I said and I'm still going to hear about it. I'm about to step back into the room and close the door when I notice a

uniformed officer from the precinct coming down the hall. There's a serious expression on his face and I step out into the hall to meet him.

"Are you looking for me?" I ask.

"Agent Griffin, I need you to come with me," he starts.

"What's wrong?" I ask.

"I was sent to get you," he says.

"One second," I tell him with a finger raised.

I step back into the room and Bellamy looks at me with her eyebrows
knitted together.

"Is everything okay?"

"Um, I don't know. An officer just met me in the hallway and said he
was sent to get me," I say.

"Did you see his badge?" Eric asks.

"Yes," I say. "And I know I've seen him at the precinct before."

"Let us know what happened."

I nod and leave the room. The officer and I get into the elevator and
head down to the ground floor. I'm expecting to follow him out into the
parking deck, but instead, he directs me toward the emergency room.
John Wheeler and Wendy Simon are in the waiting room, standing close
together like they are in intense conversation. Simon sees me first and
nods toward me.

"What's going on?" I call over to them as I hurry to the crowd.

Before she can answer, an ambulance pulls up into the bay outside.
The doors open and several EMTs pour out, bringing a gurney with them.
On it, a female EMT kneels at the edge and performs CPR on a prone
patient. A doctor runs out of the back and meets the gurney before it is
all the way in.

"We've been working on him since we got to the scene," one of the
EMTs tells him.

"Any luck?"

"Nothing."

I walk over to the doors and watch the doctor place a hand on the
back of the EMT still desperately pumping at the patient's chest. He feels

for a pulse at the man's wrist, then steps forward. I can't see the front of the gurney, but I assume he's feeling for the pulse at his neck. When he steps back, he's shaking his head.

"Call it."

"I'll keep trying," the EMT says.

"You did everything you could," the doctor tells her. "He was gone before you got to him."

The doctor comes inside and the gurney slides in after him. I catch a glimpse of the patient's face just before they pull the sheet over it.

"Marini."

CHAPTER FORTY

"**H**IS ATTORNEY WAS SUPPOSED TO MEET HIM FOR BREAKFAST AND to talk about the case before he surrendered," I tell Sam over the phone from my hotel room that night. "When he didn't get to the restaurant and didn't answer his phone, the attorney was worried and went to the house to check on him. He said his first thought was that he had changed his mind and gone on the run."

"That would have been my first thought," Sam says.

"Me, too," I admit. "But when he got there, he looked through the window by the door and saw Marini sprawled out on the floor. He called the police and they went inside and found him. He apparently had a heart attack. They tried to work on him and bring him back, but they couldn't. The doctor said he was dead when they got there."

"I guess the stress was just too much for him. It might have seemed like a good idea at the time to tell the truth and come clean about everything, but I can't imagine how it feels to wake up the morning you know you are going to prison and are going to face a cascade of charges that will keep you there for the rest of your life."

"I know. I'm sure that was really difficult and he was under stress, but I just don't know."

"What do you mean?"

"Something about it just doesn't seem right."

"It wasn't. It's never right when somebody doesn't face justice for what they've done."

"I agree with that," I say. "But that's not what I mean. I mean with the situation. The body. The way they described it. There was something off, but I can't place it. I didn't get to actually see the scene, obviously, but what I heard sounded strange."

"Babe, I think you're overthinking it."

"Maybe I am. It just seems like everything just hit a wall. It felt like things were going to work out. That all these victims were finally going to get justice. Marini was going to have to walk into a courtroom and stand there listening to what he had done. Then be told by a judge and jury that he was guilty and have a sentence imposed. It was going to tie up so many loose ends and be such a comfort to so many families. Now that won't ever happen."

"I'm sorry."

I rake my fingers back through my hair and let out a breath that feels like my lungs have been holding onto it for weeks.

"There's nothing I can do about it now. I just wish Dean had been able to get more answers. He still can't remember what happened to him. And now he'll never know." I let the thoughts settle for a second, then shift gears, wanting to get away from the tension and weight hanging over me. Even if it's just transferring over to something else. "How is everything going there?"

"Not a lot is happening, to be honest," he sighs. "Marie is still missing. Right now we're just trying to figure out her movements leading up to the last time anyone saw her so we can go from there."

"Does that mean you won't be coming home any time soon?"

"Probably not," he says. "I'm sorry."

"It's alright. I guess it's my turn to be the one to sit home and wait."

He laughs softly. "I'll be home as soon as I can."

"I will, too. I love you."

"I love you."

⌒

Emma is looking for you.

"You still are?" Jonah asks when I pick up the phone.

"Are you going to turn yourself in?" I ask.

I don't mean it playfully. I've done my part. I fought to have his name cleared. I found out who murdered Serena and the others. It's time for him to repay me.

"I'm not ready to go back to prison yet," he says. "There are still things I need to do."

"He's dead," I say.

"What?"

"He's dead. Marini is dead."

"What do you mean he's dead? He just confessed. He was going to go to trial for killing Serena."

"I know," I say. "He had a heart attack at home this morning before turning himself in."

"Son of a bitch," Jonah growls.

"At least it's over," I say.

"It isn't over," he tells me.

"Why not?"

"What happened to Miley Stanford?"

"You don't know what happened to her?" I ask, stunned at the revelation.

"No," he says. "I don't know where she is."

"How did Serena end up taking her place?" I ask. "You said you know that she didn't have anything to do with Miley being gone."

"She didn't," Jonah insists. "I put her into Miley's life. But I swear to you, I don't know what happened to her."

"Jonah, who was Serena? I need you to tell me the truth. How did you find her?"

He hesitates, then I hear the breath slip from his lungs as he seems to give in.

"She was the daughter of a crime family I encountered several years ago. She impressed me immediately and when I mentioned it, her brother offered her to me for the night. I learned she was used as currency to foster goodwill with other criminal enterprises. I declined the offer but kept my eye on her. I watched what she did and how she handled herself. We didn't get much of a chance to speak because of how protective her family was of her—in their own way, mind you—but from the little we did interact, I knew I couldn't leave without her.

"Soon after, I joined a poker game with her oldest brother. Another offer of a night with her was among his wager. Instead, I traded for her. Her family was less than happy at the arrangement and I've been protecting her since. I know she was concerned Marini had uncovered that part of her life. He was known to have dealings with some of the crime families. If he had found out, she would have been killed. Or far worse."

"She still was," I point out.

"Yes," Jonah says. "She was. But she died for her love of Leviathan rather than the hatred of her family. She died with her tattoo on her back, knowing she was who she wanted to be."

"How can you say that? Do you really not understand the incredible cruelty of taking a woman who had already been abused, trafficked, and forced to do horrible things to other people, and weaponizing her?" I snap.

"That's not what I did, Emma," he protests. "I didn't rescue her because she was innocent and sweet. I chose her because I could already see who she was in her own eyes. She was efficient, calculating, and exceptional at understanding exactly what another person needed to get them under her control. She was born to be in the body of Leviathan."

"Yet, she wasn't an equal," I say.

"Why do you say that?" he asks.

"The men in Leviathan earn sea monsters with scales and claws, flames, destroyed boats. The more they do, the more gruesome and intimidating their tattoo becomes. You gave her a mermaid and added sparkles and bubbles and hair and starfish. It's condescending."

"It's accurate," Jonah says. "Of the two, the mermaid is far more

257

frightening. It's beautiful, enticing. People are drawn to it and don't know what they've gotten themselves into until it's too late. Mermaids aren't gentle creatures, Emma. They aren't sweet. They're derived from sirens, who loved nothing more than to lure men in with their beauty and singing so they could smash them onto the rocks.

"Anyone seeing a sea monster knows it's intimidating. They know they are meant to be afraid. A mermaid doesn't have the same effect. Think of this. Which is the more frightening prospect—a vial clearly labeled as lethal, or a piece of candy that's been soaked in poison? They are both deadly, but the vial warns of its brutality and can be avoided. That piece of candy is lovely and delicious. A delicate, singular confection too perfect to resist."

"Where are you, Jonah?" I ask. I'm completely done with his riddles. His games. His nonsense.

"I'm where I'm meant to be. And tomorrow I'll be where tomorrow intends me to be," he evades.

"You need to come back. You need to face the consequences of what you did."

"Not yet. And for now, I need to keep moving. You know how to reach me."

"Jonah?" I ask before he can hang up.

"Hmm?"

"You said that you traded for Serena. What did her brother get in exchange?"

"A grave. Goodnight, Emma."

EPILOGUE

Four days before…

S ALVADOR MARINI STRUGGLED AGAINST THE LEATHER STRAPS TYING his arms to the wooden desk. He hoped if he struggled enough, he could snap them. Twist them enough to create enough room to slip out. Maybe even if he moved enough, the table would flip, and he could carry it on his back and get away.

He would have to remove the cloth from his eyes, though. The cloth was tied so tight that his veins bulged on the side of his head and his head throbbed in pain. It would be the first thing he would do if he could get his hands free. Then he could look into his captor's eyes. And spit on him.

A door shut in the distance, and footsteps echoed across the room. The man walking toward Marini grinned. This was what he enjoyed most. Using his talents for something worthwhile. Something that would please himself, and others. Especially Emma Griffin.

The wet rag in his hand was one he stole from a laundromat. Some silver-haired old man would find his basket missing a rag, but with a twenty-dollar bill at the bottom. Jonah thought that was a fair trade. Fair enough.

Salvador had stopped struggling, aware of the footsteps in the room and who was making them. He also knew that any sign of struggle would only make his torture worse. He wished he had something to pray to.

The rag went over his nose and mouth in one quick motion, and the faucet was turned on immediately after. It ran for a few seconds as Salvador sputtered and coughed. Tears streamed from his eyes and his lungs burned. It was a brand of torture banned by governments around the world. One that Salvador knew was designed to break him down, but not kill him. Jonah wanted him to do something for him, not die.

Not yet.

The water shut off and Salvador coughed. Blood came with the water coming from his chest and Jonah sighed as he waited for the noise to stop. When it did, he turned the faucet on again for just a second and then shut it off.

"You will go to the police," Jonah growled. "You will confess to being the Emperor. You will tell them you attacked Dean Steele. You will confess it all."

"No," Salvador sputtered. "No."

Jonah rolled his eyes and turned the water on again. The rag was stuffed down into his mouth, keeping him from closing it. The water burned in his nostrils and down his throat. He was sure he was going to drown this time. He couldn't breathe. His fingers dug into his palms until they bled.

The faucet shut off again.

"You will," Jonah said quietly. "You will say that you hated Serena for betraying you. You will tell them *the truth*. The truth about how she worked with me to blackmail and extort you for money and power. That she was Leviathan." He leaned close to Salvador's ear, nearly whispering. "That you killed her."

Salvador coughed, spitting up blood that fell back into his throat.

"No," he heaved, his voice muffled by the rag as he tried to move it with his tongue. He had it halfway out now. He could almost breathe.

Jonah calmly placed his hand over Salvador's mouth, pushing with two fingers on the rag. Salvador tried to bite down, but the rag kept his mouth open too far. He could taste the leather of Jonah's glove but couldn't bite him. He choked and snorted.

Then the water started again.

Salvador screamed, his voice echoing in the room and bouncing back to him.

"You almost got away with it," Jonah continued. "You got me accused of the murder. It was clever. It was realistic. But it was a lie." He turned the faucet off and waited for Salvador to take a deep breath again, gurgling as he tried to force the water out of his body. "But I will not go down for it, Salvador. You will."

Jonah slid his fingers up to the cloth over Salvador's eyes and pulled them down. The light made him squeeze them shut momentarily, but he blinked them open, forcing them to look Jonah in the face. Jonah smiled.

"You will do this, Salvador. Do you understand? This is the way it must be."

"Please," Salvador begged through the muffling rag. "Please."

Again, Jonah sighed and reached for the faucet again. Salvador screamed for him to stop. Screaming "no". Screaming "please".

"Please is not a 'yes', Salvador," Jonah said, holding the rag deep in his mouth. "This will end when I hear a yes."

"Yes!" Salvador screamed against the water and the rag and the blood. Jonah shut off the faucet and leaned down again, close to his ear.

"What was that?" Jonah said. "What did you say?"

"Yes," Salvador repeated. "I will."

"Good," Jonah grinned. "Very good."

Jonah stood, pushing the fabric back over Salvador's eyes and yanking the rag from his mouth. He tossed it away and it smushed against the wall with a wet, spongy sound.

As Jonah walked away, the whimpering sound of Salvador Marini was the only thing to be heard for miles. Jonah would let it stay that way for a while. Just to let it sink in. Then he would have him taken away to do his job. To tell the truth.

The way Jonah told him to.

AUTHOR'S NOTE

Dear Reader,

Welcome back to Emma and the crew, I hope you enjoyed *The Girl in the Woods*, the first book in season 3 of Emma. I can't believe we made it this far! Thank you for your continued support with the Emma Griffin series, I hope you continue to love it as much as I love writing it! If you can please continue to leave your reviews for these books, I would appreciate that enormously. Your reviews allow me to get the validation I need to keep going as an indie author. Just a moment of your time is all that is needed. My promise to you is to always do my best to bring you thrilling adventures. I can't wait for you to read the next book!

Yours, A.J. Rivers

P.S. If for some reason you didn't like this book or found typos or other errors, please let me know personally. I do my best to read and respond to every email at aj@riversthrillers.com

ALSO BY

A.J. RIVERS

Emma Griffin FBI Mysteries by AJ Rivers

Season One
Book One—*The Girl in Cabin 13**
Book Two—*The Girl Who Vanished**
Book Three—*The Girl in the Manor**
Book Four—*The Girl Next Door**
Book Five—*The Girl and the Deadly Express**
Book Six—*The Girl and the Hunt**
Book Seven—*The Girl and the Deadly End**

Season Two
Book Eight—*The Girl in Dangerous Waters**
Book Nine—*The Girl and Secret Society*
Book Ten—*The Girl and the Field of Bones*
Book Eleven—*The Girl and the Black Christmas*
Book Twelve—*The Girl and the Cursed Lake*
Book Thirteen—*The Girl and The Unlucky 13*
Book Fourteen—*The Girl and the Dragon's Island*

Season Three
Book Fifteen—*The Girl in the Woods*

Other Standalone Novels
Gone Woman

* Also available in audio

Made in United States
Orlando, FL
06 April 2024

45527413R00161